P9-CAR-152

THE PAPER MAN

ALSO BY BILLY O'CALLAGHAN

In Exile
In Too Deep
The Things We Lose, The Things We Leave Behind
The Dead House
My Coney Island Baby
The Boatman and Other Stories
Life Sentences

THE PAPER MAN

A NOVEL

Billy O'Callaghan

BOSTON
GODINE
2023

Published in 2023 by
GODINE
Boston, Massachusetts

First published in 2023 in England by Jonathan Cape, an imprint of Vintage, part of the Penguin Random House group of companies.

AUTHOR'S NOTE While Matthias Sindelar and the basic arc of his life story told here are real and true, the other half of this novel—that is to say, the story of Rebekah and Jack—is purely fiction.

EDITOR'S NOTE Godine's edition of *The Paper Man* has retained the author's U.K. spelling and punctuation so as not to water down the text's unique vernacular.

LIBRARY OF CONGRESS CONTROL NUMBER: 2022942740
ISBN 978-1-56792-785-6

First Printing, 2023
Printed in the United States of America

For my mother, Gina,
who'll forever be what love is

THE PAPER MAN

Anschluss

Vienna, 3 April 1938

After a long cold beginning to the year, a surprise mid-March thaw brings actual heat. Even with the fresh-seeming feel of summer, though, fires across the city continue to be lit, and those who have known such false ends before remain cautious of a last wintry bite, so that by noon most days, if there is not a good breeze blowing, the skies above Vienna are greased with smoke and turned the fatty buttermilk pallor of church candles.

There is a game that nobody wants to miss. Tickets have been given freely, because this isn't just a sporting contest, it is an event, symbolic of so much. The *Anschluss*; more than a handshake, more than an embrace, a unifying, of brothers and of blood. And from today, in the instant that the final whistle is blown, Austria as a national team—and to all intents as a nation—will cease to be.

Those without tickets have no choice but to turn to touts, so the city's criminal element gets forging, understanding the killing to be had. The trick is not to gouge, and to have youngsters do the selling, put them on street corners or the least-lit booths of those cafes and bars who might be willing, for a modest skim of the profits, to allow such business to be done, with all due discretion and the guarantee that there is to be no trouble and not even so much as a raised voice. Keeping things to just two or three marks, reasonable and affordable, in the fortnight ahead of the game; then bumping the price to five for the couple of days before, and then, in the hours immediately preceding kick-off—once the thought of missing out has turned people sufficiently desperate, and because suspicions will be aroused if those who can take advantage, and are practically expected to, should for whatever reasons choose otherwise—going to as high as ten. Sixty thousand genuine tickets will pack out the Prater Stadium in Leopoldstadt, sixty thousand fists clutching small legitimate stubs of paper or constantly patting the pockets into which they've been tucked; and at least as many again and by some estimations as much as twice that number, will arrive at the turnstiles with their forged scraps and be directed unceremoniously away. Many in the waiting line laugh openly and gloat at the idea that anyone could be so gullible as to pay out good money to a tout, but others who look on shake their heads in sympathy, and even some sense of brotherhood, probably feeling their own stomachs stir in dread that a similar fate might await them once they reach the entrance gate, because even though they've received their tickets freely and in an apparently legitimate way nothing feels quite guaranteed any more, that level of certainty has slipped from life as they know it.

Hours ahead of kick-off the streets heave with people, and soldiers stand by, squads of eighteen or twenty-four, grey-coated despite the brightness of the sun, and armed. A strange day, the air within the city trying for happiness, and bluster, but hazy with some pervading melancholy. Kids run, men stride on, eager to be inside the stadium for a good position on the terraces, a central spot behind one of the goals and halfway up the decks or higher, for the fullest possible perspective and so that there won't be too much displacement when the crush inevitably happens, when the big gates are thrown open the fifteen or twenty minutes after the game begins in an effort to clear the surrounding roads of latecomers and the ticketless and a surge takes place. Beneath the surface joviality, there's a darkness about the mood that soldiers and citizens alike are aware of, and if a few in uniform attempt to exchange banter with those passing by, even with rifles held across their chests and that much more throat to their accents, a kind of barking edge that jars against the languid Viennese lilt, it is because they are still, for the most part, just young men keen on fun, and because, in theory at least, football remains a game for everyone. This won't be an open match, but no one wants to talk today about the shameful side of things. Instead, there is teasing, from the Germans but from the daring few among the Austrians, too: *So, this is why you boys have come to Vienna, is it? To see how the game is meant to be played?* Or, *Try not to take today's beating too much to heart now, soldier. The Paper Man makes shreds of everyone. Your lot just happens to be next in line.* Jibes, all that remains to the Viennese, to be met with shrugs meant to gesture grace in defeat even before a ball has been kicked, since this is a submission so slight as to be practically devoid of meaning. And on it goes, this fun taunting, many hundred times an hour, a harmless last release but knowing where the line is and careful not to cross it. Restrictions are starting to hurt, curfews are being enforced in certain areas of the city and taxation is on the rise, and there is widespread talk that Jews have been deliberately snubbed, by orders from on high, in the distribution of the match tickets. A number of Jewish families have already gone and more still are planning to, making for Switzerland, France or Hungary, wherever their familial connections lie, the arrival of the soldiers in the streets enough to convince them that bad days are coming. But not everyone has the wherewithal to run or the courage to abandon so much, and those who haven't fled hold to the hope, probably more wishful than believed, that things have already bottomed out and can't possibly worsen, because who in the world wants all-out war? Who stands to gain from that?

But while the future writes itself in ugly jagged crosses on walls throughout the city, a pretence or masquerade remains for now in place, as if this change is just a governmental shift and nothing to fret overly about. Being deprived of a ticket might seem a mean blow, with the game such a banner moment in the life of the city, but for those in the know, Jew or not, there are still ways to get the door open, because as sprawling as Vienna is, it is also close-knit. The ticket will come at a price, but the cost, in this instance, is only money. Tomorrow is another day, with other challenges to face, but for this afternoon, there is football and nothing else.

By two o'clock, a couple of hours still before kick-off, the stadium is already crammed. Gustav Hartmann is on the terrace behind the goal at the eastern end, halfway between the goal's right-hand post and the corner flag, and halfway between the terrace's top step and its bottom. He'd have preferred a more central position but this is not bad. The friends with whom he'd breakfasted earlier at Annahof, on warm rolls and lashings of coffee spiced by a passed-around hip flask just to get the ball properly rolling, have all been lost on the way in, taken by the tides of crowds flushing the streets around the Prater. The atmosphere even outside the stadium was vicious with expectancy, and all around him now, people are running their mouths, helpless against standing easy, and the sun feels warmer than it has in an age, the first basking after a whole half a year's stretch of winter. Talking and shouting over one another about games seen, massacres and great victories, the facts vociferously disputed but the arguments part of the purpose. Most of what is said recollects Sindelar, of course, the one they've taken to calling the Paper Man—still, on his good days, the game's colossus. Goals, wonder-touches, demonstrations of skill unimaginable up to the very second of their execution. And the talk on this part of the terrace plays out in variation around the stadium until all is collage, a rain of white noise.

The sky is a pale but brilliant blue, and Hartmann lifts his face to feel the heat against his skin and for half a minute closes his eyes. And into the darkness of his mind Sindelar glides, ball at his feet, alert to onslaught and opportunity, shifting step against sliding tackles with a practised feint, a drop of the shoulder and the shove of one hip, until he is past and clear, into space. So, there are two Matthias Sindelars. There's the man he's known forever as Mutzl, his dearest friend since childhood, since before school was even a thing to be skipped, always ready with a smile for him at the Annahof cafe or in one of the dance halls, laughing, recounting tales of places he's been and women he's kissed. And there is this one, out on the pitch with a ball at his feet, a man apart, a colossus, imperious and untouchable, maybe the greatest there's ever been.

Now the stadium, which an hour ago had already seemed full, looks packed to splitting, and with the new intensity comes an elevation of noise and, somehow, a brightening. The pitch is not pristine—months of winter football have taken a hard toll, leaving the surface torn and the grass across both goalmouths as well as through a wide stretch at the centre of the field trampled out of existence—but the glare of the day makes the most of what greenery remains. For the final time, he is about to see his great friend in the colours of their nation, a thought he can't bear to face, with so much already to be sorrowful about. But he pushes all of that away, because these couple of hours are what they have now, sliced free from future and past, to be seen, felt and savoured. The rest is silence. His surroundings are a small hillside of his people; most here will have been to the Prater before and experienced heaving crowds at big games; but for the sheer sense of occasion and the rawness of energy, few will have experienced anything like this.

'Bastard,' someone shouts, a woman's voice, from a position behind and to his right, and the word, a stabbing bleat, almost a scream, penetrates the wider noise. Those who understand the intent of it cough cheers of hard, angry, supportive laughter, but among the rest along this increasingly compacted section of the terrace there is only confusion until, down at pitch level, the nearest soldiers stiffen ahead of readying their rifles. Then another voice, very close now, probably within an arm's reach of where Hartmann is standing, suggests that the Führer is here, in the box reserved for dignitaries, and that it's this that has the soldiers on edge. Lining up the German boys against the *Wunderteam* is an obvious mismatch; but with word of Hitler's attendance filtering through now from all sides, with some claiming to have actually seen him, and Goering, too, behind some barricades, on the way in, and others insisting on having got confirmation of it directly from soldiers outside the stadium, it seems a certainty that orders will have been given, of the kind which won't bear disobeying. 'Bastard is right,' another shouts, 'if it's the bastard of a whore,' and in response more cheers go up, making mob truth of it, the rising white-noise din of restlessly babbling thousands reaching something suddenly akin to the rapture of a hand-clap or a firecracker going off. Hartmann listens, absorbing everything, but can't make himself part of that pack. His stomach heaves as, down in front, on the strip of grass this side of the touchline, he watches the soldiers massing in response to the crowd. The eight who'd been initially spread across the width of the field behind the goal double in number and continue to gather until they are standing just a few paces apart and studying the crowd with expressions of stone, the earlier joviality gone or buried, rifles eager and at the ready.

A part of him wants to run. There's been talk of some kind of camp going up, in Mauthausen, not far from Linz, where he has relatives, for the internment of prisoners, criminal types. Those friends of his who are talking of getting out insist that the next few years will mark the end of the Jews across this stretch of Europe. For weeks he has sat in the cafe while friends indulged in such speculation, but as upsetting as such talk could be, its reality has remained at a distance. Seeing the soldiers so close and at the ready changes that. Even if today goes better than he anticipates, he suspects he'll no longer breathe with any kind of freedom.

Around him, again, the crowd stirs and finally a deeper roar begins, a war cry at first felt more than heard, registered as an irresistible pounding from within, that same directionless immensity. His eyes are wide open and huge in anticipation, knowing what is happening or about to but even so wanting it confirmed, the explosion sourced, and now the roar is a swelling boom, feasting on individual voices and the heavy tannoy static of some announcer trying impossibly to speak his piece. In an instant he exists within the monstrous, threshing chorus of sixty thousand baying voices, that number and who knows how many thousand more, with maximum capacity an ideal rather than a truth.

THE TWO TEAMS come out onto the pitch from the far left corner, the Austrians, no matter what the scoreboard insists on calling them, at Sindelar's behest forgoing their usual white tops and black shorts for red shirts, white trunks, and red socks in representation of the flag that, after today, will fly no more. Most of the players on both sides run but the Paper Man, distinct even from a distance in his appearance and gait, strolls into view, his left hand holding a shabby brown ball against his ribs.

The German players, full of nervous energy, hit the sunlight and fan out like scattershot before charging in a full-blown dash to the far end of the field, Hartmann's end, then fall without pausing for breath into a vigorous warm-up routine of sprints, stretches and scissors jumps. But as impressive as their display might be, it is made quickly inconsequential because Sindelar, who has taken up a position in the centre of the field, sends a long sweeping pass back to Sesta at the edge of the penalty area, leaps to take the slightly overhit return on his chest and, with bored nonchalance, sets about juggling the ball from foot to foot, and onto his knee, and now and then up onto his head, keeping it alive and moving in gainly loops, even after the referee's whistle sounds the call to order. The players of both teams trot to the right-hand sideline and form an orderly arrangement either side of midfield ahead of the various official presentations and the playing of the anthem, but Sindelar keeps on with his private game and for a full minute more the fun continues, the ball leaping as if a thing alive from his boot, knee or forehead, never for an instant beyond his control. His audience watches, restrained despite itself, as if afraid to disturb the spell being cast. And then, abruptly, he nudges the ball high, sets himself for balance and, as it drops, connects on the half-volley, sending a shot the remaining half-length of the pitch and into the empty German goal just beneath the crossbar. The net ripples and the crowd, reading the gesture for what must surely be its intent, once more explodes.

Finally, Sindelar joins his teammates, moving to the end of the line beside Platzer, his goalkeeper, to take up the captain's spot. His restlessness is apparent. While the others hold still, facing the stand and feeling themselves overlooked from the high decks by the array of dignitaries and officials who have crammed into four or five rows, the area cordoned off entirely from the public by SS guards, Sindelar bounces and jumps, rolls his neck and stretches out his hamstrings. He raises his arm as the others do when the anthem begins but stops short of straightening the gesture of salute and keeps his head and gaze determinedly and noticeably averted, and before the music has played itself out he drops away, down into a stoop to undo and retie the laces of his boots, giving the task a surgical concentration, taking his time even when the referee's whistle blows again to draw the teams into position. His teammates pat his shoulder or ruffle his hair as they pass, so that he is immediately and comically dishevelled, and Stroh leans in and says something that with the crowd noise having lifted again is mostly lost but which seems to refer to balls. Typical of the big man. 'These sons of bitches have you marked,' he shouts, his mouth nearly to Sindelar's ear in an effort to be heard. 'So, nothing stupid, all right? Don't give them the excuse.' Stroh's grin pulls wider, which only intensifies the worry that is tightening his expression. 'And make sure to keep well in from the sidelines. That's where the gunners are.'

The game itself is a frustration and, after such a build-up, anticlimactic. Within ten minutes of play it is obvious to all in the stadium that the Germans are deeply outclassed, that they can't live with the speed of Austria's passing and movement, and if this plays out as it should there can be no right outcome but a double-figures massacre. The clearness of the afternoon has stripped the field entirely of shadow, leaving nowhere to hide and no blushes spared. Desperate to avoid outright humiliation, the visitors try putting two of their toughest players on Sindelar and for a while the game turns predictably rough, and even, in a few instances, violent. But after a long and arduous career spent enduring such attention, for most of the first half Sindelar dictates the pace with a striking display of one-touch efficiency, opening up the full width and span of the field with deft flicks, lay-offs and long, raking precision passes, pulling the German defence apart and giving his wingers fullest rein on either flank, Stroh out on the left side, Pesser down the right wing. The tackles that come at him, even the late and dirtiest ones, are easily anticipated, and when he finally allows one to get close it is only so that, in drawing the foul, he can fall into a certain heap and in the process bring a hard knee to his opponent's groin, the knock apparently entirely accidental but enough to restrict his marker's ambitions for the remainder of the game.

The first half finishes scoreless, forty-five minutes defined by several wasted Austrian opportunities; Stroh going close with a header at a corner and then, again, with a strike from the edge of the box after cutting in from the left flank, and the normally clinical Franz Binder also twice firing wide when unmarked and in space from just six or eight yards out. But it is a moment shortly before the half ends that speaks most loudly of something underhand at play, when Sindelar collects the ball midway inside the German half and instead of switching possession out to one of the wings, as he's been so far doing, sets off on a run, weaving in and out of lunging tackles, driving into the box and entirely wrong-footing the goalkeeper with an audacious dummy. Then, with the goal at his mercy and the entire stadium awaiting a simple tap-in, he hesitates as if for effect and strokes the ball a few inches the wrong side of the near post.

Hartmann is at this end, but across the goal, packed into the terrace maybe thirty yards away, and even after the ball has gone wide he can't quite accept what he has seen, the display of skill elegant to the point of sublime and then, somehow, the incomprehensibility of the miss. The crowd noise lifts, full of anguish, but before the ball can even be put back into play the half-time whistle sounds and the teams trot off for the far corner and a temporary escape to the dressing-room area.

With the players' departure a kind of deflation follows. All that's just happened is considered in shouts, scrutinised and somehow made sense of, or at least justified, and only then, finally, laughed about, such a blatant miss declared obviously intentional and, what's more, savage in its goading. There's no predicting what Sindelar will try in the second half. Maybe stop the ball on the goal line and sit on it. After what the crowd have already witnessed, it'll take something that extreme to further salt the wound. And it's anyone's guess, too, what the newspapers will write about today, assuming that the articles haven't already been written.

In the Austrian dressing room, nobody has much to say. A pair of soldiers guard the propped-open door, seeing and overhearing everything. Barely out of boyhood, trying to make themselves staunch by clenching their jaws and avoiding everybody's eye, they know of Sindelar and have likely even seen him play, cheered his skills and out in the street or on some piece of waste ground with their friends, probably even attempted to replicate, feebly, his more audacious flicks and movements. But that excitement is fixed firmly in another time, and now they stand here with guns, facing into a different world. Tomorrow, if Sindelar wants to be considered as such, they'll view him as a brother, but today, while he is putting them to the sword, there can be no smiles, no ease. He sits against the dressing room's far wall, facing them but with his head lowered, hunched forward, socks rolled down around his ankles. The team coaches pace the floor, cautious about what instructions can be given. One of them, a heavyset man with wild flaps of hair the colour of which, despite his obviously advancing age, reminding of nothing so much as autumn leaves, russets and browns, talks of keeping the game tight and the passing fluid, the way they've been doing, controlling the tempo. Let technique stand as the difference between the sides. And as for goals, well, a no-score draw won't be the worst scoreline. None of the players react, not even Sindelar, since these are words that in one variation or another have been repeated over and over in the weeks prior to this game's commencing. Sindelar studies the floor, in absent-minded fashion kneading his bad knee with both hands, and when the team stirs once again to life, the others readying themselves to get back out on the pitch, he remains still. And within half a minute he is alone.

AT FIRST NO one notices. The players take the field again, the Austrians making for the goal they'd in the first half attacked, and after a few routine warm-up stretches fall into their various assigned positions. Hartmann, at their backs now, only registers the absence of the Paper Man at the same moment that the rest of the crowd does, and there is an audible gasp that quickly stirs into a discontented rumbling. With the team set out in formation, his place on the pitch, the deep-lying forward spot, has opened a chasm. But before the jeering can turn properly rancorous, he appears, strolling at leisure onto the German end of the pitch and pointedly ignoring what remarks the opposition defence, out of duty or obligation, start hurling at him. Though it may also be that he simply doesn't hear them, such is the racket of welcoming applause, a huge, relieved wall of sound that builds and sustains itself at a level that smothers all other noise, that obliterates thought.

He moves up into the centre of the field to where Franz Binder, his strike partner, stands waiting, ball beneath one boot, alongside the referee, and without disturbing his easy amble takes, following a single shrill blast of the whistle, the touch that gets the second half under way.

This second period proves even more of a mockery than what has gone before. As fit as the Germans think themselves, the opening forty-five minutes spent running and harrying has left them badly off the pace, and in a central channel between the halfway line and the edge of his opponents' eighteen-yard box, Sindelar owns the ball. Roughhousing doesn't help, even with a Berlin referee calling the game, double- and in desperation sometimes triple-marking only exposes new gaps in the defence that Sindelar exploits effortlessly and at will. Within the first few minutes of the second half he has hit the right post twice with shots from the edge of the box and from just inside, and dropped the ball onto the crossbar from all of thirty yards, efforts that have him smiling and waving to the crowd behind the goal. On the third occasion, after the long-range strike, he actually stops and takes a bow, much to the approval of everyone packing the terrace at this end. The crowd would rather count goals but are happy enough to sing loud, appreciative support for the kind of game their maestro has chosen to play, this exercise in grand humiliation. Most here must already know—though they'll resist speaking of it, not wanting to give it air in the world—that a limit is set on just how many more times Sindelar will be seen in fullest pomp, which makes this performance so worth savouring. When he runs, even at thirty-five, it is like watching a great dancer, that same godly elegance of power, grace and musicality, and against it the Germans have no choice but to abandon their strategy of hard tackling and instead fall back, trying, since nothing else is working, to pack the defence and with sheer numbers block his route to goal. Still, he glides and slaloms among them, and with scoring seemingly no longer the intent or motivation, every touch, pass and dribble becomes a small glory in and of itself, an exhibition in the purest sense.

Why he waits until twenty minutes from the finish to put the Austrians ahead, nobody can say. After witnessing a wondrous, flaunting hour-long demonstration of virtually unmatchable skill and dexterity, the Prater's crowd have begun to abandon all hope or expectation of a goal, and when it does come, it is a chance so quickly taken that many see nothing but the instant aftermath, the bulge of the net and the ball nestled in its bottom corner, and Sindelar, in that familiar way, throwing his hands in the air and wheeling away in leaping delight. Those few—Hartmann among them—who do catch it see the merest glimpse of a deflected shot breaking hard and fast from the left side of the box to where Sindelar is standing in space by the penalty spot and, without even setting himself, he smashes home a volley to break the deadlock. It is a strike as instinctual as any of the several hundred he's scored in his long career, and given the enthusiasm with which he celebrates, to him clearly more precious.

Now the stadium's volume lifts to deafening levels, and on the terrace behind the home goal the jumping and heaving threatens a stampede. But nobody cares. Penned in as they are, there is nowhere to fall, and because of the compaction the ecstasy has no escape, except upwards. Hartmann shouts with everyone else and feels himself letting go, disconnecting into rapture. In this moment, the thousands crammed together on these concrete steps under the studied glare of Hitler or Goebbels or whoever it is that holds the most senior rank here today, jump and scream and sing at levels previously unknown to their voices and throats, and they embrace as brothers and sisters and feel, within the seconds' beating, free.

There can be no return to any kind of calm, but for reasons of formality the match must resume, and the Germans, although now eviscerated, get things under way again, only to quickly lose possession and fall back, their single intent now being to brace against what can fast become a rout. But the Austrians, too, seem stunned, and they move the ball only by rote, ceding to years of honed technique, passing, slipping into space, keeping possession at times at a saunter and then in bursts suddenly shifting direction, one-touching the play back and forth across the field, toying with their foe like picadors around a weary bull, lancing and weaving away, moving as wind moves. And among them, the Paper Man conducts the onslaught, young-seeming again despite his harried look, his baldness and his spidery body, floating almost, rather than running, a dancer still but a prizefighter too, with stone in his punches. He doesn't try for further glory, attempts no more shots, though this is now simply a matter of choice since it is clear that he can do so at will, the Germans having backed off to such an extent, surrendering the field to him until he gets to within twenty-five or twenty yards of their goal. Instead of strikes then, the crowd is presented with a show of vision and touch, passes no one else would attempt to make. And as time runs down there's no sadness, no more sorrow. Tomorrow will bring a fresh tide of that, and all who are here will weigh the joy of now against the falling away of everything that is solid, and some then will weep, when alone and with a chance to properly think and count the cost. But out here, with the game still going, there is no tomorrow, there's only the world as it is, with a bright sun warming a clear day after so many bitter ones. And for Sindelar there is the alive feeling of running, the particular sense of capability with the ball at his feet.

Shortly before the end, a rare German advance brings about a foul, an overeager collision but with the attacker's studs left in out of frustration after a long, wearing day, and Sesta launches the resultant free kick forward from deep in his own half. Sindelar is loitering just inside the German box, with Binder a few yards beyond him. As cursory targets they move in and jump with their markers, challenging more out of duty than ambition, but the ball is high and the goalkeeper, impeded by his own climbing defenders and maybe, too, by the brightness of the day, can get no more than a touch on it. The long kick drops behind him and rolls into the net, by accident doubling the scoreline.

At the final whistle, nobody celebrates harder than Sindelar. He runs to each teammate and shakes hands, embraces Stroh, Sesta and one or two others, those players he's closest to and who he has lined up alongside for years, and applauds the crowd who rise in ferocious appreciation, making a cauldron of the stadium. Understanding that the cheers are for him, he breaks away from his teammates into the centre of the field and for twenty, thirty seconds accepts the acclaim. Then something in his demeanour turns steely, and after drawing and releasing a long, quivering breath he turns and jogs to the sideline where he'd earlier stood, arm so grudgingly raised, for the German anthem. Hartmann watches from the terrace with growing disquiet, and the wall of cheering turns markedly heavy and starts to sag.

How the dignitaries, the top brass, react is open to speculation. They are likely appreciative of being singled out for such broad public acknowledgement and probably stand and smile, in the moment deciding to overlook the insult of the scoreline, since this makes up for it, this is what people will remember. They watch—Hitler, if he is here, watches—surely expecting a wave, a bow, possibly even a salute, some expression of respect and due subservience. This is conjecture; while in the months and years to come it will be discussed and dissected in relentless fashion, not one fan who was present this day in the Prater can report with accuracy on the reaction of the Nazi elite. Instead, every gaze is bound tightly to the star of the show, the Paper Man, every breath held in dreadful anticipation of what will happen when he reaches the sideline: will he fall in humbling genuflection from his heroic height, or throw himself down as Austria's martyr, ready to sacrifice himself to the lions and be torn to pieces? Either way, it has the feel of a Colosseum moment.

The consensus view of what happens is that he stops on the sideline, looks up without fluster or hurry, having apparently found some state of peace. He takes his fill of the watching faces and recognises some from pictures he's seen in the papers, noting even from his distance how their smirks stiffen with the hatred that defines them and underlies everything of who they are. Then in a measured and yet seemingly entirely natural way, he extends his left arm to its fullest from his side, brings his right hand loosely to the centre of his stomach and, as his eyes fall shut and some inner music overcomes him, begins to sway in a slow and stately waltz. There is noise again, huge in greeting and growing ever more immense, but it remains for him at a remove. In his mind there is only the dance, the canting one-two-three rhythm as innate to him in darkness as a ball at his feet in daylight, and in his arms, if the world could only see, there is Rebekah, his love, gliding with him, the thought of her filling him with strength and hope. He dances at ease along the touchline, turning as the steps dictate, fifteen paces along and as many back, and he is not even halfway through when the racket that he has been holding at bay surges through and over him with the force of a dam breaking. At first he tries to stand against it by squeezing his eyes more tightly shut, but after a moment, understanding what the tumult is, what it means, the defiant howl of it for those roaring him on, he smilingly turns and weaves, letting the waves pass through him but drawing the thought of Beka all the closer.

When the dance ends he can hardly breathe. For several seconds he stands there, left arm still extended, his mind washed of thought and his chest on fire. He is afraid to open his eyes because he understands that nothing will have changed, nothing can have, the same few faces will be gazing down on him, scowling or stoic in their disdain, and the sun will still shine with lying brightness, as if everything is all right and everything is going to be, giving false warmth to a day that is still more winter yet than spring.

He is alone. The other players hold back from him, counting on safety in numbers, the Germans and Austrians alike since survival comes at a price, not quite brothers, not as the politicians like to insist, but certainly more alike as men than different. But he *is* different. He's the only one dancing.

The stadium seems set to collapse, the volume now like bombs going off. If this is to be the last reason the Austrian people have to cheer then they seem determined to make the most of it. Because he hasn't planned any of this he is at a loss as to how he should proceed. For an instant there still seems the possibility of a way out, some gesture that'll make the waltz a gift, all part of the pageant, rather than a barefaced slandering. A bow could make some strange formality out of what he has just done, and perhaps cause the Nazis in the cordoned-off area to second-guess the intent of what they've seen. But except for the thought of Rebekah, who is somewhere in the stadium looking on, cheering with all the strength she has and most likely weeping with fear and excitement for him, everything feels fragmented. In this instant he wishes for nothing more than to have her out here on the field with him for all the crowd and all the world to see, her hand in his, her smile damp and warm from his greeting kiss. And then, all at once, the feeling of solitude turns him heavy, and he knows for certain what to do. Without a further glance up at the dignitaries that he has already so thoroughly snubbed, he turns away and starts off at an unhurried walk that seems a mirror image of how he initially entered the fray, disappearing down along the sideline towards the dressing rooms. Smiling, apparently at peace, he is in fact more worn out than he's ever been, his legs barely with strength enough to keep him upright.

He bathes in dirty, tepid water, the last one into the tub, and remains soaking for so long that when he finally emerges the others have all dressed and the doorway is crowded with newspapermen and fans eager to catch a glimpse of their stars and maybe, if they are fortunate, to grab a few quotable words. Making himself deaf to the doorway crowd's haranguing, and content to be ignored by his teammates and trainers, none of them knowing quite what to say, he moves into the corner and stands naked, towels himself dry and gets into his best suit, the one he's had cleaned and pressed ahead of today, thinking it might be the last time he'll get to wear it. Then he sits, reaches for the newspaper that Stroh has left badly folded on the bench, smooths it out and leafs through the first few pages. He flicks past reports of the Nationalists gaining the upper hand in Catalonia and on to the kind of article that today he decides is the only one worth reading: how Joe Louis retained the heavyweight title last Friday night in Chicago with a fifth-round knockout of Harry Thomas, a win that will now surely set up a rematch with Max Schmeling, the former champ who, just two years ago, had taken the Brown Bomber in twelve rounds. This rematch, with talk already of it taking place as early as June, is set to be a fight for the ages.

Two men push in through the doorway, the crowd quietening and parting without fuss for them. Young but possessing a distinct air of authority, they are tall and lean in finely tailored dark grey suits. They wait in the centre of the floor until a soldier steps in behind them, clutching a rifle, and without fuss clears the onlookers. A few other players are still idling in chat over beside a window, but because they pretend to ignore what is going on they are let be. The two men approach Sindelar and stand before him. He looks up only briefly from the newspaper, and nods to acknowledge them. 'No autographs,' he says, returning his gaze to the print and turning the page lazily. Neither man reacts, or softens, and finally Sindelar lowers the paper with a sigh and considers them again, this time with more formality.

'Congratulations,' the man on the left says.

Sindelar looks from one face to the other, trying to appear unconcerned. The stares coming at him feel nailed in place, punctures in the surface of the day. 'Thanks,' he says, fighting off an urge to clear his throat. 'But the score should have been five times what it was. We hardly broke a sweat.'

'I am not referring to the game.' The man on the right holds out an envelope, which Sindelar glances at but doesn't move to accept. 'This is to inform you that you have been selected for the German national team's upcoming games, against Portugal at the end of the month, and, three weeks later, against England. Both are to be played in Berlin, in preparation for the World Cup.'

They wait, seemingly expecting some show of gratitude.

'An honour, indeed, gentlemen,' Sindelar says, matching the formality of their speech in a teasing, mocking way. He straightens and folds the newspaper with exaggerated care and sets it down on the bench beside him. 'Unfortunately, as of half an hour ago, I've retired. It's this knee. After twenty years of having lumps kicked out of it, I'm lucky to still be upright. I mean, I can manage well enough against your lot, but I couldn't survive five minutes on the same pitch as England. So it's time to stop. Sorry to disappoint, but my decision has been made.'

Perhaps it's the assurance of his tone that disturbs them the most. They remain standing, not speaking but glaring, until he reaches once more for the paper, shuffles through the pages and returns his attention to the piece he'd abandoned at their interruption, reading with thorough focus until, after a minute or so, understanding they have been dismissed and all of a sudden not so confident of their authority, they turn and leave. At the sound of the door being slammed, he lowers the paper and with a continued air of calm meets the stares of those teammates who have been watching from across the room, but their expressions surrender nothing and nobody has anything to say.

SHORTLY BEFORE NINE o'clock that evening, Hartmann locates Sindelar in one of the Favoriten cafes, sitting at a table with Rebekah at his side. Across from them is Viertl, with a companion who can be no older than her late teens perched crossways on his lap and with an arm draped limply around his neck. She is Hungarian, she says, even though no one asked, from a small village near Budapest. Hartmann can't recall having seen her before, but Viertl, admittedly already somewhat drunk, refers to her repeatedly as his fiancée, possibly because he is unsure of her name. The victory celebrations are well intentioned yet muted, a distinctive melancholia present beneath the surface joviality.

'Weren't you tempted, at all?' Viertl is asking, pouring a new round of schnapps from a half-empty bottle. Absently, he serves the new arrival too. Still standing and before he has taken off his coat, Hartmann drains the glass at a hard swallow and holds it out for a quick refill. Then he settles on the bench beside Rebekah, in the place to her left that has been reserved for him, smilingly accepts the welcome kiss that she plants on his offered cheek, and waits like an obedient child while she rubs away the smear of lipstick with her thumb.

Sindelar, on her other side, shrugs. 'I'd have liked to face England again, and go against Matthews, see if he's as good as they say. But not in a German shirt. I'd rather cut off my foot than play for them.'

The girl on Viertl's lap—Ana, her name is—has a chunky silver charm bracelet that sags from the thinnest wrist Hartmann has ever seen, and when she caresses Viertl's cheek, trying to keep his attention close, the metal's shifting links catch the lamplight. Her hair, the stained redwood shade of iodine, is cut up in a mess around her shoulders, as if she's been dragged by it, had fistfuls of it pulled, yet Hartmann knows there's intent behind such a look, a new young style of wild delight that only seems out of kilter to men of his age. She leans in with laughing kisses but Viertl, also of the older generation himself, ignores her.

'They probably felt you'd had your day,' he says, still watching Sindelar, his eyes bright with sudden fun. 'Otherwise they'd have tried talking you round.'

Sindelar reaches for his schnapps. 'It's true. I am past it. Ten years ago, five years ago, I'd have taken that team apart.'

Hartmann catches the attention of the waiter across the room and raises the bottle to signal his request for another. While they wait for the fresh schnapps to arrive, he tops up the glasses on the table with what little remains, attending to the women first, then

Viertl. The final half a shot's worth, he pours for Sindelar, who swallows it without hesitation.

'What was that, today, if not taking the team apart? Plenty are getting it in the neck for far less than the stunt you pulled. It's a wonder they didn't shoot you while you ran from the pitch.'

'The sixty thousand witnesses probably made them think better of it.'

'Maybe. But there won't always be a crowd watching. If you want my advice, Mutzl, you'll keep a low profile. Get out of town for a while.'

Though there's the chance of bravado, or passing such talk off as a joke, Sindelar doesn't smile. And Rebekah, beside him, looks on the brink of tears. She has slipped a hand inside his arm and is holding on.

Across the table, Ana is kissing Viertl. He seems embarrassed, and is gently trying to push her away, but the schnapps has peeled back her inhibitions. She writhes on his lap for better traction and turns her upper body square to him to tighten the embrace. The waiter arrives with the bottle and begins to pour, doing his utmost not to stare, though he is young himself, probably of an age with her, and it may even be that they know each other. Rebekah watches him work, reading the run of his mind that he masks behind stiff movements, but it's only when he has half circled the table and leans in to fill her own glass that she realises he probably assumes she and Viertl's girl are the same age. As a waiter in a bustling coffee house, he is used to seeing girls and young women desperately seeking affection in the company and form of older men. The thought of being so reduced, in the same instant noticed and dismissed, hurts her, partly because she recognises the truth of it. With her tears close, she lifts her glass, and when a flare of passion so overcomes the pair across the table that they have no choice but to force themselves apart, the group as a whole sets its focus on the schnapps. They take turns pouring and raising toasts, to glory days and various absent friends, drinking fast, all of them wanting oblivion but—except possibly for Ana, who is new to this scene and who might at some point fall by the wayside—unable to properly let go, aware that the night stretching on from here will be a long one and that, with the morning's eventual dawn, the Vienna awaiting them will be a far cry from the city they've always known.

Jewtown

Cork, 1980

THE AIR IS cold, those raw streams of it that come slashing through the separations between the rows of old brick terraces, and Jack Shine has to brace himself against the sting. When a gale is blowing in across the Lee, Jewtown, the cluster of small homes tucked in behind the city's docks, feels like the edge of the world, the last of the landfall, with no place left to run. His jacket is too flimsy for the sleety cold of a Sunday afternoon in February, and facing into the maw of the wind, whenever the lane bends in that direction, fills him with faraway tastes until his eyes sting and start to water.

He has already walked these same steps half a dozen times over the past two hours, traipsing back and forth the two hundred yards of street-maze between his uncle Joe's small Hibernian Buildings home—the house in which Jack had been born and reared and which is now, finally, after so much talk, up for sale—and the even smaller house that he is currently renting with his wife and child, over on Marina Terrace. For more than a century, this discreet corner of the city has been referred to, casually, as Jewtown, a settling place for those who'd fled the Lithuanian shtetls ahead of the marauding Russian army. Those who didn't or couldn't carry on to Ellis Island, or who, caught out by the language, so the old joke went, had mistaken Cork for New York, spilt from the ships out into the nearest slum area of a place whose name most of them probably didn't yet even know, and took root amid the tenements on the south bank of the River Lee. Not much perhaps, but safe, offering hope at least, and shelter. Sanctuary, at worst. A lot of the original families have moved on, but the area retains its nickname, because Cork is a place of long memory, and if the slums have progressed to something better in the hundred years since then the majority of these terraces continue to house modest types: men and women who roll up their sleeves to work and who keep their horizons close and their ambitions small.

At the request of Liz, this Sunday is all about hauling boxes and black plastic bags packed with old lives lived and spent, using the one house for storing in order to empty the other. Liz, his mother's cousin but more like a sister for her during the time they'd had together. Even acknowledging the modesty of the age difference, with just sixteen years separating her birth date from his own, practically a second mother to him, not only when he was a child and most in need of one, but in the years since, up until her husband's job had taken them initially to Dublin and then, some five years back, to Aberdeen. For the first couple of hours he had worked steadily and well, holding up against the inevitable emotional heft of the task at hand, the sheer finality of stripping bare a house that has really been the only proper home he's ever known. Until a chance discovery narrowed in a stunning instant the divide between the present and the past and turned his mind chaotic. But because it's all too much just now, and with such a lot still to be done, he has pressed on, refusing it the space in his head and concentrating instead only on the bleak coldness of the day and the slow physicality of his movements, the sheer bodily satisfaction of this manual labour.

A few boys, stuck between the ages of seven or eight and early teens, are playing football in the street, their game without shape or seeming purpose, but keeping nonetheless to some quick-paced one- or two-touch order that makes the orange rubber ball seem a thing alive. They hesitate in order to let him pass, but otherwise pay him little heed, locked as they are into their lit-stadium fantasy beneath a littering hail of ticker tape. Jack is too much a part of this place, too comfortably familiar, for them to even acknowledge him, and too out of shape to join in. And just beyond the boys, a couple of girls, again probably twelve or thirteen years old, have a game of pickie going, taking turns with a palm-sized, disc-shaped shoe-polish tin that, given the clunky sound it makes when tossed down into one of the road's white-chalked hopscotch boxes, has obviously been weighted by a stone. It is a game they know by heart, and their play is inevitably cursory, their attention, betrayed in little covert glances, fettered to the running boys. The taller of the two girls skips from one foot to both and back onto one again, following the pattern of the play and singing along in breathless rhyme, then bends like a crane, skirt flapping around her white legs and skinned knees, and scoops up the tin can for another go. Her sand-coloured hair swims in the wind, and it is clear to Jack from the backward glance she steals as she lowers herself with impressive balance that she is hoping the boys, no doubt one of them specifically, are watching or will happen to look her way, and notice her.

Aside from the two large plastic bags that have him struggling along, Jack is carrying, wedged under one arm, a twine-bound grey cardboard shoebox. It's what he discovered, bearded in dust and probably decades hidden, tucked away on top of a wardrobe, pushed right in to fill most of the ten inches or so of space beneath the ceiling, in the bedroom that Liz and his mother had once shared—his mother, Rebekah, who'd come over from Vienna just ahead of the war. Personality-wise, where Rebekah was timid, silent to a fault and easily cowed, the kind to hold herself to smallness in any room, Liz had a confidence, and at times an aggression, that made her precious as an ally and which kept most people on edge around her. That was survival, she'd explained, more than once over the years, usually whenever Jack raised the subject of his mother. Coming up as she did put brass in her neck, and you were either born to that or you weren't. Cork of the thirties and forties might have been modest by most standards but its dockside areas in particular still possessed all the sins and shadowy corners typical of such places the world over. And while it was true that Rebekah had arrived here from Vienna, as vibrant and cosmopolitan a city as any in Europe, especially in those years before the war, she'd originally been country born and bred and had kept her preference for silences and slower ways.

Jack has left the front door of his home on the latch, and entering after such bombardment of breeze feels like stepping close to a blazing fire. Through in the living room, Hannah, his little girl, on her knees on the floor and using one half of the settee as a desk, is busily colouring in whatever she's just drawn, while his wife, Rachel, perched alongside, oversees the work with a contented smile.

'Hi, Daddy,' the child says, without lifting her attention from her art.

'Hi, love,' he says, feeling his voice far away from himself.

Rachel looks up at him and starts to speak, then registering something in his expression, some element of strain, seems to bite down on her words.

The hearth is a neglected redness, and he crosses the room, shifts the cinders in the grate with a clod of turf until he can get it well bedded and adds a split block from the half-sack of birch logs that he bought on the docks from one of the men whose brother or cousin has a line going in firewood. Then, satisfied, he drops down into the armchair left of the fireplace, putting the window at his back with its net curtains diffusing the light, sieving it of its sharpness and turning it frail ahead of first dusk. The cardboard box rests on his knees, held in place by his two flattened palms, and it is only when, after some seconds have passed, his wife clears her throat, that he is drawn out of his distant trance.

She stares at the box.

He notices and nods, as much to himself as to her, as if granting himself permission, and he slowly picks undone the knot of the binding string and after just a heartbeat's hesitation lifts away the lid. The contents are neatly bundled, wrapped in red velvet cloth and meticulously tied in broad white ribbon, which he unfurls and spreads with care out across the old teak coffee table. The cache comprises four badly yellowed newspaper clippings, a pair of faded hand-sized photographs, and a sheaf of letters—twenty-three of them, once counted, not as straightforward a task as it might initially seem since several of them run to two or even three front- and back-filled pages. For the next few minutes, while Hannah continues with her drawing, they sift through the pile, passing pieces back and forth between them and handling everything with the utmost care, particularly the newspaper cuttings, which are heavily creased and made so brittle by time that it feels as if the least wrong touch will see them crumble to dust.

The room is silent apart from the ticking of the old tambour mantel clock, gifted to Jack some six years earlier as a memento of his mother's first cousin Joe, Liz's father, following the old man's sudden passing. It was one of the few possessions that Joe had carried across to Ireland from Cham, the small south-eastern German town close to the Czech border where he'd first seen the light of day, a piece even at that point already generations-old and, therefore, precious, its movement forged and shaped within yards, supposedly, of the family home, its oak casing drawn from the nearby Bavarian forests and carved in beautifully decorative shoulder scrolls. Jack can't recall a time without its beating, and often marvels at the knack it has of lifting its voice in seemingly random moments up out of the general white noise of the world to encroach hard on the listener's consciousness, forcing him to wonder what there is about it, when its running has been in no way altered, that has him all of a sudden registering its presence again. And becoming so sharply aware of it now turns this Sunday afternoon strange because a memory breaks in his mind of how much Rebekah, after she'd fallen ill, had liked to sit in the stillness of an early morning, slowing herself to an almost prayerful tranquillity and simply absorbing the steady rhythm of the clock's ticking. *I am watching time run*, she told him once, when he'd asked what she was doing. *And listening to it all pass by*. He has many recollections of his mother, and his head teems with details grabbed and held on to from the eleven years they'd had together, but this particular memory is one that he'd either all but forgotten or hadn't known he'd even packed away. And hearing the clock now, contemplating where each second goes and where it stacks all of the things it carries, he can't help but feel her somehow attached to the sound, the steady heart-beating quality of its ticking, and still, in this small, odd way, with him and with them all. When he meets Rachel's stare, across the coffee table and the spill of old words, he has the strangest sense that she is reading his mind.

'German,' she mutters. She again trawls the sentences of the letter she is holding, her lips moving slightly and in silence, trying to feel their shape. Then, finally, she returns it to the coffee table with the spill of others and slumps back into the settee, her frustration evident. 'I know a little, but the old ink is hard to make out, and the handwriting is shocking.' She takes a breath and hesitates with it. 'But I think they're love letters, Jack.'

The way they have been kept and obviously treasured, with the ribbon and velvet wrapping, certainly suggests the precious keepsakes of a sweetheart, or at least someone more than just a passing fancy. Having grown up without a father, or even, really, the knowledge of one, Jack has long since learned to keep those empty parts of himself shielded, to a point where he hardly thinks in those directions any more. Now, without understanding yet the full implications of what he's found, it's as if he's been struck and knocked askew. The stillness of the afternoon seems mocking. He picks up the largest of the four newspaper cuttings and studies the few emboldened inch-high words of headline: DER PAPIERENE TOT—loud-seeming beneath the paper's header, *Neue Freie Presse*, and leading on to several dense paragraphs of text laid out in three columns, but the only detail he can properly comprehend is the date, *24. Januar 1939*.

'You should speak to my father.' Rachel's own expression has tightened—in response, he knows, to what she is seeing in his face: the sadness and dread at having uncovered something quite possibly easier left hidden. Her mouth, usually so pretty, tucking in as it does at the corners to dimple her cheeks, has this time drawn itself slatted, and her pale blue eyes glisten silver in the heavy glare of the light. 'His mother was from Lübeck, and he was reared speaking German. He'll know what to make of all this if anyone will. We'll have a better sense of it once he takes a look.'

Jack nods but doesn't answer. She's right, of course, but what she has said doesn't begin to cover all that he is feeling. The details of the letters seem actually somehow separate from this moment; for now, simply holding them is significant in itself, and enough. A quick perusal has assured him that none of what's written here is in his mother's hand, yet he can hardly breathe for the unexpected sense of connection to her, the tangible intensity of it, so suddenly after so long. She'll be dead thirty-one years come May. An eternity, a chasm wide as galaxies and yet somehow, also, a mere gasp ago. Over the years he has often registered the scale of her absence, feeling the hole it put in otherwise precious moments—his wedding day, for example, or the morning of his daughter's birth, having them incomplete and that much short of perfect without her being there to kiss his cheek. In this instant, though, it's as if she is once again beside him, and he can almost believe that if he were just to turn his head he'd see her, smiling with pride and full of love for what she has helped create, but sad, too, in that accepting way at having had to miss so much. The shadow of loss never completely fades, though he is not entirely sure whether the twinge of grief he feels is genuinely for her or for that long-ago part of himself, the ten-year-old boy so innocent yet of the world. His young days remain with him in striking detail, and against that reality the relative stasis of adulthood often stands in pale comparison.

He rises from the armchair with the sense of having slipped his moorings. But because he can feel Rachel's eyes on him, and her concern, he sets his shoulders in his usual strong way, assuring her that there is nothing wrong, that he is still in control. It's a lie, but one that he has honed to mastery, and it makes the day easier to bear, for both of them, at least on a surface level.

From the small cabinet in the corner by the window, he stoops and takes out two heavy Waterford Crystal glasses. The set, completed by an accompanying decanter, was a wedding gift from Rachel's mother's sister and, really, apart from the clock, their family's only truly quality possession. The cut design is sharp against Jack's fingers, and the glass itself has a coldness that presses deep. There is a bottle of Jameson tucked away in the same cupboard and still half full, probably six months on from having been initially opened. Jack is not much of a drinker, unlike so many of the dockers who go at it both-handed at the Sextant or the Harp Bar and are perfectly capable of pissing away a full week's wages on a single Friday night, if their wives don't show up in time to salvage part of the pay packet. Some of them jibe that it's a Jewish problem, the reluctance to prise open his wallet, but he just laughs such talk away because, at his age, forty-one, and having spent the entirety of his working life among the crates, he is well used to it and worse. What he has in his life is more than he ever wants to risk. Stevedoring is low-paid and physically trying, and while Rachel is adept at managing on what he earns to cover the cost of food, basic necessities and a rent stiff enough even on so modest a home as theirs, come the end of the week there is usually not a lot going spare, and something as trifling as alcohol feels like an unjustifiable indulgence.

He pours the drink, attending to Rachel first, offering her just a drop, because even though she'll barely touch it, whiskey being far too raw for her taste, he wants and needs her to feel part of this. The afternoon has a sense of ritual about it, the silence and rainy brightness carrying the significance of something worth raising a glass to. The old house going up for sale marks the end of an era, but these letters, dragging back the past as they have, feel like the start of something more. As he splashes a careful measure into his own glass, the crystal is kissed by the bottle's mouth and sings out a piercing birdsong note that sustains itself for long seconds until awareness of the clock's ticking once more pervades the room. He lifts his glass and drinks, and Rachel, after a hesitation, does the same, sipping in tiny whispers.

The two photographs lie on the settee cushion beside her, where they've been carefully set down. In unpacking the bundle and thumbing through the letters, Jack had purposely avoided them, not yet prepared for the face they might depict, but with the whiskey hot in his chest he has a sudden desire, a need, even, to see. He holds out a hand and Rachel passes them across.

His throat has that constricted sense, that same painful throbbing that you sometimes feel when you need to cry but don't want to give in to it. But after the anticipation, there is, at least initially, a degree of anticlimax. The pictures, little more than cigarette-box-sized and faded as they are, dirty tobacco shades of brown and grey, thunder-clouded from clarity, seem so slight and inconsequential as to be hardly worth saving, much less treasuring. The first is a simple head-and-shoulders portrait of a middle-aged man in collar and tie, hair greased back in a style that emphasises rather than conceals his advancing baldness, and with a face full of angles and hard edges, thin going on for gaunt, hawkish. His demeanour is stern, except for eyes that even on dulled paper bristle with the good mischief of life, and the tease of a smile plucking at the corners of his thin mouth, not there exactly, or not obvious, but suggested if you look for it, a detail that hints at hidden depths and other stories. The second photo is an action shot, just as staged as the first, though made to seem less obviously so, and really such a strange-seeming thing for Jack's mother to have in her possession. It depicts the same man, this time in a full-length pose, in running stride across a pocked and muddy field, a lumpish leather football at his feet. He looks too old for the game, and for the outfit he is wearing, a dark long-sleeved shirt, white shorts and matching knee-length socks, and yet there is an ease, too, about his posture. The camera, set to waist height or lower, makes something towering of him, but even without the angle tricks there's a clear assurance, an elegance, of the sort possessed or displayed by the best acrobats and dancers when a camera catches them at the high point of some leap or pirouette. Jack scrutinises the images, not sure what else he is looking for or expecting to find but unable to help feeling that there is more to be had. For now, though, the mystery holds.

'Do you think he could be . . .' Rachel's voice is a whisper, and lets the thought go unfinished.

Her husband confronts her gaze but doesn't try to answer. She can see his upset, some suffering fusion of anger and hurt. She half rises, leans forward across the coffee table, accepts the pictures back and shuffles them in restless, clumsy fashion, almost as if she is waiting for a third, maybe some shot of Rebekah, to complete the story. 'This must be the man who wrote the letters,' she says, studying the portrait shot. 'Otherwise, why would they be kept together?'

Jack sips his whiskey. 'It's hard to see, isn't it?' he says, after several seconds. 'I mean, she'd have been so young. Early twenties, if even that. And look at him. He's an old man. He looks fifty if he's a day. Don't young women usually fall for the handsome types?'

Rachel smiles to herself. 'Yes, they do. Usually.'

He ignores this, not in the humour to be teased, drains his glass and holds the dregs in his mouth, feeling the sting of it in the nerves of his back teeth, before swallowing. There is all of a sudden too much in his mind, thoughts pulling him in too many directions. He tries to remember if he properly locked up the other house and decides it will be his excuse to go and check. But later. For now, he just wants to sit. He glances around him, seeking solid ground, and registers that Hannah, unnoticed, has abandoned her drawing and slipped out into the hallway. After straining to listen he is able to catch the sound of her playing on the bottom few steps of the stairs, as she often does, talking in that funny voice she likes to use when addressing her doll. He sighs.

Rachel's glass is on the table and as empty as his own, but when he unscrews the bottle's cap and gets up to pour a refill she leans forward and flattens a hand across the mouth. 'Thanks all the same, love,' she says, 'but if I have any more I'll be out for the count. And who'll make the supper?'

'I can do it,' he says, knowing she won't let him. 'I'm not that bad, am I?'

She shrugs. 'No. Just out of practice, I suppose. The last time you cooked for me the fried egg looked—and fairly tasted—like a bit of scrap from an old saddle. And you made shit of my best pan.' Still smiling to herself she gets up, comes around the table and kisses his cheek and then, with slow energy, his lips, but when after a few seconds he attempts to draw her down into his arms for more and better she wrestles free and laughingly hurries from the room.

He almost follows, then doesn't. Again, the letters on the table catch his eye, the flattened drag of the handwriting across the old paper still keeping its secrets close. In response, not knowing what else just now to do, he takes up the bottle and pours himself another drink.

At First Sight

Kaumberg, 1935

THE THREE FOOTBALLERS had entered the tavern a little after six, all of them young, mid to late twenties, perhaps thirty at a push, the first two through the door tall and big across the shoulders, the third, trailing after a few seconds' delay, smaller, and slight, not only by comparison. That early the place was empty apart from two old men, one settled at a table beside the front window with a newspaper fully unfurled across it, the other over by the empty fireplace transfixed by his train of thought, his fingertips slowly twisting and turning a shot glass of some strong, clear liquor. The new arrivals paused in the doorway, looked around and, seeming to turn easy all at once, made for the bench seats along one end of a long tarnished oak table that filled most of the tavern's floor space.

The sound of new voices, and laughter, brought Rebekah through from the back room. She recognised them in an instant. In a town like this and of this trifling size, where little of note ever happened—except, perhaps, behind closed doors and drawn curtains—anything beyond a local kickabout amounted to a big deal, one of the year's highlights, even a meaningless exhibition game against a regional eleven. And because, in this case, spectacle far outweighed significance, for weeks the talk in Kaumberg concerned itself with very little else. Austria Vienna was a side known and renowned across Europe, and everyone within probably a ten-mile radius had gathered to watch, even the women, most of whom had never in their lives seen a ball kicked in any kind of organised fashion, and let themselves be caught up in the excitement.

After a hesitation, she hurried to their table, straightening the half-apron across her hips and front as she came. At this hour the air was sweet still with the fresh gluey smell of newly spread sawdust, shadows gathered in the corners and sheltered sides of the room, and the glare of the evening's slow-fading light pressing in through the high, west-facing windows gilded part of the table and a span of one wall. Spring had rarely felt as brilliant.

Of the three, the one called Viertl, the team's centre forward, seemed the most at ease. A hulking type, he stretched in a peculiarly graceful slump across the bench seat, with his back to the windows, holding himself mostly upright against the table's edge on an elbow and thick forearm. The second man, Stroh, almost as tall as Viertl but not as broad and seemingly quietened by the gregarious manner of his friend, perched opposite, his big hands grinding at one another in a way that caused the muscles of his bare arms to bulge and shift. But it was the third man that properly caught Rebekah's attention. When she'd first appeared from the back room but had yet to be seen, he'd still been standing, holding the door ajar, clearly unsure about surrendering the wonder of a bright evening on an hour or two of idle drinking. When he did step fully inside, he moved across the floor as if wading chest-deep against a tide. Her initial impression of him, especially when measured against his more athletic-looking teammates, was one of frailty. He was older, too, distinctly so, and not just in appearance but demeanour. While the others sported casual open-necked short-sleeved shirts, he was meticulous in a charcoal pinstripe suit and carried, pinching the crown between fingers and thumb, a matching homburg. He slipped off his jacket, folded it carefully lengthwise, draped it across the bench beside Stroh, lay the homburg brim-down on top and, moving as if not even a charging bull could hurry him, took ownership of the position at the end of the table.

'Beer, sweetheart.' Viertl was smiling with a hardness that strained his face. He considered Rebekah slowly and with emphasis, but in a way that was neither unfriendly nor intimidating but seemingly going for exaggeratedly boorish. 'And a bottle of schnapps. The best you've got, since Stroh here is paying. Touch up the glasses of your other customers while you're at it, only leave them until you're done with us.'

She returned with the beers first, carrying the three large steins at once, two in her left hand, one in her weaker right, moving slowly in order to better bear the heft. The third man, the slight one, saw her coming and made as if to rise, but the movement passed in an instant once it became obvious that she was capable. Nevertheless, the shifting, however slight, was a glimpse of something, a rare and unexpected litheness that dismissed any apparent lethargy as an indulgence. She fought to concentrate on her work and kept her eyes lowered even though she could feel him watching her, and he waited until she'd set down the glasses on the table, then murmured a barely heard 'thank you'.

Those were his first words to her, and the first time she heard his voice, and while she would soon come to know that gentle, breathy tone as his natural one, his true self or at least the version of it that he revealed when around her, especially during their most intimate moments, a part of her continued to hold on to this initial encounter, for its heightened quality, as something innately precious. The signs that would have given away her anxiety and excitement were minimal, a certain stiffening of her posture and a small catch in her breathing, and easily overwritten by the pragmatic way she wiped her wet hands on her apron and without lingering took quick leave, making for the bar counter across the room where she could pause and properly compose herself before reaching for a new bottle of schnapps and gathering three freshly rinsed shot glasses, so small that they fitted easily together in the palm of one hand.

When she looked back again in the direction of the table she saw the two big men leaning towards one another in conversation, Viertl, slightly the more animated, waving his left hand in jerking time to whatever he was saying. The smaller one sat back, as if distanced from what was being discussed and untouched by it. A little of his vagueness remained but his demeanour had softened from how he'd initially seemed and she was surprised to note that in the seconds or minute she'd had her back turned to them, he had already put away almost half the beer in his glass. At roughly that same moment the others seemed to notice this too, and in response both reached for their own steins and began to drink hurriedly.

She returned with the bottle and began pouring, the schnapps a local wild raspberry blend harvested and distilled within the Kaumberg limits, not the most expensive that the tavern stocked but considered, by those whose tastes ran in such directions, to be the best. She poured each glass slowly to the brim, giving the task her full concentration, and when she'd topped off the third glass, Stroh cleared his throat and said that she should just leave the bottle, that they'd help themselves so as not to be disturbing her all evening. 'But you'd best keep these coming, my dear,' Viertl added, and raising the stein to his mouth in wet slurps drained the last of the beer down to its froth. The effort drew a level of gasping that seemed to embarrass him, but rather than trying to conceal it he offered her instead a grin so big and open, so sweetly ugly, that she couldn't help but smile herself in response. And she was still smiling when she turned and met the third man's stare, and now it was her turn to blush. Her voice, when she could bring herself to speak, sounded small and girlish.

'You played wonderfully this afternoon, sir.'

'You were at the game?'

'The whole of Kaumberg was there. I went with my father. I wouldn't have missed it, but he'd have dragged me along even if I hadn't wanted to go. I enjoy football, but he lives for it. He even goes down into Vienna for games. And he was like a child, watching you today. I had a running commentary the entire time and he'll be talking about your second goal for weeks. We'll be sick of hearing about how you twisted out of a tackle, went past the second lunging centre half and sold the keeper with a feint that turned him very nearly inside out. To hear my father speak, you're Mozart, or Picasso. An artist.'

'What about me?' Viertl took a swallow from his shot glass, and gasped another wet heave, this time overly exaggerated. 'I knocked in a hat-trick today. Doesn't that count for anything?'

She looked at him, took up the bottle and poured him a refill. 'The first two were headers, from close in, and the third was a goalmouth scramble. The papers are always full of how good you are in the box, the best in the business from six yards, so that's expected of you. Those goals are your bread and butter.'

'She makes a fair point.' Stroh smiled. 'And she knows her football.'

His big teammate pretended to think about it, then shrugged a concession, feigning disappointment.

'We can set aside the formality, I think,' the other man said.

'What?'

'I'm just Sindelar. That's enough of a name. And my friends, the ones I can bear, anyway, call me Mutzl.'

She looked at him again and for a few seconds nothing moved, and the air, as if filled with a fine dust, hurt a little to breathe. The light in the room was starting to lose its sharpness, and she didn't quite know what to say or do. But he held out a hand to her and repeated his name again, Mutzl, and then somehow her hand was in his, feeling the papery coolness of his strong but gentle grip, and she heard herself, in a voice that came from her throat and mouth but which still felt somehow separate from her, whispering her own name, in full and with a quite absurd formality, Rebekah Schein, in answer to the question he'd not asked.

As evening tightened towards night, she busied herself with lighting the lamps that quickly gave the tavern a snug feel. Other men came in from time to time, singly or in small groups, and each in turn approached the footballers to say hello, shake hands, raise a glass of schnapps with them and praise what they'd earlier seen. At some point, when she had arrived at the table with a fourth round of beers, Sindelar put his hand very lightly to the small of her back, signalled with a tip of his head for her to lean in and discreetly asked whether the tavern was in the business of letting out rooms for a night or, failing that, if she could possibly advise him on suitable guest houses in the locality. Stroh and Viertl were taking the coach back to Vienna with the rest of the team, he explained, and would need to be leaving shortly, but he'd driven up here himself and didn't want to face the road back with so much alcohol in his system.

She finished distributing the refreshed steins, her mind and heart racing, then straightened up, untied her apron, folded it neatly and set it down on a vacant stretch of bench and announced, to whoever might have been listening, that she was just slipping out on an errand but would be back long before anyone died of thirst. Within ten minutes she had returned, a little out of breath. She came directly to Sindelar's side to assure him that a most suitable arrangement had been made, that Kroll's guest house, just a few minutes' walk from the tavern, had their best room available. They would be honoured to accommodate him, without charge, in appreciation of him bringing his talents to Kaumberg and as a demonstration of the town's hospitality.

HIS REASONING SEEMED plausible, and it only occurred to her later, once she had given the matter some consideration, how easily he could have taken a place on the bus and had a teammate or member of the coaching staff drive his car back. She'd felt through her cotton blouse the solidity of his touch and recognised the gesture as a signal of intent, but in electing to stand so close, coming to his side with the beers when she could have just as efficiently delivered them from across the table, there was also no denying that she'd encouraged his interest and felt flattered by it. At nineteen, she was not a thoroughgoing innocent. Some slim volume of love poetry lay always close to hand as a way of occupying the free moments, the lines of Goethe or Rilke or Shakespeare's sonnets in translation, time spent easily on dreaming, and over the past couple of summers she'd stepped out with her share of boys, enjoyed fast polkas and slow waltzes around local halls and even a few kisses—mostly of the snatched variety, having been led hand in hand up some leafy lane or avenue into a moment of unexpected privacy; but on a couple of occasions, too, bordering on the passionate. This, though, whatever this was, seemed different.

Standing close, feeling his hand against her back, caused her skin to bristle as if racked with shivers, and in attempting to stem the wild hammering of her heartbeat, she could only breathe in sighs.

On the surface, they seemed such a mismatch. Aside from him being nearly twice her age and looking probably ten years older again, by even the most generous estimation he fell a notable stretch short of handsome. Kaumberg had no lack of decent prospects, strong young men who'd have been an easier and far more natural fit for her, hard workers with heavy jaws that nevertheless held smiles well enough, who could keep their ideas to a sensible eye level and never above, and whose big dirt-baked hands were capable when necessary of softening to caress. And Rebekah, in turn, had more than enough about her to turn their heads and hold their interest. Girlishly pretty, with long, slightly chaotic hazel-blonde hair and eyes the teasing greenish-gold of harvest afternoons, she stood a little above average height but with a sapling litheness that seemed likely to keep rather than turning thickset and which marked her out from the crowd of her peers as, if not necessarily better, or even more attractive, then at least different. Working in a tavern, she'd grown easy with the flirtations and double-talk of certain types of men, and had become adept at fending off the occasional drunken grab. But what was going on with Sindelar felt like more than that. Watching him made her think of the sudden darting movements of birds when on the ground, that manner of bursting to life from an entirely frozen state. Considered this way, it might have been the difference between life and death that she was weighing, or different states of being. And he was more than Kaumberg could ever have offered, sweet though this town was, and secure. Any hesitance in making herself too easily available for him was due to natural shyness, in addition to her age, lack of real experience and a certain insecurity about her place—her station, as her mother called it. But when the time came for him to call it a night, somewhere around eleven o'clock—a couple of hours or so after Stroh and Viertl had hurried away to catch the team coach, lumbering him to their great amusement with a considerable bill—she'd gone outside too, under the pretence of showing him the way, insisting that he'd never find his guest house in the dark, and in one of the unlit lanes leading down from the tavern let him take her hand. Nothing was said, no games played. When he stopped at the corner, in the last of the utter blackness before the well-lit street began, she understood why, and when he turned to her and leaned in close she let herself be backed gently against the stone wall and lifted her face a little for his mouth to more easily find hers. He took his time, until her breathing turned as thick and heavy as his own, and if at that moment he'd gone up under her skirt she probably wouldn't have resisted the advance. Tonight, though, there was only the kiss.

His lips tasted of schnapps, and the breath he put in her mouth was all heat, making her think, in some distracted, swooning way, of winter days spent standing at a roaring fire in damp clothes. His body pressed against her, his frame strong as a young tree, and when he broke from her, finally, she was able, even in the darkness, to make out a little of his expression, a seriousness heightened by the alcohol.

'It's late,' he whispered. 'And I'm always beaten flat after a game. But I want to see you again.'

'I'd like that,' she said. 'But tomorrow you'll be going back.' She knew it was ridiculous, but the thought, and voicing it, made her want to cry.

'I can stay until lunchtime. It won't matter if I miss training. I'll make an excuse. If you like, meet me for breakfast, and afterwards we can walk in the woods.'

'No,' she said. 'I couldn't. That'd set the whole town talking.'

'So, let them talk. We'll be doing nothing wrong. Breakfast is no sin.'

She felt herself wavering. A cup of coffee, some bread or fruit, maybe fresh eggs. Let them say what they liked. But it wasn't just herself she worried about.

He let go of her hand and without awaiting her response stepped out into the centre of the lit street. The cast of the gas lamp turned him spectral. She remained at the wall, hidden by the dark, frozen.

'I've never even had a real boyfriend,' she said at last, managing no more than a whisper.

He looked back in her direction, and shrugged. 'Even so, you're not a child. Meet me for breakfast. That's all it has to be. Can we say half nine?'

AFTER THIS, SLEEP came in shards. Because the room that until just months earlier she'd shared with her now married sister, Gitta, was stifling, she slipped out of her nightdress and lay with nothing but the thin cotton covering of a bed sheet to her waist. For hours the night was silent but her mind thundered. She'd been kissed a few times by boys of her own age but never like tonight, and lying in her bed, her body singing out with want, hands together across her flat stomach, she strained to recall the press of Sindelar against her and the hot beery sweetness of his mouth. Gitta was living now in Graz, but there'd been a night last summer, similar to this one, that they'd spent wide awake while she confessed in murmurs to Rebekah how, earlier that evening, after weeks of his pleading and of her wanting to but being afraid, she'd given her virginity to Franz. She'd wept in confessing, though only, she insisted, because her emotions had been so wildly flung, and tried to assure Rebekah that she was happy, ecstatic, about what had happened, since she loved Franz and knew that he loved her, too. Because of how tightly the sisters embraced, the spilt tears soaked Rebekah's cheeks and neck, and the whispered words branded images of themselves into her, until it felt as if she herself had been right there with the loving couple, in the small back bedroom of Franz's father's house on the edge of Kaumberg. The actual sex, beyond the usual petting, wasn't exactly one for the books, but even though it had hurt at first because neither of them really knew what they were about, it did feel sort of good, too, Gitta said, once they settled to it. And if she'd maybe spoilt things a bit, at least for herself, by warning him over and over not to get her pregnant, then that was still the right thing to do, and afterwards he'd taken a fresh handkerchief from the drawer of his bedside locker and very gently cleaned her stomach and between her legs, and they held one another and kissed for a long time and talked about how it would only get better for them in all the years they'd have together as husband and wife.

Rebekah stretched in bed, throwing her arms wide and letting her feet reach for the mattress's lower corners, and wished that she had Gitta to confide in now. But her situation differed significantly from that of her sister's. Franz and Gitta were at least of an age, they'd known one another all their lives and had been stepping out together since school. And Franz was from a good Jewish family. Sindelar, in contrast, was a stranger. *Der Papierene*, the sports pages called him, the Paper Man, illusive, full of guile, but a story, a kind of fiction. The little she knew of him had been pieced together from insinuations. He was famous, yes, but for her not yet quite real, a man of too many shadows, and what hope had she of finding something true with him when the age gap was so wide and the lifestyle he enjoyed so obviously hectic?

She turned her head to watch the blackness of the sky beyond her open window and resolved to keep the past evening as a good and happy memory but to ignore, for the sake of her own well-being, his invitation to breakfast.

Yet she was out of bed as soon as she felt the dark start to soften. By the glow of a lantern at the kitchen table she washed herself from a large ceramic basin with tepid water that she'd intended at first to heat until impatience got the better of her, daring to stand stripped down to just her skirt because she was certain that neither of her parents would wake for another hour at least, scrubbing her face and body with a wet flannel cloth and rinsing out her hair with a piece of carbolic soap that she'd been saving. Then, after tidying up, she got the fire going and made a start on breakfast, putting on water for coffee, boiling eggs, slicing bread and cheese, laying out a bowl of pickles and the jar of gooseberry preserve. Her father was always at the shop by eight, and when he finally appeared, followed a few steps later by her mother, everything was ready to be eaten.

He sat at the table, bowed his head above his plate and more out of habit than belief mumbled a few quick words of prayer, then tapped and picked clean an egg of its shell and proceeded to slice and mash it onto a piece of bread. 'We'll get rain,' he said, between bites. 'There's thunder coming. Heat like this isn't right for March.' In the thin early light, and without his bifocals, he had to squint to see what he was eating, the years of needlework, often against only the tallow glimmer of a candle or kerosene lamp, having all but ruined his eyes. But at his age such things no longer seemed to matter; his fingers knew the way well enough.

While the elders ate in their usual dreamy fashion, Rebekah took only a cup of coffee, which she held just beneath her chin cradled between the fingertips of both hands, her elbows set on the table, and drank from it in little hissing sips. Her mind sought offhand words for how, in the tavern the evening before, the footballer, the one everybody talked about, had asked if she'd help arrange a night's stay for him at one of the guest houses and in gratitude, nothing more, had invited her to eat breakfast with him this morning; but the half-sleep state still cloaking the room made speaking difficult, so she remained silent. Then, after ten or fifteen minutes, her mother got up and began to clear the table, a move that had forever in their house signalled the beginning of the working day, and her father finished the last of his coffee and roused himself, too. She remained where she was, breathing the heat of her replenished cup and listening to the differing weights of the footsteps around her and in other rooms, until finally the front door opened and her father called back a 'so long', making it already too late for her to confess or explain.

Because her own work didn't begin until afternoon, a four-to-midnight shift, it being a Friday, that would keep her busy the entire evening, mornings were allowed a level of idleness, either to sleep on or to sit and read and moon over all the poems she couldn't properly begin to understand. But this morning she was too alive to settle with a book.

'I'm going for a walk,' she said, passing her mother in the kitchen doorway, and Hilde looked at her but vaguely, muddled with the list of chores that needed attending, and muttered to herself something from her distraction about how, if Izaak was right and they really were set for thunder, hanging out the washing would be a move foolish in the extreme.

As soon as she was outside, Rebekah started off in a direction away from town, moving at a brisk pace. The air was ablaze, the sky over Kaumberg and its surroundings lowly banked. She wanted to get herself lost but even straying into the woods couldn't achieve it, the simple undulations of the land keeping her well tethered, and after an hour of struggling to be away she heard the church bell, still somehow impossibly near, ringing out its chimes for nine o'clock, and in frustration but perhaps also with just a modicum of relief gave in and started slowly back.

The roads along the town's outskirts were deserted, and she walked without hurry and persisted in denying her true intentions until she'd turned onto the street leading past Kroll's guest house and from fifty yards away saw Sindelar waiting, his back against the side of the building and a newspaper held wide open before him. Her breath, by now quite strained, stuck in her throat, and she gave serious consideration to slipping into a side lane and hurrying back home. Running, if necessary. But then, as if he'd felt some disturbance about the morning, he lowered the paper, looked around and, noticing her ahead of him in the distance, raised a hand in salute. And she had no choice but to go to him.

'I hope you slept well.'

Sweat lacquered her temples and chased runnels down her sides from her armpits, and she was glad that she'd worn her summer dress, even so early in the year: her favourite buttercup-yellow cotton with narrow shoulder straps and a skirt that fell in pleats to just above the knee.

He stared without seeming to, taking everything in, and could laugh and still seem serious. 'Is it always like this in Kaumberg, with all the pretty girls dressing for July when it's still only spring? Because that's enough to make a man want to abandon Vienna.'

'Don't give up on Vienna yet,' she said. 'My father says it'll thunder before lunchtime.'

◆ ◆ ◆

ALTHOUGH THE STREET was empty apart from them, she kept a modest arm's distance apart, fearful of nourishing gossip, and held her hands loosely together in a way that protected the hem of her dress from the lift of an unexpected breeze. He'd dressed casually but well, in slacks of some metallic shade and a crisp white shirt worn open at the neck and with the sleeves rolled to his elbows, and looked younger than he had in the tavern, with the limpid solidity of a fighter about his slender frame.

'Well,' he said, his serious tone a clear tease, 'if there's thunder due, I'm surprised you came.'

She shrugged. 'When it comes to rain, my father's right nearly half the time. I decided it was worth the risk.'

The Letters

Cork, 1980

IT RAINS THE entirety of Monday, a bleak lashing that settles in over the city during the Sunday night and persists through the following day. A Danish ship has docked early and needs unloading, quarter-ton crates are lifted off by crane and forklifted onto waiting truck trailers, but the sixty-pound sacks of cement that line the second hold have to be hauled ashore by hand.

Jack turns up early, while it is still dark, and finds that the foreman on duty today is Lewis, the one who doesn't like him and who considers it a kind of sport to mock, calling him 'Jackie the Jew' whenever the opportunity arises and if there happens to be an audience present who'll laugh along out of duty. A big man, four or five stone at least overweight, with tufts of red hair curling clownishly over his ears and a large bald head made beige by continents of freckles, he has often come into the canteen cabin during the lunch break and, as a joke that amuses no one, tried to find some way of bringing Hitler into the conversation, or the concentration camps, knowing that these are the most aggravating buttons to push. Once, he'd started mouthing off about how the IRA and the Nazis were natural allies and had actually colluded—or attempted to—during the war, how through a series of top-level meetings they'd even discussed plans for a possible invasion of the country as a way of distracting the Brits. Going on from his place in the centre of the floor, like a town crier or a politician in full oration mode, until Reilly, a man from Carrigtwohill, one of the older stevedores, probably late fifties, looked up from the newspaper's crossword puzzle and in a small, tight voice that made its warning clear, told him that even idiots knew better than to talk of things they knew fuck all about.

This morning, though, standing in the rain in a huge green set of oilskins, Lewis has nothing to say. He considers Jack, shakes his head at some inner thought, but scratches the name down at the top of his clipboard's empty page. Mondays are often short-handed, especially when the weather is as dirty as this. Sick heads lift from the pillow only long enough to check the heft of the sky beyond the glass. And with so much work to be done, prejudices must be set aside.

For hours then, Jack goes at it. The work is the very definition of tedium, a slow repetitive monotony of trudging up the gangway, heaving cement sacks up onto his shoulder, staggering back down onto the dockside and stacking the loads in a corner of Warehouse 2. Once he becomes accustomed to the rain the discomfort ceases to matter.

The night before, needing some fresh air, and with everything—pictures, letters, cuttings—packed away again in the box beneath his arm, he had crossed the couple of hundred yards of Jewtown to Monerea Terrace, the nice red-brick houses over towards the old gasworks, where Rachel had been born and where her father, Samuel, a widower these past few years, still lives.

Samuel met him at the door with a handshake, as he always did, brought him inside and listened, mouth tight, eyes like small charcoal scuds behind round, wire-framed bifocals, while Jack, leaning with one hip against the kitchen counter, explained in broken sentences, still trying to make some sense of the whole situation himself, what had been discovered and what was needed now.

'Jack,' the older man said, after pouring them both coffee that had been percolated to the consistency of treacle, 'I don't know about this. I can translate, yes, of course, if it's what you want. You know I'll always help in any way I can. I'm here for that. But these letters were hidden away a long time. Their world is gone. I just want you to be sure, that's all.'

After a long pause, Jack lifted his gaze from the floor's apparently transfixing pebble-patterned linoleum, a dominating avocado colour with shade effects of browns and greys. He sipped the coffee and winced at its bitterness, but Samuel, used to it, drank with more fluency, holding mouthfuls for long seconds at a time before swallowing. 'What choice do I have? Wouldn't you want to know, if you were me? Wouldn't you need to?'

His father-in-law looked at him in a serious way, then sighed. 'All right. As long as you're sure. Can you leave them with me? The newspaper clippings especially look interesting. We're obviously dealing with somebody of note. And I can speak to a few people from the synagogue, either here or above in Dublin. The old men. There's always a chance that someone will remember something.'

After returning home, he'd stayed up late, sitting at the fireside with Rachel until she began to fall asleep and had to turn in, and then, for a couple of hours more, alone, nursing a last glass of whiskey that eventually became only the second-last, his mind racing too fast for proper focus. But today's exhaustion, accumulating from the hard physical labour and the lack of sleep, does achieve a degree of peace.

The lunch break that interrupts is a quiet one, with those men who've turned up tired from the weekend's exertions, and what little talk there is keeps to football, and Cork United, which everyone still refers to as Albert Rovers. It's the name the club has had, in one form or another, since its inception but which was altered last summer following the folding of Cork Celtic, leaving them as the city's only representative at League of Ireland level. The Alberts are enjoying a decent run in this year's Munster Senior Cup but have struggled badly in the league, never getting better than three or four places from the bottom of the table all season, and few among the dockers are impressed by the point picked up against Home Farm over the weekend. A scoreless draw up in Tolka Park would have been considered a solid result, but over in Turner's Cross, in front of a fair-sized and fairly vocal home support, more was expected, especially since Home Farm have themselves been in poor enough form over the past few months and in most people's estimations were there for the taking.

After all the early hauling, the afternoon proves less of a hardship. Because the long morning has done for most of the work, a few who can't otherwise shift their hangovers take the chance to slip away for a couple of curing pints, either at the Sextant or down at the Harp Bar. Lewis isn't blind to their leaving but, with the rain coming down the way it is, decides not to cause a fuss, knowing that those who stay can manage whatever slack is going spare. And by four or so, the ship has been stripped to its bones, and Jack and a couple of others, having nothing else to do, take shelter in one of the sheds at the back of the yard, dry off as best they can and indulge in a few games of pitch-and-toss until the five o'clock whistle sounds to officially end the shift.

'You'll catch your death, out in that all day,' Rachel says, meeting him at the door, her expression full of concern, a fresh towel in her hands. 'Get those wet clothes off you. I have dinner waiting.'

'Only dinner?' He smiles, lifts his eyebrows in teasing fashion and grabs her around the waist. 'Who gets naked for dinner?'

'Jack,' she says, slapping his chest and trying not to laugh. 'Stop it. The child will hear. Anyway, it's skirts and kidneys.'

'What is?'

'Dinner.'

'Oh, I thought that was another invite.'

'Will you behave?' She wrestles free, exaggerating the struggle. 'Also, my father was here a while ago, and he wants to talk to you. He'll be in the Sextant at six, he said. But he's in no hurry. I've run a hot bath for you. It'll help get a bit of heat back in your bones.' She leans in suddenly and kisses him, but her movement is so entirely unexpected that before he can ready himself to make something more of it the chance is gone. Her smile, in recognising this, is triumphant but also seems to suggest that the ceasefire need only be short-lived. 'Go on. Have a quick wash and I'll start taking up the food.'

THE LOUNGE OF the Sextant is almost empty at this hour. Jack hurries inside, bringing shut his umbrella behind him. Two soakings in a day is too much. The pub is so heavily gloomy that for a few seconds he can only stand there, just inside the door, while his eyes try to adjust. At first he takes the place to be deserted, apart from Marie, behind the bar, drying a pint glass with a towel and lost in thought, her expression sullen. Everyone carries their problems around with them. But then, sensing his presence, she looks up, smiles, immediately becoming somebody else, and knowing instantly who he is here to see, gestures with a glance in the direction of the corner snug. Jack looks across and recognises his father-in-law by the staunch shape of his head and shoulders. He approaches the counter, takes a pound note from his pocket and calls a pint of Beamish for himself and whatever it is that Samuel is drinking.

'I'll give you a shout when they're ready,' Marie says, handing him his few pence of change, which he counts almost unconsciously, out of habit and in a casual way that can't cause offence. She has long thin fingers, with many gold and silver rings crowding her left hand but with none at all on the right, and her inch-long nails are painted a red that looks nearly black in this gloom. In handing him the coins she has tickled his hand and the sensation of her touch lingers. He feels as if his palm has just been read, and hints of his future revealed.

Samuel is so engrossed in what he has on the table before him that he doesn't react to the voices across the pub floor and doesn't look up until Jack settles on the seat alongside.

'Ah, Jack. Good lad. What will you have? A pint, a drop of something? This was some day to be out on the docks, I'd say. It's a wonder you weren't washed overboard.'

'I got them in,' Jack replies, nodding vaguely in the counter's direction, but he is distracted by the sight of the shoebox uncapped on the table and his voice barely sounds above the lashing of the rain against the window.

'So, you've been through them, then.'

On the table, beside the shoebox, is a yellow foolscap notepad, the page on display smothered in small, spiky writing, but Jack doesn't attempt to reach for it. Apprehension causes his stomach to churn.

'I have,' says Samuel. 'I was up late with them, and then again this morning. There's a lot to take in. I'm not quite there with it all yet, and it's a job trying to get the chronology right because so few of the letters are dated. But I am starting to get a sense of their story, I think.'

'And do I want to know?' The dread is obvious in the pitch of Jack's voice. But at that moment, Marie, the barmaid, calls out to him and he gets up and collects the pint of Beamish and the glass of Powers, neat, from that end of the counter, and the interruption gives each man time to compose himself so that when he settles again at the table they are able to act as if the question had gone unasked.

He takes a deep swallow from his pint and steels himself for what is to come. 'All right,' he says, softly. 'Let's hear it. What have we, so far?'

What they have, it seems, is a romance of some significance and depth, even with the voice on the page exposing little of itself beyond the inevitable professions of love. The writing has the striking confessional quality of deep intimacy; with the intended recipient so obviously versed in what is being written of, personal details, when alluded to at all, prove spare and almost determinedly lacking in specifics. Far from achieving revelation, the one-sided nature of the letters, especially when considered in total, only raises further questions and deepens the sense of mystery. But since her name appears numerous times—most often truncated to Beka—in lieu of *darling* or *sweetheart*, they can feel assured, at least beyond a reasonable doubt, that Rebekah is indeed the lover being addressed. Because his strongest recollections are of a woman so often tired and unwell, Jack struggles to connect his mother with the object of these scribbled yearnings. Yet this is what there is, letters, fragmented and incomplete, that seemingly piece together a love affair in sad waning: the earliest of the pages passionate but uncertain, holding to a note of caution as if anxious of the wrong eyes scouring these words and finding some advantage in them; the later notes more relaxed in their intimacy, and the best and most unfettered of them those written on the road, from Paris, Milan, Budapest, Berlin, on headed hotel paper, describing sights seen, people met or encountered again, trying to make something of sharing the words but serving only to magnify their loneliness. Wistful at times, and occasionally bordering on the explicit, remembering moments they'd had together, embraces, kisses, dance-hall movements treasured, every step and touch.

By the final few letters the tone has turned increasingly resigned, lamenting the fact of their separation, though attempting to reiterate it as the right decision. The writing speaks of soldiers patrolling Vienna's streets, curfews in place, and spies and informants everywhere. There is mention of others getting out, names who seem to be friends either of the letters' writer or of Rebekah's, and news shared of places that clearly hold significance for the lovers, favoured cafes, bars and restaurants, either shut down due to the new ownership laws or redressed as places for SS men to congregate. The Hotel Metropole now serves as the official Gestapo headquarters, arrests are widespread, with Jews in particular being hauled in for the least infringement, and there's talk of a forced labour camp set to open just outside of Linz. In these last letters, all romance is gone, though not the sense of love. The writer struggles gamely, with questions about Cork and how she is settling, how she is feeling, whether she is being well looked after and whether the country really is as poor as it had seemed to him when he'd paid a fleeting visit to Dublin a couple of years earlier for a game against a team called Bohemians. If his impression of Ireland is at all accurate then at least the money he is sending will help and that she shouldn't be afraid to spend it, or to help out her family with it, those people who have taken her in, because as long as he has money, she'll have money, too.

Samuel finishes his whiskey, and ignoring the fact that Jack's pint is still half full, turns towards the bar and raises a hand to catch the barmaid's attention. Marie has the *Evening Echo* spread open on the counter and is hunched forward on her elbows but still catches the movement.

'Two pints of Beamish, when you're ready, love. And put a drop of Powers beside each of them, will you?'

She nods and, setting herself to the slow task of pulling the pints, watches idly as Jack finishes off the stout he has remaining.

Samuel is leafing through the letters again, setting them back into their approximate order. 'They're not signed,' he says, 'apart from the few that sport what looks like and what might be an S followed by a longish dash. But it's plain to see they've all been written by the same hand, and the newspaper cutting and the photos give us plenty to work with.'

Jack reaches for one of the photos, the one of the man with the football. 'You think he's the S, then? The bit of a signature?'

'I do, yes. I mean, he must be. And it makes sense of that mention in one of the letters about playing a friendly in Dublin against Bohs.' He hesitates. 'The German is a bit rough and the handwriting fairly childlike, so I doubt our man had much in the way of schooling. But there's enough here to suggest that this was more than just a fling. These could have been typed, fixed up, but they're not. They're raw. That takes trust.'

THIS TIME, INSTEAD of calling for one or the other of them to come and collect the glasses from the counter, Marie brings the drinks to their table, the pints first, setting them down on cardboard beer mats, giving all her attention, exaggeratedly so, to what she is doing, then returning with the glasses of whiskey. Because of the rain, the pub is still otherwise empty, though in the next hour or so men will start arriving, their thirsts and other needs outweighing any discomfort the weather can inflict. Just now is the calm ahead of whatever storm might be set to blow. She picks up Jack's empty glass, but lingers a minute, leaning a hand on the backrest's corduroy upholstery. 'Were you out in that all day, Jack?' she asks, already making a face of sympathy. 'You've earned your few pints tonight, then. It's been a desperate day even from this side of a window.'

'Fine cut of a girl, that Marie,' Samuel says, watching her saunter back across the floor to the bar, and then, after a few further seconds of appreciation, considers his son-in-law, seeking perhaps reaction, perhaps something else. 'She is.' Jack meets the look and smiles. 'But don't worry, I'm already taken.'

Samuel laughs quietly, showing teeth. But his nonchalance is a thin act. He reaches for his pint, and swallows a deep draught. 'That's good, lad. That's what a father-in-law needs to hear. Because over the years, I'd say that one there has turned plenty of heads.'

'Ah, no. It's part of the job, that's all. A bit of friendly talk is probably as far as it ever goes. She's a nice girl.'

Behind the bar, Marie has once more settled herself above the *Echo*. One hand rests on the counter, crouching in a spidery way, her many-ringed fingers now and then rolling out little tapping arpeggios, the sounds of which are too small to carry across to the snug, especially through the beating of the rain.

'Did you really not know any of this, Jack?' Samuel asks, after a pause.

Jack shakes his head.

'Not a bit of it. Hand on heart. I don't know, maybe if we'd had longer. I was only ten when she died, and at that stage she'd already been ill for so long. And for most of what time we did have, there'd been the war. Joe and Ruth must have known, because they'd have had to, but even though I was close to them, we rarely broached the past. That's how we were, always going around things rather than through them. The bits and pieces I did get, in the years after, once I was of an age to understand, were mainly about my mother's family. She and Joe were cousins, so all of that was closer to the bone. Even then, though, it wasn't much. Too painful, I suppose. And there was nothing at all about the other side, who my father was or might have been. As I got older I had moments of curiosity, and maybe they were waiting for me to ask, but I never did. As far as I was concerned they were my grandparents, at least in all the ways that counted, and whatever I am, whatever good there is in me, is due to them and the rearing I got. The love. I'd have gone to the bottom of the river before causing them a moment's hurt.'

He sighs and lets his stare fall on the shoebox. 'And then I find this. Letters from a stranger who apparently loved my mother, and who I suppose we must assume, since she held on to them the way she did, she loved in return.'

Samuel goes into his coat's side pocket for his pipe and his small leather tobacco pouch, and takes his time packing the bowl and getting it lit. There's a meditative quality about watching him, and the earthy smell of the pipe smoke hangs with pleasant heft in the warm pub air.

'Based on what I've gone over, and bearing in mind that there's not been time to thoroughly scrutinise everything, I'd say you're safe enough in your assumptions. Also, we still have the newspaper clippings to consider. If we take the S of the letters to be this man, Sindelar, in the news articles—and that doesn't seem such a stretch, given how all of this was found parcelled up together—then the picture starts to grow clearer.'

'Sindelar.' Jack repeats the name, hissing it almost, feeling the shape of it against his teeth.

'You were born, when, Jack?'

'October of '38. The 23rd.'

'We'll have to check, because there must be documents and records somewhere to prove it, but if I have the dates figured right from the letters, your mother had arrived in Cork in May of that year.'

The pause that follows underlines this detail. Jack sips his whiskey.

'Yeah,' he says, slowly. 'I suppose I assumed that. I couldn't have told you exactly when she got here but I did know it wasn't too long before the war.' That she'd carried him to Cork also isn't a thunderous shock. The fact that there'd never been anyone local to wonder about had to indicate that his origins surely lay elsewhere.

Until the shoebox's discovery, he'd long since accepted his lot. *Count your blessings*, one of the teachers at school used to say, often enough for the instruction to have embedded itself. He'd suffered loss, the worst kind for any child to have to endure, and if, growing up, there'd not been a lot of coddling then he'd also been raised in a relentlessly loving home and gifted that particularly precious sense of security and belonging. Ruth and Joe never had much going spare but they'd have lain down before lions for him. And knowing that, being able to believe it, was strengthening. In Jewtown, you worked hard and tried to get by. That was it, and most of the time that was enough. The past hung its shadow across everyone's back, but you bore what you had to. The missing piece of him, the father he's never known or known of, and being deprived that entire lineage, has troubled him at times but kept itself largely to the more reflective moments, to be walked with on early mornings or to toss and turn with in bed once the lights were out. Only rarely has it impinged on his actual daily living, like when he'd been required to produce a birth certificate at the time of his marriage, and once, earlier, while in hospital to have his appendix removed, faced with questions about his family's medical history. If not knowing who he's come from made a hole in him, then he's learned, by necessity, how to live around the void. The days have to be passed, regardless, and if his world these past forty years has kept to a square mile or two—Jewtown and the dockyard; Saturdays in the synagogue, when he was of a mind to attend and more for the feeling of belonging than for faith; and Sundays spent watching the hurling in the Park or football over at the Cross—then that's been, for the most part, world enough for him. There is contentment of a kind in settling, just as there's turmoil in finding himself suddenly on the brink of revelation. According to the Ketuvim, he that increaseth knowledge increaseth sorrow. But what choice has he? When faced with potential understanding, ignorance can no longer be an option. Turning away now would feel like too great and overwhelming a sin.

And yet, hearing it broached aloud, just shy of actual words but with the intent clear, causes anger, illogical but real, to burst within him. He stares hard at the shoebox and, beside it, the yellow jotter.

'What about me, then? Where am I in all of this? Am I even mentioned? Hinted at?' A grin twists his mouth, revealing clenched teeth. He reaches for his glass of Beamish and swallows deeply from it. 'You'd think she'd have told him, wouldn't you? That's what I can't get. I mean, what was to be gained by keeping me a secret? Was she ashamed? Afraid? What?'

Against such a tide, Samuel can only bow his head. 'I'm sorry,' he says, his voice a murmur. He recognises the signs of shame across the table, and is careful with what can be said. 'I don't know, Jack. We don't have her side of the correspondence. And some of his letters could have been lost. It's possible this is not all there was.

And try to imagine how tough a place Vienna must have been to live in after the annexation, with the threat of war so immense. She might have feared that the information could be used against him, or that there was no hope of a reunion. Who can say? But that kind of speculation is unhelpful. We need to concentrate on what we have, what we know.' He reaches into the shoebox and lifts out the newspaper cuttings. 'And these,' he says, with something like triumph, 'are what we have.'

THREE OF THE four cuttings are reports of football matches. The earliest, under a heading that Samuel translates as: A THURSDAY EVENING STROLL, dates from the end of May 1935, and recounts a rampant 5–1 National Cup final victory for Austria Vienna over Vienna AC, singling out Matthias Sindelar, who was collecting his third Cup winner's medal, for particularly lavish praise, not only because of the two goals he scored but also for so immaculately controlling the tempo from his deep-lying forward position that the Violets had the game won practically from the kick-off.

Following this is a longer cutting, dated from mid-September of the next year, detailing something called the Mitropa Cup final, and a harrowing two-legged single-goal win for the same club over Sparta Prague, their second time lifting the trophy in four years. Again, much of the report concentrates on Vienna's diminutive playmaker, Sindelar, the Maestro, *Der Papierene*—the Paper Man. Light as a breeze, slight-boned but fearless, his mind seemingly half a dozen moves ahead of the play at any given moment, the range of his passing and his impeccable ball control, even on a desperately heavy pitch, as natural to him as breathing.

'I made a few enquiries at the synagogue,' Samuel says, his expression almost apologetic. 'I'm about as fluent with football talk as I am with Swahili, and to make some sense of what I was reading I felt I needed to speak with a few of the old-timers. Rubin Leibler vaguely remembered the name, but says that he has a cousin still living in Graz who's getting on for eighty and he'll know if anyone will. And Toby Ullmann told me that this one, the Mitropa Cup, was a big deal back in the day, a kind of forerunner of what became the European Cup.'

Jack continues to drink, concentrating on the cold weight of the stout on his tongue and in his throat. By now, their table is in deep shadow, the plain upper section of the big window beside them, the pub's main source of light, is so ruined with rain that its texture almost matches the heavily opaque, disc-patterned style of the glass's lower half.

'If he was playing in those kinds of games then he really must have been a somebody.'

'Reading these—' Samuel puts a hand on the small heap of cuttings—'it would seem so, yes.'

'Sindelar. You'd think we'd know the name, wouldn't you? Like Puskás, or Pelé.'

'I suppose he was just that bit early. And there was the war.'

The last of the football-related cuttings is of an international match, also from 1936, with Austria defeating England by two goals to one in a friendly played in front of some sixty thousand fans at the Prater Stadium in Vienna. It is a nothing game, a casual exhibition match, with the home side due to age and attrition already noticeably past their prime, but no triumph over mighty England was inconsequential, especially back then, and the report, clearly looking for an angle, chooses to paint the result as sweet revenge for a famous 4–3 defeat they'd suffered at a packed Stamford Bridge some three and a half years earlier. The actual facts and statistics are dealt with in perfunctory fashion, with most of the piece dedicated to recalling that earlier game, and how, after struggling through much of the first half, possibly due to a sense of awe at the occasion, the Austrians, known at that time as the *Wunderteam*, the then reigning Central European champions and on a fourteen-game and almost two-year winning streak, rallied in spectacular fashion and were in the end unlucky not to secure a result.

'According to Toby, prior to the war England were football's superpower. The ultimate unmovable object, they'd never lost on home soil to a team outside of the home nations. So any side that ran them close would have made major headlines.' Samuel holds up the piece of old newspaper as evidence. 'I've read this over and over, and it seems that the *Wunderteam* that day at Stamford Bridge had a chance at achieving footballing immortality and very nearly took it. But just as not all victories are sweet, not all defeats are tragic. And the place seemingly erupted when Sindelar jinked between two lunging defenders and slotted the ball past the despairing keeper to put Austria within touching distance of a draw.' He leafs again through his foolscap notes, holds the page close to his face, resettles his glasses on the bridge of his nose, and reads: 'A goal afterwards described by the match referee as "a masterpiece such as no one ever before accomplished against such opponents". Even the British newspapers acknowledged that everyone present on the day had witnessed a genius at work.'

They sit for a while, finishing off what drink is in front of them. Samuel looks embarrassed again. On his own these past few years, he tends to veer between long silences and, whenever he finds company who'll listen, gluts of talk. Neither state is quite who he is, yet this, it seems, is what he has become.

'We'll stay for another, will we?' Jack says, sucking the last drain of whiskey from his glass. He has fallen seconds out of time with the day and is dragging to catch up. A lot has been said, but plenty also hangs unspoken between them, and he needs time to process all he's heard. 'Isn't there one more cutting to look at?'

But the older man is already getting to his feet.

'I haven't had time to go over that one yet.' His voice sounds forced. 'Like I said, there's so much here. And getting them ordered had me up half the night. This last one is the longest of the cuttings so I'll need to take a bit of time with it. And I've a couple of phone calls that I want to make before it gets too late. One or two people above in Dublin who might be able to shed a further bit of light on things. You remember Moshe Gerbult?'

'From Greenmount? I know Jacob and Lenny who worked in that garage on Victoria Road.'

'Right. Moshe is their old man. He must be ninety if he's a day but he was born in Switzerland and lived all over Europe when he was young, and he was always stone mad altogether for football. I'd bank on him remembering something. Another Powers will put me on my ear, but if I go now I can still speak without having to chew my words.'

Jack gathers the glasses, and carries them to the counter. A couple of men he knows to see have come in and are standing at the far end of the bar, laughing in a low way with Marie about something probably off colour. Still smiling, she turns and is about to start in his direction when he raises a hand, thanks her for the drinks and wishes her a good night. She nods, her grin unflinching, and tells him to mind himself.

Then Samuel is at his side, gripping his arm above the elbow.

'I've kept you out late enough, lad. Let's call it quits for now. Otherwise I'll hear all about it from Rachel. But I'll call over tomorrow evening. And you might tell that daughter of mine that if she wants to put an extra kipper or two in the pan, I wouldn't object. I'll have the last cutting translated by then, and we'll see what comes from the calls I make.'

'About that,' Jack says, going into the left front pocket of his jeans for his wallet. 'Calling Dublin isn't cheap. I need to fix up with you.'

But the older man waves such talk away. 'Ah, would you stop.'

They hesitate a moment in the Sextant's doorway. From here, the world looks to be in fast decay. With the confluence of weather and falling night, everything in view seems forbidding. The Lee's tide is running high and washing up against the port warehouses on the city-centre side of the bridge, and the rain, torrential, chases eastward in sheets across the front of the pub, yellowing the dusk where it catches and making flecked coronas of the street lights.

'Come on,' says Samuel, sounding already in pain, his eyes slitted, his large front teeth clenched. 'You can walk me home. We only have the one umbrella, and at my age I could really do without a drenching.'

Falling

Kaumberg and Vienna, 1935–1936

SOMETIMES, DURING THE stretches between his visits, which could run to as long as three weeks or a even month at a time, if he was caught up with business obligations in Vienna or had to be away on tour with the team, Rebekah couldn't help diminishing in her mind what it was that they had going, reducing it to something simple and casual, a romance, yes, but not a serious one, not one that could lead anywhere good. The mismatch was instantly apparent: at the time of their initial encounter she had only just turned nineteen and was every bit the country innocent, naive and wildly under-educated in the workings of the world; by contrast, in both appearance and life experience he seemed already firmly banked in middle age. The thirteen-year difference felt like a hurdle impossible to overcome, yet when they were together, either in shared solitude savouring an intimate moment or as part of some larger group on those evenings when he arrived in his car and carried her away to a party at one of the coffee houses or dance halls in or around Vienna, he invariably left her swooning. Just being near him was such a thrill, watching him move, glide, somehow finding space to exist and tower even in a packed room. And, in a similar way, while she was there to be seen, he had eyes for no one else.

After breakfast that first time, they'd gone—at his insistence—up into the woods to walk. Aside from a little further kissing there'd been no great impropriety, nothing unseemly, and she decided later, once she'd relived it all sufficiently in her mind, that it was during those couple of hours spent hiking the densely forested slopes to Araburg Castle, the area's highest and most scenic point, that she must have fallen in love. Given his extreme level of fitness, the climb for him would have been nothing, but he set his pace to what she could manage and kept to her side, taking her hand when the ground turned challenging, talking all the while. Easily, of simple things and nothing, yet somehow telling her about his life, opening himself to her so that by the time they reached the high clearing, the skin of their brows glistening from the exertion and the warmth of the day, she felt as if she'd had him around her forever and knew all there was to know.

Those moments would remain with her, the sheer happy weight of them, with everything an onslaught to her senses—the sweet, earthy reek of the woodland, the splashes of penetrating light a silver thick to shimmering with dust, the comforting mire of the shade, the way her body held itself in such awareness of him and how it sang out to every jolting touch, however slight. When they stopped to rest, at some rough halfway point in their trudging, she leaned her back against the nearest birch trunk and smilingly closed her eyes, trusting in his presence and feeling her heart bang in such anticipation just before the shift of his shadow, a coolness almost, fell across her. For a full second the gentle brush of his breath against her mouth was like a kiss in itself, and then his lips found hers and opened her up. His hands held on to her, her hips first and then loosely clasping her arms above the elbows, and when one hand came to her cheek she gave herself over to the touch and swayed to his direction, kissing, breaking to breathe in soft heaves and then kissing again, her eyes shut all the time but not clenched, swimming in that darkness just to hold back a while the explosion of day awaiting her.

In his company all background paled. His teammates were invariably tall and strong, athletic in the honed, ferocious style of warriors, and beside and among them he should have seemed at odds, slight to the point of brittle and, a decade or so out of time, badly dated. But in fact, it was they who for all their bulk and muscle became lessened by some inferred elegance of pose. A kind of irresistible electricity, another of the women explained one night while a party heaved around them in fullest swing—a film actress of at least moderate renown who'd for a time been romantically involved with one of the other players. Meaning her words casually, simply passing remark, but staring with a certain compulsion, Rebekah saw, and unable to look away.

For Sindelar, living as he did, keeping a lifestyle of such broadness, what he and Rebekah had could have been a mere fancy. Every night the cafes and clubs were full of women who with their low-cut dresses and allusive smiles likely turned his head. But there was something about what he'd found with her that held his interest enough that he kept returning, and wanting to, initially a few days on from that hike to the castle, and then, after, with once- or twice-weekly regularity, getting away whenever he could and driving the hour and a half of bad road just to be near her, even if that meant having to sit in the tavern nursing a beer or two while she finished her shift. On other less impetuous days, when plans were properly laid and he'd been able to free himself for a couple of nights, usually after a game on the Saturday or Sunday, or if he'd picked up a knock bad enough to keep him hobbled for some short stretch, he took a room with the Krolls and he and Rebekah spent their time together exploring the surrounding areas by car and on foot, or just strolling around Kaumberg. They stopped to chat with people, men and boys keen to recount specific games or talk tactics, but with some of the local girls and women, too, since his face was well known from advertisements in the papers pushing everything from hats and overcoats to sweeping brushes and varieties of soap, and his name, less flatteringly—though none of them dared speak of this—featured all too regularly in those same newspapers' much-scrutinised gossip columns. When, in the evenings, they ate at her home, Mr Schein—'Izaak, please'—struggled to curtail his torrent of football-related questions, and if Hilde was somewhat tight in her demeanour, having from the beginning made clear to both of them her disapproval of the relationship, not just because of the age difference but that, undeniably, chief among the reasons, then she was also still polite and welcoming, treating Sindelar with the formal respect due any visitor to her house, and probably understanding that whatever was going on between the couple lay far beyond their control.

Often, after they'd finished eating and if the weather was especially fine and the stars were out, they'd take a stroll before bed and stop in at either the tavern or the local cafe for coffee or a glass of wine, Rebekah linking him openly now, or holding his hand, since they were already the talk of the place and being upfront about what they had going seemed the best way of facing it, to demonstrate that there was nothing untoward or shameful about their love. She lived for such nights, the feeling of being so calmly grown up, so all of a sudden, after all the years of girlhood, womanly, and so valued, cherished, by someone whose love still made no logical sense to her but who she believed to be entirely true and honourable in his behaviour. And when, towards the end of the summer, he asked if she'd consider moving to Vienna, she hardly hesitated, though when she announced the news at home her mother wept openly and got down on her knees for drama, and her father moved around the room in a silence that seemed set to crush him, before settling at the window with his back turned to them and refusing to face her again that night or even acknowledge her. A week later, her belongings—dresses, skirts and cardigans, mainly, but her books, too—stuffed into an old army duffel bag at her feet, she stood at the same window, with it open just a crack so that she was better able to listen for the sound of an approaching car.

It had to be this way, a clean break. 'If you go, you won't be able to come back,' her mother said, that morning, echoing one last time the argument she'd already acknowledged as futile. There was no more crying now, only the stoicism of grudging acceptance. Rebekah's father had left early for his workshop. 'Even if your young man is honourable, the whole of Kaumberg knows of your leaving. You can visit, and we hope to see you often. But that's all. And of course, you must write to us, so that we know you're safe. And happy. Because that's what we want for you, all we have ever wanted.' Rebekah knew her parents were saddened at the thought and manner of her going but, after sleepless nights spent discussing the situation in whispers, had come to understand that the life she yearned for was bigger than the one she'd find in their village with even the best of the local young men. She was going to be in her own apartment, she'd explained, and they accepted this and believed her, never having known her to be deceitful. 'I have a job waiting, in the office of a department store. Filing, dealing with correspondence, answering the telephone. And I'll be independent. We're not sharing a room, Mama. There'll be nothing improper. But it's Vienna. If I stay in Kaumberg, my life will only ever be small.'

WHAT AWAITED OVERWHELMED her. Shortly after arriving, finding herself alone in the cramped, stale-smelling second-floor room once Sindelar had slipped out to a corner shop for a few essentials—milk, bread, coffee, cheese, eggs, sausage, as well as a bottle of schnapps that they'd open to celebrate—she sat on the corner of the bed with her duffel bag on the bare floor between her feet and, trying to feel optimistic, dismissed her tears as silly homesickness. With a bit of effort, a feminine touch, the apartment would feel more welcoming, she decided, and as a modern woman she'd embrace this new life with an excited heart and be ready for the challenges it set her. When he finally knocked again on the door an hour or more had passed. Apologising at having been waylaid, dragged into a nearby cafe by some people he knew, a couple of Simmeringer players and their wives, he looked around in small astonishment at finding that she'd already made a start on transforming the place. She had mopped the floors to a reddish sheen in the lantern light, cleared out and cleaned the kitchen cupboards, utensils drawer and stove, and was busily scrubbing the pans, pots, cups, plates and cutlery, left behind by the apartment's last tenant, which were a tad grubby but otherwise quite usable. To mark her first night in town, he'd planned on taking her out to some nice restaurant and maybe, if she wasn't too tired from the stress of the day, a spot of dancing after, but she shrugged and said that they could wait until the weekend to celebrate her big move, because getting the apartment straight and made comfortable felt more immediately important. So while he sat and poured himself a little of the schnapps, helping her only when she asked for his assistance in moving heavy things, the armchairs, the table, the bed a little towards the window, she fell happily into cleaning and tidying, easy in work that she'd spent her life about, humming snatches of songs she knew and talking, to herself as much as to him, about what colours would go well on the walls, or how a nice rug would really tie the room together. When she finally did sit down at the table, which she'd pulled a white cloth over, for greater effect, supper was a cold but welcome plate of bread, cheese and sausage, with pickles taken straight from a jar for spice, and good rich black coffee that he made, insisting that she let him, since it was one of the things he could do particularly well. Then, once she'd cleared and washed the dishes, he suggested a short walk, to give her a sense of the neighbourhood and to get a bit of air before bed. He was still at the table, turned aside from it now with one arm outstretched across its edge and his legs crossed tightly at the knee, left over right, and he watched as she moved across to the bed and began pulling items of clothes from her duffel bag and folding them neatly before putting them away. And, eventually, with the same unhurried ease, she began to undress, peeling down to her underwear, a grey cotton slip that was only thinly strapped at the shoulders and fell in a kind of lace frill to just above her knees. 'Let's skip the walk,' she said, without turning, though she must have known how intently he was watching her. 'You can open the window a little, if it's air you need.'

THE CITY WAS not only so much more than she'd dreamed, but seemingly everything at once: the public parks, gardens, museums and monuments immaculately sculpted, the tucked-away backstreets of the poorer corners fetid where sewers stood open and rats thronged. The main thoroughfares heaved and bustled to deafening levels during the working day but stood eerily quiet at certain early hours, the time of morning that Sindelar liked to take his run. And half a world away in everything except miles, the tranquillity of beautiful spring could be felt at any time of day or night out around Schönbrunn, where the air was at its most clean and fresh. The job that Mutzl had arranged for her felt too big at first, the department store an enormity unlike any place of business she'd ever known, the offices above it, a warren of them tucked away behind the second-floor storerooms, all windowless and at a loss to any sense of time, always hectic and overrun by secretaries, office boys, delivery men, and management types who floated back and forth between doorways and desks and who were immediately identifiable by their white shirts and braces, neatly clipped moustaches and slightly traumatised expressions, everyone it seemed an underling to someone else and with the same pallor of relentless harassment.

The first day, her heart chased whenever anyone glanced in her direction, terrified that she'd be tasked with something beyond her capabilities. But by afternoon, after eating a sandwich in the canteen and drinking a tall cold glass of milk, she found herself settling better to the pace of things, and shortly before the finish of the shift one of the other women in the office, a girl named Elsa, of about her own age and with an accent even more country than her own, having originated in the Tyrol, a small mountain village called Sölden, asked if she'd like to come with a few of the others for a spritzer or a glass of beer after work. It was a warm day after all, and it would give her a chance to get to know her workmates in an easier setting than the one surrounding them. They met again at the top of the stairs after signing out of the same register she'd that morning, as instructed, signed into, and walked together the couple of blocks to a small tavern with wooden benches to its rear where some women, varying between youth and middle age, and also a couple of young men, sat or stood around drinking and discussing something that seemingly required a considerable waving and gesturing of hands in order to be better explained. The group smiled when Elsa introduced her, a few shook her hand in welcome and a couple stared, but everyone was friendly and she answered the bombardment of questions as best she could, even the most forthright ones, without going into her actual reason for having moved here and without making any mention of Sindelar beyond acknowledging that yes, she was involved with someone, and no, there'd been no talk of marriage yet. She drank the glass of cider that Elsa put in her hand, and watched for her opportunity to reciprocate the kindness, not wanting to be seen as a type too quick to take. But even before her second glass was finished, seeing that the others were just getting comfortable, she made her apologies to any who cared to hear, explaining that unfortunately she had already made plans for the evening that couldn't be cancelled but looked forward to other such days as this, when she would be more prepared.

For all the apparently casual nature of what she and Mutzl had going, it was quickly clear to those who knew them that the connection they had was real and went beyond easy definitions. Team duty took him frequently out of Vienna—sometimes, when they were touring abroad, for weeks at a stretch—and if the trip fell across a weekend and required only a short stay, a one-off friendly or the away leg of a Mitropa Cup game, and was no further distant than, say, Prague or Budapest, then she joined them, the only one of the wives and girlfriends to do so. More often, though, she remained behind, and if the few friends of her own that she'd managed to make never rose to higher than the level of acquaintance then they were still people she could call on, to meet for coffee and to chat with for a couple of hours of an evening. At the beginning she put in more of an effort in this direction, but after a while found it easier to pass the time alone, reading in one of the parks if the weather was fine, visiting the Belvedere to enjoy the works of Klimt, Schiele and the various French Impressionists on show, or simply improving conditions at the apartment, wallpapering or painting, cleaning surfaces that were already by now well scoured but which seemed to come up that much brighter with every fresh pass. Sooner or later some ache for Mutzl struck, usually as she was undressing for bed or lying awake in the dark with time finally to contemplate, and often in feeling the emptiness of his side of the bed, she gave in to tears and had to throw an arm across her eyes or else turn over and press her face into the pillow that smelled of him. Because while there should have been contentment in knowing that as soon as he made it back home it was into her arms he'd be returning, it was still possible to trust someone with everything and still hold on to doubt, and the thought of other women in his life remained difficult to suppress, the hordes of hard beauties just waiting for the chance to offer themselves up to him at parties or in dance halls. Not only in towns across the country but probably right here in Vienna, too, the sprawl of this city so crammed with the kind of secret corners and alleyways that she, as a stranger, didn't dare even think about exploring but which he surely knew by heart from having spent so many years tucked away among them. Little things were said, by teammates, mainly, their intent teasing rather than hurtful, about who he'd been before she'd entered the equation, how he'd lived, and as open as the couple were with one another in almost every other way, so far there'd been no denials, though perhaps only because, in so dreading what the answer would be, she lacked the courage to ask. In their moments of togetherness all of this faded into the background and ceased to matter, but while they were cities or even countries apart, what they had going felt lessened, compromised. Occasionally she'd come across names, scrawled in handwriting that wasn't his on pieces of paper he'd evidently thought enough of to want to tuck away and save, though she had to concede that he may also have done so mindlessly and out of simple politeness, having them pressed upon him in a crowd situation. Intimate notes, in languages that she knew only a few words of, if at all, but which she seemed to understand, just the same. Unable to help herself, she thought about some of these women and tried to picture them, even faceless to her as they were, standing smiling at his side in nightclubs or cafes, in his arms for fast and slow dances, and later, whether paid to be or simply coaxed, lying naked beneath him in some hotel bed, and the pain she felt made her cry out and in her lowest moments want to die.

But all of that was for the night-time. Waking with the skin around her eyes raw from having cried herself to sleep and even through it, there was always the calm of a new morning, a fresh start, sunlit or rainy but with some element of brightness. If she had work that day she'd usually return to find him waiting, having let himself in, sitting at her small foldout dining table in his usual pose, one arm outstretched along its most convenient edge, body half turned away from it for the freedom of the room, legs folded one across the other at the knee. Not doing anything, just sitting, in perfect pent-up stillness, waiting. She tried to play casual, offhand. 'Oh, you're back. Did you have a good trip? Did you win?' Moving around the apartment as she talked, acting in charge, pretending not to even hear when he told her how much he'd missed her, and how beautiful she looked, slipping out of her coat and hanging it up on one of the hooks behind the door, hanging her hat up too, if the day was wet or snowing and she happened to be wearing one, her wool cap or tan fedora, smiling but as if to herself, at some inner thought, and giving him no more than glances. At the same time, though, thrilled yet again at how intently he was watching her, logging her every movement, however inconsequential, but not himself stirring, suffering the stillness even when it became unbearable, waiting, heightening everything, until she happened to notice the parcel on the table, the brown paper wrapping, strung in twine or bowed in ribbon. Nylons, usually, or a silk scarf, maybe a lace nightgown of the sheerest variety. And once, a small box, which had her heart beating so hard she thought she'd either pass out or be sick, brimming as she was with the mistaken assumption that it must carry the ring that would in some official way signify their engagement instead of the beautiful gold love-heart locket that it actually contained. The gifts quickly came to feel ritualistic, a kind of making up for all that went unspoken, and she was appreciative of the gestures and told him so but insisted that they were unnecessary, that just having him back to her was enough and all she really wanted. Still, she did admit to adoring the locket, at least once the disappointment at his lack of a proposal had passed. She'd lifted it from the box and, when the delicate chain's clasp proved too challenging for her own excited fingertips, had had him stand behind her and fasten it while she watched herself in the wall mirror and admired the necklace settling into place against the skin below her throat. Hardly an hour later, before they'd even sat down to eat or waited for night to properly fall, she wore it to bed with him, and as invariably happened after the initial moments of awkwardness following his return, tides washed in to scrub and salt their surfaces clean of grudging thoughts. Those other women, whether imagined or real, were not enough, she decided, to break what they had going, whatever that was. *Love*, for want of a better word, because it was the word he used, the promise he made, whispering and swearing it, his eyes, usually so sharp, falling half-lidded above a daze while his hands traced the contours of her body from shoulders to hips; and choosing to believe him she repeated her response to it over and over in her mind, *I love you, too*, breathing it, feeling its give and take, and held on as he drew himself against her. And even if in giving so much of herself so easily she was selling herself terribly, sinfully short, the truth was that nothing else seemed nearly as important or completing. When she put her arms around him and held his chest tight to her own there was neither past nor future but simply the instant, and the sense of being, within it, wildly and entirely alive. Vienna lay beyond the window, a world that was not hers and never would be, but for those twenty or thirty minutes there in her room, and even more so confined to the margins of her bed, all of that ceased to matter.

SHE WORKED, AND he did too, approaching his day job with the ferocity of focus common only to those who achieve levels of success beyond the merely ordinary. Trying hard to be good and then to be better, he said, on those cold mornings when it was still dark outside and snowing and when they had one another to hold on to in bed, with no pressing need to be anywhere else but where they were. Kissing her, smiling away her protests, and acting as if he wanted more than anything to stay but slipping from the bed to dress in old shorts and a sweatshirt and maybe a woollen cap against the weather, to run. Through the quiet streets, crossing the city out to more rural stretches, asking ten or fifteen miles of himself, even though his knee hurt almost all the time and that kind of distance was often asking too much. It's what it took, he explained, later on, in some cafe or restaurant, the pair of them happy and holding hands. There was a level that he had to keep to, and at his age now he needed to fight for it, because it was no longer given freely.

On the pitch there were few still who could stand comparison. Whenever Austria Vienna had a game in town, Rebekah went and stood on the terraces to watch. Supporting the Violets, of course, and always wanting them to win but attending really with eyes only for her man, thrilled at being able to see him in his element and in a certain way at his best, the truest and most natural version of himself, separate from his connection to her. Sometimes, in a rival stadium, she dared to lurk anonymously among the enemy fans for the chance to savour the vehemence of their baying vulgarity. When it came to Mutzl, though, they tempered their bile to applaud his skill even when it cost their own team dear, cursing him but with smiling admiration and shrugging to one another that there was simply no accounting for genius when it flashed. That had, after all, been some pass to split the defence, some display of vision, some goal. With the ball he seemed to float, even through quagmire, elegant and full of grace and almost never harried, not even when the marking was tight and overtly physical, confidently trusting his touch and passing technique, seeing threat from yards away and seconds in advance. In effortless fashion, he set the tempo and moved the pieces of his team, leading even when hobbled, when some hatchetman had him lame and bloodied from the knees down with relentless hacking until one of his teammates, usually Viertl or Stroh, stepped in to exact retribution with a well-hidden elbow or headbutt, leaving his assailant as pulp in the mud, the nose, jaw or cheekbone smashed nearly irreparably. That was the game, he told her once. Even the most beautiful river was nothing without a stony bed. But while that was the game, indeed, it was not his game, and not what the crowds bought tickets in their tens of thousands to come and watch. They came to see magic, and to have their breath taken. And that, almost without fail, even if just for a heartbeat or two a game, was what they got.

In terms of skill and an ability to read the game he had few equals. There was the Italian, Meazza, who'd been thoroughly outclassed when Sindelar, with a magisterial performance that culminated in a blistering hat-trick, took Ambrosiana Inter apart in the Mitropa Cup final of a couple of years before, but who, since then, had led Italy to World Cup and Central European Cup glory, and was universally regarded as a special talent and a genuine star. And in England, a young player, Matthews, a winger for Stoke City, one of the sport's founding clubs, had already been capped a few times for his country, and according to those most in the know about such things seemed to have all the attributes for greatness. These two, then, and if arguments might have been made for one or two more it was still only against Sindelar that they could reasonably be rated, he being regarded as the standard, the brightest star of the once- and perhaps forever-fabled *Wunderteam*. Even now, in what had to be considered the twilight period of his career, at thirty-four and with his prime some half a decade already behind him, still in the estimation of most, the game's maestro.

The press loved him because in everything he did he was pure story. Mozart with a football, they'd write, putting it in headlines. *Der Papierene*—the Paper Man, suggesting that a stiff breeze could carry him away, yet meaning it as complimentary, as if he were something elemental, only suggestively real and the purest make-believe, a fiction dressed as fact. That Austria Vienna didn't dominate their division year after year was almost beside the point. Art is flashes, the sportswriters suggested, especially those more given to poetry than statistics, which might have explained why the long grind of an entire league season held less appeal than the more romantic spontaneity of a National Cup run, or the grand stage of European competition, or even the easy-going excitement of taking his talents beyond local borders, acting almost in an ambassadorial role in the dozens of exhibition games his side played yearly across the entirety of Europe. By the late twenties, fans, even those of rival teams, and players too, were flocking to pay homage, many among them there purely to study his movements and bear witness to touches that seemed impossible until seen, and even then scarcely believed. There was a goal against Brigittenauer that saw him dribble through six tackles in the space of barely ten yards in a frozen, badly cut-up penalty area before entirely wrong-footing the goalkeeper for a tap-in finish. And a moment in a home game against one of the Italian sides when with a piece of absurd skill he took the ball out of the air fully a yard above his own head with a kind of upside-down scissors movement that for months after had other players, including many who'd simply heard tell of it, nearly breaking their necks in futile attempts at emulation. In every game, it seemed, he came up with two or three small tricks that had never before been seen on a field in Austria: a certain way of trapping the ball, an astonishing pass or flick, a shot—whether it scored or not—that looked to have come from nothing and nowhere. To witness him playing, even in the most meaningless local exhibition or fundraiser, and regardless of the final result, was to receive, at least in glimpses, a lesson in what the game could be.

Football was his way of impacting the world and, consciously or otherwise, staking his claim towards a place among the immortals, but as far as the newspapers were concerned it still amounted to only half his story. Because during those long nights after the games had been put to bed, fresh intrigues were so often set in motion. In coffee houses and dance halls all around the city and in nightclubs in cities abroad, particularly back during his prime years, the late twenties through to the mid thirties, crowds made up of dignitaries and other notables, genuine stars, joined in the same pressing pack as the rabble, ordinary men and women, and swarmed to him, just wanting to be near. And he was a firework, all the light in any room. People couldn't speak to him without reaching out and touching his arm or patting his back, as if there was something holy to be had from the connection. The thirstiest among them—beauties mostly, with chiselled smiles and even harder stares—did what they could to linger and hang on his every utterance, laughing at the least and most throwaway of his remarks, living to catch his eye, having decided on him as the gift they wanted to give themselves. And on those nights when he decided that he was feeling lonesome too, and once all the photos had been posed for and the offered hands shaken, these were the women who invariably won out, they wanting a piece only because he was what so many others seemed to crave, and finally, for a while anyway, an hour or two ahead of dawn, getting their fill, though nothing more and certainly nothing that counted.

That was one reality, but it turned frail as smoke when set against the nights he had Rebekah standing alongside. Those other women were barely noticed then, if at all, and he was able to distance himself, and his lover, too, by putting up a kind of wall around them. Nothing about his demeanour changed, his friendliness and swagger didn't shift; hands were still shaken, cheeks pecked and all expected duties fulfilled, but it was clear to all that a boundary had been decisively set and was not to be broached. With his hand holding on to hers or curled in a relaxed way around her waist, Rebekah felt like somebody too, even when in her heart she understood otherwise, and on such nights they drank champagne as fast as their glasses could be filled, his appetite as usual unquenchable, and when they danced, floating to the music, it was as if the whole room stopped to watch, looking on with envy and with awe. Later, hours on, when they were again alone together, strolling back towards either her apartment or his with the morning at its smallest, huddled to one another against the cold and filling the stretch of road by counting the spill of stars above them, they talked in murmurs of love and little things and, in the easy, laughing silences, stopped once in a while to kiss. Everything else then, all the rest of it, the parties and the flash, the other women, dropped away, reducing the entire world down to the square yard of ground on which they stood, and making forever of it, a permanence. Embracing beneath a talcum spill of street light or in shadow, breathing deeply of one another's air, Rebekah let the moment fill with what mattered and decided again and for certain that whatever this was, whether love or something other, it was all there would ever be for her, and all she needed.

The Marina

Cork, 1980

WHAT SLEEP COMES to Jack is fitful and disturbed, and for most of the night he lies awake, listening through the darkness for murmurs. Alongside and turned in towards him, Rachel dreams on, her raven hair spread out in wild feathers across the pillow, lips slightly parted, showing the pale edge of upper front teeth, her slow exhalations warming the skin of his bare shoulder. Even now, it astonishes him to be sharing a bed with her. There's no shyness between them, and no secrets, at least not on her part. She told him once, during some intimate moment, not long after they were married though probably long enough for the first blush to have faded, that she didn't believe she could ever be happy unless he was happy, too. That had bothered him. He'd grown up with love, but this was of a different magnitude. For a while he had struggled with the notion of having to give quite so much, believing that everybody, at their essential core, consisted in at least some respect of lies, and his deepest dread was that by revealing the darker corners of himself he'd be somehow lessened for her. The fact that they had grown up together should have soothed such anxiety, but in all the time they'd been a couple, from when they first started going out, just ahead of her seventeenth birthday, through their initial fumbling efforts at sex and on into the early stages of their marriage, he couldn't look at her without feeling a tinge of inadequacy. There would have been plenty interested in her, if she'd only taken the trouble to look around, but the few times he mentioned this she'd made a joke of it, laughingly insisting that nobody got to decide who they were going to fall in love with and that it was never for her a question of having to settle—if that's what he was implying—but of wanting to. As the years passed, and especially after Hannah was born, his insecurities faded into the background, but there are still moments, such as this one now, lying here in bed, studying her face while she sleeps, when the old dread seeps once again to his surface.

A little after five he gives in to his restlessness and slips from the bed. Registering even in her sleep-state some shift in the equilibrium, Rachel spills over onto her back and throws an arm out across the space he has just vacated. Light from the street, sullen tangerine, uses the cast of the window's blinds to lattice her face in this new position with alternations of shadow and glow, and in response to this annoyance a tightness creases the skin across her forehead and around her eyes. He dresses quickly, pulling on his work jeans and doing up the buttons of his heavy wool shirt, but drawing the blinds does nothing to ease the stress in her expression. He studies her, and can't help wondering what it is within her dreams that's causing her concern. Almost immediately, though, he decides that he's better not knowing. A marriage without hidden places is a fine notion but doesn't take into account that, when all is said and done, everyone is still an island unto themselves and that even the most willing and eager hearts can only ever be prised so far open. He leans down again across the bed and presses a kiss onto her cheek, high up near the corner of her eye. She reacts without waking, something like a smile quivering her lips and a heavy breath that seems to hum with laughter, and such a burst of affection overcomes him that he kisses her again, this time on the mouth, not a peck, and after a moment she pushes against him in response and after a few seconds more opens her eyes. He leans back while she lifts herself up onto her elbows.

'What time is it?'

'I don't know. Early. I just feel like getting up.'

'Can't sleep, is that it?'

He shrugs. 'I keep playing it over in my head. I'll go down and make a cup of tea. And I might go for a walk. I've time yet before work. Let you stay where you are, love. Keep warm. You've no need to be stirring awhile.' He leans in and kisses her again, and this time she puts an arm around the back of his neck and holds his mouth to hers, letting him taste the heat of her exhaustion.

'I'll get up, too,' she says, but he holds the blankets across her.

'You won't. It's hardly gone five. The small one will have you moving soon enough. Can't you take these couple of hours while you're getting them? And I'd prefer you be awake tonight than now.'

She looks up at him, eyes shining. 'That's a date.' She laughs, then all at once turns serious. 'Don't go too far, all right? The Marina can be a lonely spot of a bad morning. Especially in the dark. And don't be killing yourself at work today. I mean it, Jack. Keep a bit of energy back for me.'

OUTSIDE, THE MORNING is full of skinning cold. Feeling foolish at being up so early but needing this air, the pummel and lash of the sharp wind thick with stones of rain, he pulls the lapels of his heavy black donkey jacket across his chest and hurries through Jewtown's maze of lanes before turning eastwards and crossing over onto the entirely deserted Centre Park Road. The first mile is a dead-straight stretch, ground laid down with trucks in mind, carrying as it does past several gated industrial businesses, furniture warehouses, paint and plastics factories, before doglegging at a shallow angle back north again towards the water. After the first couple of hundred yards the road turns tree-lined, with mature oaks, sycamores and, further along, magnificent old European limes leaning in on either side, and the street lights are interspersed in such occasional fashion that they offer almost no relief against the darkness. While he knows the way well, having walked it all his life, in every kind of weather and in all seasons, he keeps his hands fisted inside his coat's side pockets, just in case. For wrong types dark corners make good hiding places. But at least the rain has cleared, and aside from his footsteps on the wet pavement the only real sounds are the whip of the gusting wind and the tree branches overhead, stripped nearly entirely bare after a long and frequently stormy winter, moiling with all the relentless fury of waves breaking across shale.

By the time he reaches the road's shallow bend sweat has begun to lather the skin of his back and neck and he is conscious of his heart's quickened beating. His mother is more than thirty years gone, and in many ways it's almost as if she'd never existed at all. These past few years especially, unless he can be specific with his memories, he's had difficulty recalling what she even looked like, at least beyond the couple of photos he has of her, the same face watching from small cheap wooden frames on either side of the mantelpiece, her expression serious as a schoolteacher in one, slightly scolding, and in the other smiling ever so sadly, young still and undeniably pretty but frayed along her edges, and weary.

These paper images are, to a large extent, who she has become, sepia lines and curves, eyes already devoid of life, personality and soul a flatness that has her reduced to simple surfaces, and it hurts him that he does not have more of a hold on her. Occasional reminders, of course, have her in unexpected moments storming his mind, something said or glimpsed, the little tucking gesture that Hannah, his daughter, makes with her mouth when thinking aloud, or hearing a song come on the radio, Ella Fitzgerald, Bing Crosby, or Sinatra, who she loved, whose voice she used to say made ruins of her. Songs like 'The Way You Look Tonight' or 'The Night We Called It a Day' are time-slips, ripe with the heat and perfume smells of their old surroundings, and Jack only has to hear the dirty blue strains of 'That Old Black Magic' to see her jiving again around their cramped Hibernian Buildings kitchen with her cousin David, the one closest to her in age, as her dance partner, he feigning reluctance but secretly delighted to be learning such daring, jazzy steps and to be holding on to her, and she against him so caught up in the rhythms while the rest of the household, even Ruth and Joe, clicked their fingers or clapped along in laughing time. She's part of him, Jack knows, half of who he is, alive in that sense in everything he does. The same blood that ran through her veins runs in his. But the truth is, he's lived for so long without having her around, and as a way of coping kept her memory so deeply buried that, until the discovery of the letters this past Sunday, he probably hasn't thought about her two consecutive days in years.

The letters. God. At forty-one, he'd long since accepted his lot, the missing pieces just a fact of life. Growing up, most of the boys he knew had fathers, but there was scarcely a family in Jewtown spared the damage of the war, at least on some level, kin—extended if not immediate—lost to its brutalities, and in the face of such senseless horror, and the sheer immensity of its magnitude, enquiry seemed futile. In the synagogue, the men discussed it, and women in their kitchens, too, recounting to one another from newspaper articles the testimonies of those who somehow made it through; but for so long the picture of what had occurred was confused, not only during the period of the war but for upwards of a decade after, when further and worse was gradually revealed, until books started being written in an attempt to make sense of it all, the facts so scattershot and contradictory and the scale so overwhelming as to be almost incomprehensible. No family went unscathed, and a kind of universal loss was understood and held reverent, and against the weight of all that was known and whispered of, his own unanswered questions were left easily lie. The other Jewtown boys had fathers, but because he had Joe he didn't feel particularly deprived. He remembers, at ten years old, straining to understand when Ruth, the woman he'd only ever thought of as his grandmother, came and sat beside him, held and squeezed his hand in both of hers and explained, in a voice parched to scrapings from a night spent in tears, about what an awful disease tuberculosis was and how a beautiful, frail creature like Rebekah had stood no chance, really, especially with it having been caught so late. He'd felt as if somebody had taken a butcher's knife and hollowed him entirely, and to keep from having to see Ruth's face, and all the sadness in her eyes, he'd turned to the doorway and found Joe standing there, in that quiet way he always had about him, like a tree leaning with the wind but never going over. Two or three years earlier, without prompting or discussion and even though Grandad would have been a neater fit, Jack had started referring to Joe as Dad, something he'd keep up until almost into his twenties. Not at home, where it might have been embarrassing for all concerned, but if they were out somewhere, the pair of them having walked out to Douglas for a drag hunt of a Sunday morning, say, or down the Park for a hurling match or else over along the Mardyke to watch Cork United or, after United folded in '48, Cork Athletic. Even without a direct blood connection in the world, it was made abundantly clear to him from the beginning that he still had family, and was still—and always would be—adored.

All things considered, life has been full and plenty, given worth by his wife and the daughter that has become his world. Work is hard but relatively steady, and the home they rent is sufficient for their needs. Plenty have it worse, in this country and abroad. And never the most ambitious type, he's content, both with his lot and with who he's found himself to be. At his age, settled. At least, he had been, before uncovering the letters. Now, all of a sudden, peace is lost, and the cacophony of questions has him muddled. Walking, fighting hard to retain a state of calm, he attempts to list the most troubling of them as they suggest themselves: Who this man, Sindelar, was. What his story is—how he connected to Jack's mother, how they became involved and what it was that had ultimately forced them apart. Who the newspaper cuttings had been sent by, too, and whether there is further correspondence to be found. It hurts his mind to think that the letters—and whatever answers they might contain—had been tucked away all those decades only yards from where he slept and dreamed. But are the conclusions he and Samuel have drawn even accurate, given that only one side of whatever kind of relationship this was can be read and judged, and only fragments of it, at that?

So much feels impenetrable, the dark density of it all frightening. Is he reaching, making of this what he wants and maybe needs it to be, or has he in fact uncovered, as they all seem to suspect, the *one*, the father he's never had or even known of. If so, was this man, Sindelar, aware of Rebekah's pregnancy, and Jack's arrival into the world?

This last, of everything, is the question that holds most importance for him. The others matter, too, but can be guessed at and, based on the few details they do know, assumptions made, even if they can't necessarily be verified or proven; but this one is the great torment, the black hole that has been dug into his existence.

In times of upset, and regardless of rain or cold, he walks the Marina. It's what he has always done. The area's familiarity is a balm because of how it keeps his ghosts close, in particular those long-ago summer evenings spent accompanying Rebekah, strolling without sense of what lay ahead or even what was really happening in their lives, and holding her hand simply because she was his mother and he loved her. And this was the best he'd known her to be, her mood easy and languid, especially once they got out onto the riverbank. If the days were stretching long they'd enjoy how the late brightness ribbed the water's surface in reds and shades of gold, or wave at the boatmen drifting past on their slow way into port, the diesel smell of their vessels suited to the hot air. Liz, who was always so wound up about the latest fashions, had at some point persuaded his mother to put her hair, that shade of threshed blonde, in low curls and to have it back from her face, in the way of film stars like Veronica Lake and Joan Fontaine, and she liked that style enough to want to keep to it even if it presented her with the problem of looking both young and old at the same time.

Young and old and then far too quickly gone, but roused again, it seems, resurrected, by the letters. Not her voice, but directed to her, fleshing her out in ways Jack had never previously thought to even consider.

And reuniting them, a man, a stranger and at the same time perhaps anything but, and for Jack, potentially, the whole other half of himself. But it's so much to have to comprehend. 'You think you know yourself,' he'd said, the night before, in bed, just before

Rachel had drifted off to sleep. Speaking as much to himself as to her, his voice cowed and made small by the dark. 'You fill yourself up with what you can, you grab what's going and you hold on. And then something like this happens, and suddenly you're empty all over again. That's the worst of it. You can't help feeling lost.' She'd listened, held his hand and tried to reassure him that he was wrong, that nothing had changed and, no matter what was discovered, nothing could. 'I know you,' she'd said. 'I know the man you are. If you're ever in doubt, ask me.'

BEYOND THE ROAD'S dogleg the flanking trees start to thicken, but eventually the way widens and breaks out onto the Marina. After the claustrophobia of the natural cover, there is a sense if not yet an actuality of brightness. The air coming off the river has the mean chill of a winter's frost; out in the channel scuds of fog cling to the water's oily surface, keeping just beneath the breeze, but across the way, against the far bank—impossibly far-seeming, yet a distance he's known men and even boys make at a relatively easy swim—the black tide is lit by the grisly wash, yellow as exposed bone, of the Lower Glanmire Road's towering sodium lights. His own path, eastwards in the direction of Blackrock, stretches darkly on, and, shoulders hunched, he follows, moving at a steady pace rather than a quick one. The water fringes his left side and a dense wall of trees crowds his right, the cover breaking early on to reveal the low building of the Lee Rowing Club and, a hundred yards further along, rising up behind the mostly stripped alder branches, the hulking walls of Páirc Uí Chaoimh. This is where, right up until Joe's death, six years ago, he and the old man had stood together at the cost of the cheapest terrace ticket to watch hurling matches and bear witness to the masters of the game, he catching only the final playing days of Jack Lynch, the real Taoiseach, who everyone insisted had as a young man been dynamite altogether with a stick in his hand, but getting to more fully appreciate the likes of Paddy Barry, Ray Cummins, the Doyles of Tipp, Jimmy and John, Kilkenny's Eddie Keher, Bobby Rackard of Wexford, and of course the greatest of them all, the mighty Christy Ring. Walking to games or home from them, and sometimes just walking for the sake of movement, out here along the river for the fresh air, was when Joe would open up with talk, as much as he was ever able, not making mention of fathers or anything in that direction and not even really speaking of Rebekah or the circumstances of her arrival in Cork, but giving bits and pieces about Jack's people on her side. Never all at once, but letting a picture build by accumulation.

There'd been a sister, Gitta, who'd written to Rebekah a couple of years after the war, sending her letter care of the city's synagogue, not having a more specific address. And for a while they'd corresponded, not only the sisters but Joe and Gitta, too. The war had destroyed everything good. In '43, she, her husband, Franz, and their daughter, Analise, who was just three years old, were sent to Sered', a camp not far from Bratislava. Franz succumbed to pneumonia early the following year, and Analise died soon after, from dysentery, but somehow Gitta had survived, though she carried numerous health problems with her through the remainder of her short life, including the lung disease that within just a few years would prove fatal. After the war she met and lived for a short time with a cousin, Asa, the eldest son of her father's brother Jakob. Other cousins had made it to America, and this was Asa's intention, too. He hated Europe now, he said, and would cry at random moments of the day no matter where he was, whether in a shop or on a bus. He was the one who'd broken the news to Gitta that her parents—Jack's grandparents—had died in a camp-ghetto. They'd gone back to Cham, to the family home, hoping probably that there'd be security in numbers, but were soon rounded up along with other relatives and moved across the Czech border.

'What happened over there is our tragedy too, Jack,' he said once, in a way that stuck. 'And it's never the past, not really. It can't and mustn't be. You understand that, don't you, lad? They were our people, our own flesh and blood. My father and mother were both already dead by then, but I had uncles, aunts, cousins. And there were the children, too. Think of it. Lambs to the slaughter. Good God. That's why we keep remembering, Jack. Why we have to.'

WHETHER BY DAY or in the dark, it is the same along this stretch, with the rattle-calls of nesting herons and egrets from the hidden Atlantic Pond, and the constant stabbing chirp of little grebes. This morning, he longs to be able to stroll all the way to Blackrock to watch the sun coming up and on the way back to sit a while on one of the benches by the Pond, wrapped snug in his coat, and enjoy the lash and crackle of the tree branches sword-fighting in the wind or the sight of the birds on the water. But there is a long shift of work ahead, and obligations to be met, so he allows himself to continue only until he is roughly adjacent to the ruin of Dundanion Castle, Galwey's Castle that was. The dense foliage now conceals the crumbling walls and the shell of a broad tower, the facade vine- and ivy-clad and, as its entry from this side, the overgrown slipway—the very one which, some three hundred years ago, had supposedly launched William Penn towards the founding of Pennsylvania—indicating just how broad the Lee had at one time run, close to the width of a football pitch south of where the river currently banks. He turns towards the city again and the breeze settles against his back and suddenly everything about the pre-dawn feels more comfortable, except for the fact that if the sun should begin to rise now, he wouldn't immediately know it.

Why hadn't she told him? That is what he struggles with, and what he can't get over. During the time of war he'd been too young to understand, but by '49, in those months prior to her death, he was already ten years of age, and old enough to bear the truth, whatever that was. Even after falling ill, she'd had time enough to sit him down and explain the situation, if not the story in gory detail then at least some simplified, cleaned-up version of it. What had she been so afraid of, and what, really, was she concealing? His mind raved with the most terrible imaginings. She'd made it out of Vienna with the worst still looming, found sanctuary with relatives that she'd barely known about and had never met but who immediately welcomed her into their lives and hearts. Was it shame that motivated her silence to the bitter end, the stigma of unwed motherhood, or that she'd escaped unscathed while her closest family perished in camps along with millions of others? Or had it to do, specifically, with this man, Sindelar?

There'd been a brief period, just as he was about to finish school, when Jack had held the fact of her dying against her. A reaction common, surely, to all boys in his situation finding themselves on the cusp of manhood, it nevertheless hurts now having to admit that to himself. In the face of his own desperate uncertainty, he'd been angry and afraid at having been abandoned, and full of a sense that the world was mercilessly spinning him loose of his place in it. He remembers on more than one occasion lying awake late into the night while the house around him slept, telling Rebekah in his mind how unfair she'd been, and how selfish, leaving him as she had, when he'd needed her so much. That dying was the last thing she'd have desired seemed actually beside the point; at that age, fourteen, fifteen, feeling so small and helpless, so daunted by the thought of life, he was lashing out in the only way he could. Had she lived he's certain they'd have come to all of this eventually, and if she had failed to leave a note or instructions of some sort for him then surely that was because nobody ever really believes they are going to die at thirty-three, even with so much writing on the wall. And the truth was that, towards the end, and particularly during those final months, she'd been unable to focus on anything but the pain and the struggle to draw breath. Consumption was such a filthy and brutal illness, a thing that lived up fully to its name: flecking the handkerchief that she held to her mouth with its black mist, peeling away pounds of flesh, and drawing her shoulders together in a way that turned her hunched and quickly old. It squeezed and ruined her, contracting her whole existence down first to a sanatorium room, then to a narrow grey-sheeted bed, and finally to her own brittle shell, with all else but the suffering ceasing to exist.

Knowing as little yet as Jack does, the tumult of detail within the letters feels all at once too heavy a fog to navigate. They carry about them the implication, if not quite the words, of razed towns and cities, death-camp visions, bodies ravaged down to sticks of bone from fighting, marching, hard labour and starvation—too much just now, with a long shift of work on the docks ahead of him, to have to face. Tonight, he tells himself, in a kind of soothing promise, Rachel's father will have finished translating the final pieces of the story, and that will give him a chance to properly consider his options.

He starts reluctantly back in the direction of the city. The time is coming on for half past six, so there is no reason to hurry. He'll be at the dockyard gates with ease by seven, ready to lose himself in another day's labour. If nothing else, it will give him some place to be.

Separating

Vienna, 1938

THE ROOM WAS still, this far beyond midnight. During their exertions the cotton sheet had fallen or been kicked away and now, in the aftermath of their lovemaking, hung in bunches from the foot of the bed. Neither one of them had the energy to do more than breathe, he in long thin whispers, she in little silent bites. But even though sleep refused to come, there was contentment enough in having this time to share, the pair of them freshly uncoupled but remaining in a thousand ways entwined.

His apartment, on Annagasse, was more elegant than her bedsit, but without any of the softness or even comfort that she'd instilled in her space. They tended to stay here only when they had spent the evening in this part of town, at a function or dance or dinner with friends and it felt too late to be crossing the city. Hers was far better equipped to make something more than merely alcoholic of an evening, and because he could never sleep for more than two or three hours without wanting to be up and away, she preferred to have her own walls around her on waking and her own bed in which to keep warm and remember. At home she could cook while music played and he could sit and watch, and it just felt, for both of them, a better way to live. This Annagasse apartment, for all its high rent and extra room, was harder to make homely.

Tonight, though, it was where they'd ended up, the most convenient to the restaurant at which they'd eaten dinner, just the two of them, over candlelight, as if some occasion was being celebrated.

In the corner nearest to the end of the bed on her side, an oil lamp, turned to just above a glimmer, made a low umber of the dark, letting the room's shapes be traced while still hiding enough of the details for fantasies to thrive.

They lay on their backs, studying the ceiling. Because the mattress was so narrow, really just a single, their bodies on his left side and her right met at the shoulder and down the length of their arms, and then again from the waist down. Her foot, small and pale, lay across his, and she could feel the bone of his bridge nestled into the arch of her instep. She tried to feel him alive beside her, but this was downtime, and beyond the clammy fire of his sweating skin there was nothing, no movement, not even the sense of a pulse. The weeks since the *Anschluss* game had taken a toll, mentally as well as in physical terms. He had his left knee raised a little, kinked in a way that relieved some inner pressure, the one he always kept strapped during games, ever since injuring it so badly as a young man—not as a result of some particularly brutal tackle, as most might have reasonably assumed, but actually due to a fall on the slippery tiles around a public swimming baths. The damage suffered was significant, requiring extensive surgery, which cost him, at not yet twenty, a full year of playing, and for a while seemed set to finish his career before it had even properly begun. He'd shrugged when she had asked him about that, how it was that he'd coped and whether he'd been afraid, and told her that he'd often wondered if, on the contrary, it had made him as a player, in giving him something so clearly defined to overcome. The bandages were like a cross on a map for every opponent who stepped onto the field against him, a target impossible to ignore, and survival required not only great focus and drive but also a necessary guile. Stripped of what natural speed he might have at one time possessed, he had no choice but to develop his passing range and close touch, and hone his ability to recognise and weigh opportunities before they presented themselves. From the beginning of their time together, Rebekah was acutely aware of his caution, subconscious or otherwise, in overstretching or having it bear excessive weight. Even now, after three years of knowing him better than she'd ever known anyone, he remained to her a muddle of contradictions: vulnerable in moments, yet capable and generally assured; fragile-seeming, yet in other ways hard as iron bars; and ageing to the eye, fatigued by time and weathering, yet aflame with an ache to live and full still of appetite for the world. If the knee had set him lopsided or askew then there was something revealing of his true self, whether to do with hunger, determination or just blind faith, in how he adjusted and found balance. Being able to trace with fingertips and kisses the raised white welt left over from his wound's slow knitting gave her a sense, in a way she could feel if not necessarily verbalise, of why she'd so freely abandoned her reputation and good name in Kaumberg and what she'd glimpsed about him that had seemed so worth joining. Compared to where she'd come from, Vienna was monstrous, especially in and around the cafes they tended to frequent, places full of vicious smiles and with a constant silhouette of menace draping the periphery. For a girl so used to walking country roads and who'd known everybody for miles in every direction to at least the second or third generation of their stock, the sheer bleak scale of the city, particularly when she found herself alone, at times overwhelmed her. Growing up, home was an entire town, small as it was. Here, home, if it existed at all, amounted to nothing but the space between four walls, the box into which she'd lock herself away, afraid of every strange thing. And yet, within her new life there were also bright moments, when it was just the two of them, twisted together on her narrow mattress or on his, while the snow gathered on the windowsill or rain lashed against the glass, or else out strolling, savouring the open space and seasonal blooms in one of the parks, they each hanging on the other's words, in the moment needing nothing more, adoring the naturally soft way he addressed her not by name but as his *liebling*, his darling, as if the world was only them.

She had just closed her eyes when she felt him move, and she kept them shut until he eased away to settle in a sitting position at his side of the bed, with his face turned entirely from her and the weight of his bare feet causing the old oak boards to creak. Her sense was that something had slipped adrift. In the dim light she considered the lines of his back, the lattice of bones prominent beneath the skin, his slender shoulders made narrower still by the way he slouched forward, hands gripping his knees. Because there was no unsteadiness about his breathing she dismissed her initial assumption that he was suffering some pain, but from where she lay, his seemed very definitely a posture of despair, and after a moment spent considering him from that angle she turned over onto her side, reached out and ran her fingers down his back, tracing the track of his spine, as if an answer was there to be read. Finally, she shuffled a little across the mattress and pressed herself against him in a half-risen embrace. His skin remained hot against hers, and the excitement that had been slow in waning stirred in her again.

'What's wrong?' she asked, tightening her grip. But his response was several seconds in coming and, when it did, felt like a heavy stone being moved. Everything about him exuded weariness.

'I'm sorry,' he said, without fully turning. 'I've not slept in days, trying to work out what I want to say to you. What I need to say.'

She'd released her hold on him and was kneeling, settled back onto her heels. His eyes took her in, her hair a flaxen spill around her shoulders, her nakedness, the familiar wonder of her breasts' slight upturn, the softness—not weight exactly, but something, a maturity perhaps—which had begun to fill her out these past months. Sensing the worst and dreading the words of it, she stared back hard at him, not crying yet but holding her tears close, and when her lips parted to tease with the ever-so-slightly gapped upper front teeth that had always seemed to him the very sweetest of her features, he fell back to his previous pose, sitting faced away from her, as his only resistance.

She hesitated, then put her arms around him and once more held him tight. 'Come on, Mutzl. Tell me. I'd rather know. Whatever it is.'

He cleared his throat. 'I want you to go,' he said.

'What?' She started to laugh, as if playing along with a joke ahead of its punchline, then abruptly cut herself off. 'What do you mean? Go where?'

'I'm sorry,' he repeated, and leaned forward into more of a stoop, with his elbows across his knees and his head hanging low between his shoulders, taking himself that much further from her.

Rebekah sat back again, but continued to stare. The walls of her throat seemed to be closing in, making it difficult to swallow, and her heart had begun to beat so hard she could feel it echoing in her head. 'I don't understand,' she whispered, her confusion genuine. 'Did I do something wrong? Or is it that you've grown tired of me?'

He turned his head, not all the way round but to one side, as a kind of acknowledgement. 'Come on, Beka. You know it's not that. It could never be that. Didn't I tell you not ten minutes ago how I feel about you, how much I love you? Do you think that's something I say easily?'

'I don't know. Maybe. You'd have no shortage of other girls when you're on the road. I know what footballers are like. There are probably things you have to tell them, too, and that you perhaps even mean.'

'From the beginning, you knew who I was. I never lied to you, Bek. Not once. With you I'm different. You know that. You're the one who matters to me.'

'So?' She held out her hands to him, then changed her mind and dropped them to her lap. 'What is it, then? Why now? Talk to me, Mutzl. You can't just say you want me to go and not explain yourself. And if it's not me, then what is it? Something must have happened. Are you in some kind of trouble? Tell me.'

He stood, stooped to gather up the pillows that had fallen to the floor, stacked them one on the other against the headboard and lay down again on the mattress, this new arrangement serving the purpose of elevating his head and upper body. Rebekah remained as she'd been, kneeling on her side of the bed, sat back on her heels with her thighs together, seemingly prepared to give him what time he needed, her anxiety evident only in the wide strain of her eyes trawling the length of his body short of his face and the sad way she chewed at a corner of her lower lip. The skin of his chest and stomach, apart from where wiry twists of hair gathered at his sternum and in swirls around his nipples, had the pale sheen of candle wax, and his penis, thick still from their bout of sex, slumped against his upper right thigh. Once again, he kept his left knee raised those few considerate inches.

'It's not you, my love. It's this city. My family came here from Moravia when I was just two years old. Kozlov, a village that would make your Kaumberg seem sprawling. My father was a stonemason in search of work, and this is where he found it. So even though I wasn't born here, Vienna is the only home I've known. It's given me everything I've ever had and it has my heart and soul. I love it.'

'Yes, I know. Everyone knows.'

His sadness was evident in his stare. 'I don't like the turn that things have taken. Most don't want to even admit it's happening, and I almost don't want to myself, but worse is coming. And I'm afraid. I'm worried for all of us but I am afraid for you. Terrified. My father was killed by the Italians in '17. Did I tell you that? At the Isonzo front. Bad fighting that was. Two hundred thousand dead in a month. I knew men who came back from there, and none of them were ever easy in themselves again. I was young, fourteen, when we heard the news, but fourteen is old enough to remember. We all want to think that that kind of war can only happen once. But just look outside. Soldiers patrol our streets like it's the most natural thing in the world. Germans. Nazis. We're not them, but the distinctions between us are becoming less and less clear.'

'You think there's a war coming? Is that it?' She almost laughed, even though she felt sick.

He shrugged. 'Something is. And it won't be good. You already get a sense of it in the coffee houses. People used to sit and argue half the night away, drinking wine or beer and talking politics, music, literature, art, football, everything. The meaning of life. Intellect was valued. In Vienna it was always so easy to fall in love. But these last few months, you can just feel the dread. Ideas aren't spoken of above a whisper; the sense of freedom has been stripped away.'

Rebekah reached out and rested a hand on his thigh just above his right knee. He seemed to be studying her face, yet there was a distance about his focus, and in that moment she felt sure that she had never seen anyone so devoid of hope. She kept her nails neatly trimmed and earlier that day had painted them a delicate and almost fleshy shade of pink from the bottle he'd brought her from Prague, and when she lightly squeezed his thigh his gaze fell in that direction, drawn perhaps by the colour, but he did not otherwise react.

'You think I'm exaggerating,' he said, 'but it's the same all across Europe. Politics shadows everything. Changing our club name is part of it. Ostmark won't stick—to the public we're the *Judenklub*, and always will be. But it's just the beginning. There are already whispers of purges.' Some seconds lapsed, and when he spoke again his staring eyes seemed full of other rooms. 'Dr Schwarz is gone. Did you know that? Our president, forced out, though they're trying to paint the move as voluntary. He was the one who signed me from Hertha, back in '24. I've known him longer than I knew my own father. The day he left we were told that the connection was now broken and that any attempt at further interaction would be viewed by the club as an act of betrayal. I immediately sought him out, shook his hand in front of a crowd and told him that whenever and wherever we met, no matter what the situation, I'd embrace him as I would a member of my own family. I had to, because we are either men or we're not.'

Tears, scarcely noticed by either of them, chased Rebekah's cheeks.

'I'm sorry,' she said. 'I've grown fond of Dr Schwarz, and his wife, too. They're good people who've shown me nothing but kindness. But isn't his firing just bureaucracy? Why does it have to mean something terrible for the whole of Austria? The whole of Europe? I admit it's frightening to see the soldiers in the street, but that's just a display of might. Because who is there to challenge them? It takes two armies to fight a war, and I can't believe that anyone wants bloodshed. In a few months things will settle down again. You'll see. And life will go on.'

But Sindelar shook his head. 'I hear the talk, even in the good cafes, of Aryan superiority and what dangers Jews and Gypsies pose. If you doubt me, come to the clubhouse. The walls have been smeared with the most disgusting slogans, in red paint that leaves a shadow of itself behind even after it's been washed down or painted over. I've seen similar in Favoriten, and over in Leopoldstadt when I went to visit Canetti. Truly vile stuff. And the worst of it is that it's finding support. Dr Schwarz is just the beginning. No one is safe. Some of the players are already talking about getting out. They don't want to go, but feel that they're running out of options. From what I've been told, a number of the French clubs are watching to see how things develop, Racing, for one, and they'll welcome with open arms and good contracts any who want to come. But I'm not sure Paris is far enough away. There's the option of Italy too, and Milan, Rome and Turin all have good teams who'd take our best players in a heartbeat, but again, I was there in '34 for the World Cup and for games since, and I've seen how things are. It's no different to here.'

It was all too much to take in. She abruptly scrambled from the bed, went through into the kitchen and poured herself a glass of water. She drank slowly, in little sips, standing in the middle of the floor, oblivious to the rising cold pushing up through her bare feet from the tiles. In the soft dark, she felt entirely alone in the world.

For as long as she'd been in Vienna, the city remained a strangeness. Sometimes, when its noise and frenzy became too much, she went and sat in the park, needing that sense of space to return some equilibrium to her spinning life. But even on a bench with one of her poetry books or stretched out on the grass under the greenery and the open sky, there was none of Kaumberg's balm or solace. Vienna was hectic and vibrant, nourishing to every young desire, but it was also an outpost of isolation. If she were to stand up in the train station's main terminal at rush hour or in any of the five or six dozen bustling coffee houses in her district and just scream to the fullest capacity of her lungs, nobody would so much as even turn a glance in her direction. That's how it was. In Vienna each person's pain was theirs alone to bear.

He made the difference. Those days and nights when he was in town, all her troubles seemed set right. That was love, she told herself, needing to believe. In bed, from the start, he was capable and adept, gentle when that was what she wanted of him, all the time talking in a hush, of the future and how much it meant to him to have found her. She'd been initially nervous, but there was no coercion. That first night, she opened herself to him and took his kisses, finding his mouth different in the darkness than during daylight, and guided him with small throat-sounds and careful touches. Night-time peeled the years from him and uncovered for her a young man's body, supple and full of grace. Afterwards, she lay in his arms, and even as he slept his hands moved across her back and sides, tracing her undulations. Still awake when dawn broke, she watched the sky beyond her window soften and turn grey and the first sunlight spill pale and then yellow from above the neighbouring rooftops. That new morning felt blessed, and from that hour forward she considered them in their own way married.

But now, just three years on from such a beginning, he was seeing an end already in sight.

His expression was knotted with concern when she reappeared from the kitchen, carrying a refreshed glass of water for him. She handed him the glass and settled herself again at the foot of the bed, facing him, with her knees drawn up to her chest and her thin arms hugging tightly at her shins. He drank in sips, and watched her, but she kept her focus only on the lamplit details of his body.

'What about you?' she asked, finally, in a murmur.

'What do you mean?'

'You want me to go. For my safety.'

'Yes.'

'And your teammates are getting out.'

He shrugged. 'Well, planning to. Some of them, anyway. They're talking about it, yes.'

'So, what about you? Just because you're famous, don't think—'

'It's not that. But it won't be the same for me.' His silence after a moment forced her to look up. He shrugged again. 'As far as they'll be concerned, I'm Catholic.'

At first she made no response, just continued to meet his gaze. A punchline seemed to be missing. Then, bitterly, she started to laugh. 'Right.'

'It's true. We're Catholics from Moravia. It's in the records, if anyone cares to look. I might not practise but it seems I'm documented.' Her eyes fell and he followed, and understood. 'Take no notice of that. There are plenty of reasons besides the Almighty why men get cut.'

This stunned her. She tried to think, but the facts refused to line up. 'I can't make sense of it,' she admitted, when she was able to speak again. 'All your friends, the team you play for, the district you grew up in. Even your interest in me. I just assumed.'

'I don't care how people pray, or even if they pray at all. That's their business, and between them and their God, and I've never thought it the measure of a man or woman. Do you care that I'm not Jewish?'

'No, of course I don't. How could I, when you're the one I love?'

'Then you can understand.'

A sob tore from her. 'Except now you want to cast me aside.'

'It's not like that, Beka. Don't say it that way. Please.'

'Why not? What else can you call it? I gave you everything. My home, my family. All I had.'

He stared at her, and she stared back, angry and hurt, waiting for more.

'If things are really as bad as you seem to think,' she started again, suddenly placating, 'we can get ourselves away. To Paris, Milan, even London. Anywhere. The place isn't important. What matters is that we're together.'

But exhaustion, from all that had already happened and at the thought of all that was still to come, had him beaten. 'They're watching me,' he told her, his voice sick-sounding, leaden with fear. 'I've heard I'm on a list. I can't say how true that is but it's easy enough to believe. The *Anschluss* game upset a lot of people, and I suppose I crossed a line. But I couldn't just stand back and do nothing. The coffee houses and nightclubs in Favoriten are already changing hands, and people are grabbing what they can while there's still something to take. Who knows how bad it'll be a year or two from now. For Jews, especially. That's why I want you safely away.'

At the foot of the bed, she tightened the clench of her arms around her knees. Her tears came hard, blinding her, crushing her expression, and he forced himself to watch, then turned onto one elbow and rearranged the pillows behind him for better comfort. Idleness didn't suit his body. He'd replaced his mattress a year earlier, in the hope of getting better sleep, but as with the previous one, it never more than tolerated his presence.

'If they have you on a list,' she said, between heaves, 'then how can you even think about staying? Why are you being obtuse about this, Mutzl? Why do you insist on acting the fucking idiot?'

The shock of hearing such a word from her widened his eyes, and he smiled in spite of all that he was feeling. But the momentary amusement didn't hold.

'Even if they are watching me, I don't believe there's much they can really do. My profile is too high. With my knee the way it is, and at my age, I have maybe a year left as a player. But the coaching I've been doing is laying groundwork, and that's what I'll settle to, moving forward. I know the game as well as anyone. It may not be quite the same from the sidelines, but nothing about life will be, either. And I can't leave. My mother's here, and my sister. Vienna is my city, for better or worse, and I'll stay and make my stand in however small a way that has to be. I won't let them make me run.'

Rebekah's neck felt stiff, and she rolled her head in a slow circular motion and began to knead her right shoulder and collarbone with the fingers of her left hand, wincing with the effort. Then she stretched out her legs and leaned back onto her elbows. Thin shadow veiled her, not concealing but enough to keep her surface details dimmed.

'Well,' she said, 'if you're staying then I am, too.'

He sighed. 'You're not. I'm sorry, Bek, but no. Don't you see, my love? They'll go for you. Even aside from wanting to round you up with the rest of the Jews, it'll be a way of getting to me. I wouldn't be talking like this if I wasn't frightened. You must know that. But if I can get you out then I'll have at least done some good. And this might be our only chance. Moving between countries is becoming more difficult. There's so much paperwork involved now. I have some connections, so there are people who can help us, but six months from now, maybe less than that, who knows, there's no guarantee they'll still be in a position to.'

The sense of shock had made two of her—a surface that could only cry and some far removed second self.

When she spoke, the words seemed to echo for her with that distance:

'You're really serious about this.'

'I wish to God I wasn't.'

'Then tell me, where am I supposed to go?'

'I'm not sure, yet. Switzerland, anyway. For a start. Then probably France. I can get you across those borders easily enough. But further away would be better. Because Austria won't be enough for Hitler. The Nazis are already pushing for the Sudetenland, and if that falls then the whole of Europe will need to worry.' He fell silent, his mind evidently reaching for something. 'Didn't you tell me once that you had family abroad? In Scotland, was it? Or did I imagine that?'

'Ireland, not Scotland. Yes, the son of my father's brother. Josef. We're first cousins, but a generation apart, if you can imagine that. His father was the eldest of a big family, and mine was the youngest. When I was a child, and very young, Papa took us a few times to Cham, the town in Bavaria where he was born. For weddings and funerals, mostly. Josef would have been already in his twenties by then, and I have no recollection of him. Actually, my memory of those trips is vague, and fragmented. Watching from the window of the train, and coming into an old house that seemed very dark inside and feeling afraid. The faces of some old people, and playing on the street with other children, cousins, who wanted to know who I was and where I'd come from. By the age of about six or seven, we'd already stopped going back. In the years after, letters used to come, from one or another of my father's sisters who'd write with news, about who was living where, who was sick, who was marrying who. That sort of thing. There'd be an occasional mention of Josef but I know nothing about him, really, other than that he'd settled in a place called Cork. Whether or not he's even still there, I couldn't say.'

'I visited Ireland once,' Mutzl said. 'A few years back. I don't know if you remember, or if it was before I met you. It's a poor country and it rained a lot while we were there, but when the sun came out there was something beautiful about the place. The bit of it that I got to see, anyway. Is he on his own, your cousin?'

'No, he's married, with a family probably grown by now, or near enough. A son and, I think, a daughter. They'll know at home. The letters were always a big deal, and likely are even now, since I assume they still come, and my father would sit at the kitchen table and announce details as if reading newspaper headlines.'

The night had settled a grip on them, a kind of stupor. Sindelar closed his eyes. With the hour having grown so late, she watched him seeming to doze. But when, several minutes later, he opened his eyes again, it was clear by the intensity and alertness of his demeanour that he hadn't been sleeping after all.

He stared at the ceiling. 'All right,' he said, as if the matter was settled. He still sounded weary, beaten, but in his familiar darting way surged into motion, swinging his legs out over the side of the bed and heaving himself up into a sitting position, his back once again to her, though not this time in dismissal. 'I have training at nine, and I want to run some miles beforehand so I'll be away early.'

'Do you want me to go?'

'No. The opposite. I want you to stay and get some sleep. But I know how you are, and I only mean that if you don't want to be here on your own in the morning and would rather your own bed then I'd better take you home now. Whatever you decide, though, I'll come for you at lunchtime. Think of somewhere nice for us to eat, no expense spared. And we can make a proper day of it. We might even take a run up to Kaumberg, if you feel like it. Get ourselves out of the city.'

He turned and stretched back across the bed, bringing his face close to hers. Outside, rain had begun to fall, a light drizzle that nevertheless filled the room's window, the droplets in their thousands lit to shining by the lantern's golden kerosene glow. 'I'll stay,' she told him, because the thought of the streets at this hour frightened her and because she didn't want to disturb the moment. She smiled, sadly, in reaction to his smile, and having given him the answer he'd wanted, they kissed, very slowly, and she closed her eyes and then opened them again just to be able to feel her lashes brushing his skin. After some seconds his breathing turned heavy, and she set an arm around his neck and back, wanting to keep him in place and to hold on to him. Finally, though, he pulled away.

'Sleep, Beka. You need the rest. And I need to think on this. Work some things out.' He looked at her until she nodded, and using his thumb wiped away the tears that were again building in the corners of her eyes. Then he got up and began to dress in the same clothes he'd earlier discarded.

He buttoned his shirt to the centre of his chest, stepped into his trousers and pulled the straps of his braces up onto his shoulders. His hair badly needed cutting and poked like tufts of straw from the sides of his head, and he registered her stare and reacted accordingly, attempting, with only partial success, to restore some semblance of neatness.

'Don't be gone long,' she whispered, but even in forming the words had to put the back of one hand across her mouth in an effort to stifle a yawn.

'I might call on Hartmann,' he said, as if he hadn't heard her. The throat and chest buttons of his shirt remained undone, and the wings of his collar stood wide and stiff behind his neck. 'He's always up. There'll be a cafe still open, and I'll chat with him for an hour over a cup of something strong. Or maybe I'll just go home and check in on my mother, see if she needs anything. I want to sit with all of this. I said a lot tonight. Probably more than I was ready to, but it's helped get some of the details straight.'

She stretched herself out and felt small beneath his gaze. Then, again, she was overcome by a yawn. It made him smile, and she grinned too, though her eyes, reddened and thick-lidded from crying, remained desperately sad.

'For now, just sleep, love. Let me worry for both of us.'

She wanted to argue, to insist that this was impossible, and to ask that he stay, even if only until she'd fallen asleep, but she no longer had the strength. Her eyes fell shut again and in gradual fashion the world receded. She sensed him moving around the bed, and caught the light clip of his shoe heels crossing the floor, and then the darkness deepened as he quenched the lantern. In the seconds immediately after he'd pulled the door shut behind him, a scene cut through the fog clouding her mind, a small prompting flash of nightmare. She saw him sitting beside the window of a nearly empty cafe, perhaps alone but more likely playing out his charm on one of the young Czech or Hungarian prostitutes on a break between customers or else the waitress as he talked her into shutting the place down early so that they might slip out together for half an hour to some back alley or nearby park. But just as he and his choice for the night were before her eyes getting ready to move, a couple of cars pulled up outside and men came through the door, Gestapo, dressed in long black coats and backed with armed guards, asking the kind of questions that can have no good answers. She knew even in the throes of such a vision that she was dreaming, yet what she was seeing felt on some level so truthful, playing as it did on so many of her concerns, that even in sleep state her tears began once again to fall.

Revelation

Cork, 1980

Samuel enters the house with all of his usual bluster, a big man filling the narrow unlit hallway. He removes his hat, shrugs off his overcoat and muttering his discontent about the meanness of the weather presses a kiss onto his daughter's offered cheek, then scoops up Hannah, who has come running to meet him, and in a sudden way that draws shrieks of terrified delight lifts her high over his head and thrusts her almost to the ceiling.

'Don't, Dad,' Rachel pleads, through her daughter's piercing howls. 'It's close to her bedtime. You'll get her all worked up.'

'Ah, would you stop?' he says, hoisting the child again and again, throwing and catching. She bleats happy laughter and slaps in helpless fashion at the top of his head. 'I'm hardly going to let her fall, am I? Sure, don't I only have the one granddaughter?'

When he finally sets her down she stands before him, waiting while he turns back to where his overcoat is hanging on the newel post at the end of the stairs banister. Having seen this game played out so often, Rachel utters an exasperated sigh, tosses up her hands in despair of them, turns and walks off, abandoning them to their corruption. Once she is gone he sets about fumbling through the coat's pockets, drawing out the search in order to fully test the child's patience, pulling an increasingly concerned expression, as if fearing that what he's seeking has been somehow lost, then at last draws from its concealment a bar of Golden Crisp.

Hannah's face lights up and she dances impatiently from foot to foot, her gaze fixed only on the chocolate.

'Now this is for after your tea,' he says, his voice turned all the way down but still trying for authoritative. 'All right? Otherwise, I'll have your mother to deal with. And don't forget to brush your teeth afterwards.'

She nods her head keenly, drags at his sleeve until he drops into a crouch, kisses him hard on the cheek and throws her arms tight around his neck. 'Thanks, Grandad,' she says, whispering it as if sharing a secret. 'I promise I won't even tell.' Then, without waiting, she darts away into the living room, the precious chocolate bar clasped in both hands, and through the doorway left ajar he sees a television screen full of Charles Mitchell, a face somewhere between middle-aged and elderly, notably creased and made long by a balding pate, reading the evening news. He's outlining plans for the new twenty-pound note scheduled to enter circulation from the end of the month, blue in colour and featuring the image of W. B. Yeats over a background representation of Cú Chulainn, hero of the Ulster Cycle, and the fabled wolfhound from whom his name was drawn.

In the kitchen, Rachel has returned to cutting and buttering thick slices of white batch bread. The kettle on the stove is whispering towards boiling point, alongside kippers poaching above a low flame in a large blackened pan. Samuel smiles at his daughter, even though she doesn't turn away from the work that has her busy, and settles himself at the table. After a couple of minutes he hears footsteps out on the stairs, and then Jack enters, shirt-sleeves rolled up to the elbows and face looking freshly washed. He nods a greeting in his father-in-law's direction, and accepts the same in return. There's business that needs attending but it must wait until they've eaten, even though it is the thing uppermost in everybody's mind.

When the kettle starts to wail Jack lifts it from the heat and, in a manner so practised as to be almost subconscious and yet with a kind of ceremonious or even ritualistic precision, scalds the old tin teapot, spills the dregs down into the sink, shovels in four heaped teaspoons of fresh tea leaves and adds the water at a slow pour, then sets the pot down in the centre of the table on a thick piece of cork board to let it draw. Mugs have already been laid out, and they stand clustered together beside a small jug of milk and a sugar bowl. The strain of two practically sleepless nights, and two days of fairly gruelling physical work on the docks, has begun to show. Though of an age still where he can keep going, he needs activity to stay alert and it takes immense effort, whenever he sits, even if just for a minute, to resist sliding into a trance. So much has happened, in too condensed a time, and against such gales of detail, even simply breathing takes effort. He glances at Samuel and, covertly, at the cardboard folder lying flat beside the older man's right elbow, but just as he is about to speak Rachel turns back to the table from the counter, sets down a platter heaped with the buttered bread and asks him to pour the tea. He moves in close and does so, slowly pouring through a small tin strainer to fill three mugs, while she lifts the kippers out of the pan and onto plates.

Hannah enters the room again at a run, climbs up onto the chair beside her grandfather. Traces of chocolate stain her fingers, but nobody remarks on it. Together, the family eats slowly, the adults talking only occasionally and in unspecific rambling about whatever comes to mind—the recent misery of the weather, or some largely inconsequential synagogue business, or about the story that's been in the news the last few nights of the bomb on that train up in the north, in Dunmurry, and how the reports have it now that one of the dead was IRA but that the other two were just innocent passengers. Samuel's fondness for kippers has only intensified since being cautioned by the doctor to limit his salt intake, and not caring about the night of heartburn that inevitably awaits, he savours each mouthful, smothering the fish in butter and chewing in a feeling way, cautious all the time of bones, washing down every few smoky bites with a deep mouthful of tea. As he eats, and to lighten the mood a little, he asks Hannah about how she is getting along at school. The child is mostly just playing with her food, a small plate of bread and some cubes of Cheddar, and she tells him when prompted about her teacher, Miss Kiernan, who always wears nice dresses and these pink glasses with pointy corners that would remind you of a butterfly's wings, and who is very pretty except for a mark just like a blackberry smudge at one corner of her mouth. In the couple of weeks before the class broke up for the Christmas holidays, she had read them, every afternoon, a book called *Treasure Island*, and now, behind her back, some of the children, the boys especially but a few of the girls, too, have started calling her the Black Spot, even though that's terribly mean and she'd probably cry and be heartbroken if she ever heard them.

HALF AN HOUR later, in the living room, Jack and Samuel have settled opposite one another in the armchairs either side of the fire. The television is on but with the volume turned all the way down, and they can hear, from upstairs, murmurs of Hannah's voice, probably in reaction to the story, *The Wind in the Willows*, that Rachel is reading with her. A couple of nights earlier they had reached the point where Mr Toad, who had been serving a twenty-year sentence for car theft and reckless driving, escaped incarceration by dressing as a washerwoman, and so laughter has been a common sound coming from the small front bedroom the past few evenings. But now a war must be waged against the terrible weasels in order to win back Toad Hall, and the excitement is growing more intense with the turning of every new page.

Jack has made a fresh pot of tea, and pours a cup for Rachel, adding one spoon of sugar and just a drop of milk when, still smiling from the details of the story, she finally joins them. Samuel, with a distracted nod, accepts yet another refill, then opens the folder and takes out the last newspaper cutting and a couple of heavily handwritten foolscap pages. He sets the clipping down on the coffee table, smooths out the creases and takes a bracing swallow from his mug.

'What we have here, I'm afraid,' he says, 'is an obituary. The fact that it makes the front page of a national paper, and above the fold, too, as a major story, especially when we consider everything else that was happening in the world at that time, is of no small significance. The piece itself does give us some useful background and fills out our picture of him quite a bit, but it also raises more questions than it answers.'

The article is dated from the end of January 1939 and announces, in bold inch-high font just under the newspaper's front-page banner heading, DER PAPIERENE TOT, then proceeds to recount how the body of Matthias Sindelar, one of the world's finest and most renowned footballers, had been found in bed in his city-centre apartment on the morning of the 24th, beside his lover, and fiancée of ten days, Camilla Castagnola. At the time of the gruesome discovery, Miss Castagnola—an Italian former prostitute, according to the initial reports—still exhibited some signs of life, shallow breathing and a low pulse rate, and was immediately rushed to hospital but died hours later, without having regained consciousness. Sindelar, the piece goes on to say, had retired from international football several months earlier and had settled down to buy and run a small but popular coffee house, the Café Annahof, on Laxenburger Strasse in the city's Favoriten district, an area in which he'd been raised and had lived for most of his life. He'd continued to play for his club, Austria Vienna, albeit with less frequency and in a reduced capacity, and had finally called a halt to his footballing career just a month before his death, bowing out with a farewell goal in an exhibition match over the Christmas period in Germany's capital against an increasingly well-regarded Hertha side.

When the cafe failed to open on the Tuesday in question, the 24th, some of his friends, customers who stopped in every morning to chat and reminisce, became concerned for his well-being and hurried to his apartment on Annagasse. 'The official verdict had the cause of death as carbon monoxide poisoning due to a fault in the building's heating system, a cracked chimney flue, a theory lent credence by claims that other residents had complained of ventilation problems in the days leading up to this tragedy.

The older man rubs his cheek where a brush of stubble has darkened the skin. He is one of those that suffers a heavy beard growth and has to shave twice a day in order to keep from looking dishevelled, but this evening he has forgone the trouble of a second pass, and the sound of his fingertips against his face puts a buzz of whispers inside his head. He looks across at Jack and then, in a lingering way, at Rachel.

'That's about it, I'm afraid. That's as much as we've got. The outline, but not the colours. If there's more to be known then we'll have to go hunting for it.'

Jack looks in despair. When he speaks, when he finally can, his voice has almost no sound. 'So that's it? After everything that had gone before? Dead from fumes, bad ventilation. I don't know. It doesn't seem like enough, does it?'

Samuel looks at him, understanding. 'It's like I said, lad. There are more questions here than answers.'

'God. Think of your poor mother.' Rachel has reached out for the foolscap pages but doesn't even try to decipher her father's impossible handwriting. Just holding on to them, though, seems enough. 'Imagine opening an envelope to something like this. Having to read it. She must have cried herself sick and sore. Everything about this is bad. The love of her life dead, and so young, and the manner of it. But as terrible in its own way is that mention of the other woman. The fiancée. A prostitute, the paper says. Reading that would break any woman's heart.'

'We have to remember that this was, what? January '39, you said, Samuel?' Jack feels oddly defensive, and can't help himself. 'With the Nazis packing the streets and the signs of war everywhere, the world must have felt a pretty hopeless place. The rules of normal behaviour probably no longer applied. I suppose it's a matter of perspective. When you're in the mire either you keep wading or you give up and let yourself be dragged under.'

He meets the eyes of his father-in-law and then those of his wife and feels, within the moment, entirely alone. The air in the room is heavy, and the red shift of the fire spills shadows across the walls. Once they've looked away, Samuel and Rachel sit pretending not to watch him, and with their connection to one another they can be easily silent. His silence, though, is differently weighted, and he has to fight, finally, to break it down. He shrugs, as if to lessen his thoughts, or to lighten himself of them, and gives in a little.

'But yes, you're right, of course, love. It must have been devastating to read.' The words hurt because of what they excavate. 'The wrench of separation from home, giving up everyone she'd ever known, and then the news of his death and the shock of learning about the other woman. When you think of it, it's a wonder she managed to stay as strong as she did.'

Samuel scratches at his cheek again. The flesh of his face is heavy and sags darkly around his eyes, giving him an insomniac look of shame or guilt as well as long-time sadness. 'I'd hoped to be able to bring you a better story, Jack. That he'd survived, the war and everything else, and was maybe even still alive. Because wouldn't that have been something? I'm sorry it's this way.'

'There's nothing to say he even knew about me.' Jack's stare is glass, a white shine fastened to the distance. 'That's what makes all this so hard to take.'

'We can't know that.' Rachel wipes her eyes with the heel of her palm, her left eye first and then the right, drying tears. Samuel watches, surprised that her crying can hold such silence, but Jack, his focus still adrift, hasn't noticed, and certainly there is no trace of it in her voice. 'These letters are a bit like photographs. They catch moments, but the view is always limited. They say that about archaeology, don't they? How with each new bone dug up the story has to be retold? If we were to find a new letter tomorrow, everything we think we know would probably change. And who's to say there wasn't a second boxful? We're dealing with fragments here, the survivors, and the missing pieces could be a whole history in themselves.'

'Listen to your wife, Jack,' Samuel says. 'Just because there's no mention of you in these letters doesn't mean he didn't know he had a son. There may have been calls, telegrams, a whole other thread of correspondence. But even if he didn't know, it's probably just that there'd scarcely have been time.'

Jack takes a moment with this thought but misses the logic.

'What do you mean?'

Samuel shrugs. 'Well, you were born in October.'

'The 23rd, yeah.'

'Right. So you'd have been, what? three months old when he died?'

Rachel clears her throat, starts to speak, hesitates and with uncertainty tries again. 'Also, your mother might have been trying to spare him. A woman's mind is not like a man's. It's possible I'd react the same way myself in such a situation. Every day must have felt to him like having a gun to his head. If he could have made it to Cork, don't you think he'd have already done so? Maybe she was afraid the news would be somehow used against him, and was trying to be brave in not telling.'

'I'd want to know if I had a son. War or no war, and gun to my head or not. Any man would. I adored my mother, but if that's what she did then she wronged him. And me, too. Because he had a right to know. She should have told him.'

'We're just guessing,' Samuel says. He sounds all at once very tired. 'Speculating. Likely as not, she did tell him. We just don't have a paper trail to prove it. Yet. But who can say what was getting in by then and what wasn't.'

The tea in the pot is by now tepid and has stewed to a state that would be painfully bitter to taste. But nobody is thirsty for tea. For distraction, in one corner of the room, a faded mountainside clad in pine trees lingers on the muted television screen before the camera pans dreamily away to present a beautifully quaint wooden ranch house with a long wraparound veranda and three prominent upstairs windows. A title appears, in wavy yellow script, *The Waltons*, and is given a moment to impress itself on the watcher before the shot zooms slowly in on the first of the upstairs windows and, within that room, a young man seated at a desk in braces and shirtsleeves. John-Boy pauses in contemplation from his writing before his attention is snatched away bywhat they all know to be the car-horn announcement of an old Ford Model pickup arriving in a billow of dust, sweeping past a couple of children on a makeshift see-saw and into the yard. Tuesday-evening entertainment, and yet another world seeping into this living room. Jack and Rachel gaze in the screen's direction, and if little of what they are seeing registers with them then they still know by heart the story about to unfurl itself, *The Waltons* such a long-playing record that the familiarity is at once comforting and contemptible.

Rachel watches until the introduction that she's already seen a hundred times has played out, then shakes herself loose of the television's grip, gets up, gathers the cups and teapot onto the tray and carries them out to the kitchen. They watch her go, and Jack's mouth tightens, as though he has taken to chewing words, and as if they'll be like stones when he spits them out. But the silence holds almost a minute longer, until Samuel turns restless and shifts in his chair.

'I made a few phone calls,' he says. 'Last night and again this morning. And I managed to jog some memories. Morey remembered hearing about him, the kind of player he was. A superstar, he said, up there with the greats. The game wasn't yet what it would become, of course, but a player can only exist in his own era. He said that back before the war you couldn't talk about football without mentioning Sindelar.' Samuel pauses, clears his throat. 'But it sounds like he was well known for other reasons too.'

Jack's expression tightens. 'What do you mean?'

Reluctantly, Samuel continues, shrugging as if this will lessen the impact of what he has to say. 'Just that apparently he was fond of a good time.'

'How good?'

'Well, I don't think we're talking a few pints of Beamish over in the Sextant, Jack. Vienna throughout the thirties was close to what Paris had been a decade earlier. The beating heart of Europe, full of artists and intellectuals. And Sindelar was the darling of the city. They even had that name for him: *Der Papierene*—the Paper Man. I'd say the photos don't begin to paint him as he must have been. Morey, who's not prone to exaggeration, told me that there was no one like him, and at that time, anyway, nobody in his league.'

Jack stands, for no apparent reason. He just needs all of a sudden to be upright. The reflections from the television screen make something lost and helpless of him, and after a long moment, arms hanging uselessly at his sides, he drifts to the window and stares out at the lamplit street. But beyond the rain, nothing moves, no life evident.

'Thank you,' he says, still gazing out into the dark. 'I mean it, Samuel. This is a big thing you've done for me. And I'm grateful. Truly.' When he sighs, his breath whitens the glass in a fog so faint and weak that it fades in the instant of connection. 'I thought knowledge was supposed to make things clearer. But it feels like the more I learn, the less I understand.' He laughs to himself, without mirth. 'I suppose no one can ever really fully know the past. We have to be content with glimpses. And I am better off than I was. Maybe once it all settles with me, I'll have more of a sense of it. And I have the photos now, so at least I can picture him. That's not nothing. It's a lot more than I had.'

Samuel turns in his chair but to no great effect. And this is what Rachel sees when she re-enters the room, carrying the replenished tray. She sets it down, reaches for the teapot and begins to pour. There's a plate of toast, too, hot and thickly buttered. She is like her mother; whenever she has something on her mind, she feeds.

As if that's the answer to everything. When Jack's tea is poured she adds a splash of milk, stirs, and brings it to the window.

'Don't even think of giving up on this,' she says. With the words, there is no need for force in her voice. 'This is just the surface scratched.' He accepts the tea, and finds that her eyes, when he meets them, are intense with excitement. 'Think of it, Jack. You've just been introduced to a man you never even knew existed, and you've been given the start of the story, and some clues. But this only ends when you stop looking. When *we* stop. Because we're all of us in this now.'

'Absolutely,' says Samuel, catching some of her enthusiasm. 'I'll continue to ask around, because we must know people who still have relatives over there. And there are letters that we can write. The libraries and documents' offices in Vienna will have records and archives.'

'You make it sound easy.' Jack looks from one to the other, his father-in-law first and then, with more intensity, his wife. 'As if it's simply a question of deciding to find out.'

Rachel understands. In some ways, she knows him better than he'd like to admit. As much as he wants this, she knows how he can be when something frightens him or has him feeling daunted. 'Well,' she says, trying hard to smile, 'why can't it be that? We won't know, one way or the other, until we try.'

'And if we're genuinely serious about finding out more,' Samuel says, after the silence between them has been allowed to stretch, feeling that he is getting to be the one to say what they are all suddenly thinking, 'then the logical place for us to begin is at the source. There's nothing else for it. We'll have to go to Vienna.'

Arriving

Cork, 1938

REBEKAH ARRIVES IN Cork on a grey morning in May. She is on deck, alone, with the small cardboard suitcase at her feet that had started out with her as something new but which, after being dragged and bounced across Europe, stands cracked and battered now. A strong wind is blowing from the west, directly into her face and ripping at the hem and lapels of her coat. Braced against the guard rail she squeezes her arms tight across her chest and lowers her head in an effort to keep her eyes from watering. She has been out here since first light, bearing witness to the reluctance of a breaking dawn, and now, an hour on, the fatigue of yet another sleepless night has burrowed so thoroughly into her bones that she can barely keep from crumbling. To feel herself alive, she breathes deeply of the air and licks the salt-taste from her lips. The sea cannons against the hull of the *Innisfallen* in small, relentless slams that, until the first seagulls scream in the distance, makes for the morning's only sound.

Land appears, a dark pencil line, etching itself into the picture, and she rubs her eyes for better focus and gazes hard in that direction, doing what she can not to feel anxious.

Saying goodbye had broken her. He'd come to her apartment early, taken her in his arms and held her for so long it had begun to seem as if he'd never let go. He kissed her lips and cheeks and, when her tears began to fall, her eyes. Everything was arranged, checked and double-checked: the papers that she required to get across borders and the envelopes that would grease the hinges on doors and help the process along, bus and train tickets, clips of cash in various currencies. During the previous days and nights, they had talked of little else. In Basel, she would be met and taken care of by his friends Pascal and Carine, who'd get her through France, look after her and, once everything was in place, put her on a boat. From there, Pascal had trusted connections in England who'd ensure her safe passage to Cork. And as a precaution, tucked away in the bottom of her suitcase, should she run into any trouble or unforeseen difficulties, was a comprehensive backup list of names and addresses. Nothing had been left to chance. Because eyes were so continually on him—on them both, more likely, as a way of getting to him—he'd packed a simple overnight bag too, as if romance was the only reason for their trip to the Tyrol, but on arrival in Innsbruck they hadn't even taken the time to share a last meal or so much as a cup of coffee before he'd boarded her on a late-morning train. That would, according to advice he'd taken, be the easiest way of crossing into Switzerland. Carrying her suitcase while she linked his arm, he came out onto the platform with her and they stood kissing and embracing beside the door to her carriage until from up ahead a whistle blew to signal the final boarding call before departure. 'You know I love you,' he said, and she could feel by the slow whisper of his breathing pain of a magnitude that matched her own. 'That'll never change. We're too much a part of one another. I know you don't want to go, and I'd give anything for things to be other than they are. But this is how it has to be. It's the only chance we have. And I'll write. I promise. Every day if I can. This isn't goodbye.' They kissed again, with desolate hunger, holding tight to each other for as long as they could, then he opened the carriage's door for her and slid her suitcase aboard. That was the hardest moment, the release, the sense of losing touch. Her seat was on the other side of the train so that final sight of him on the platform, there below the doorway, was all she had to hold on to. She remained for as long as she could in the corridor until an influx of other passengers, some shoving past her through the same doorway, others crowding in from the next carriage, forced her back, and she had no choice but to surrender to the pushing and let herself be swept along. Within a minute they'd slipped from the cover of the station out into the open afternoon, and dazzled by the flare of a brilliant white sun she dropped with reluctance into her seat and drew her suitcase close. With the fingertips of her free right hand she held on to the small golden love-heart locket just beneath her suddenly grief-parched throat, and clenched her eyes shut in search of some ease. And it was as if a page had been turned.

She reached Zurich somewhere around three and caught a second train to Basel, with very little time to spare between changes, the task made all the more intense by the heat of the day. It was barely an hour's distance but the journey proved particularly stressful. Two police officers, stern-faced men with heavy moustaches, and pistols holstered at their hips, accompanied the train conductor through the carriages demanding to see evidence of identification along with each passenger's tickets. The aisle ahead of her was narrow, and as she watched them approach she felt sure that, being a woman alone, and obviously upset, her expression wouldn't fail to give her away. But when they reached her, the officers stood back and, as if under instructions to do so, averted their eyes, and the conductor, ignoring—if he even noticed—the trembling of her hand, simply took her ticket and punched it with no more than a cursory glance at her identification card. In a small scratched voice he wished her a safe and pleasant day, adding that the station was only a few minutes away and that, since Basel was practically the French border, she ought to watch out for the shift in scenery. She thanked him, forcing a smile, surprised at being able to speak, and that she'd remembered to respond in French.

And then, in Basel, everything became easier. She disembarked the train, struggling to carry her suitcase, small as it was, because of the heft of what she'd packed, the meagre but dense entirety of her possessions. For a few moments she felt lost and insignificant in the huge station hall, the high wooden ceiling above a convoluted apple-green spider's web of girders. Because she only had Mutzl's vague descriptions of the people he'd said would be there to meet her, she was entirely unaware of them until a hand tapped her gently on the back. She turned in alarm. A grey-haired man of about sixty stood waiting, well dressed in a blue worsted suit and tie, his brawny six-foot frame given elegance by an obviously skilled tailor; and alongside him on his left, a smiling woman, slight of build and probably fifteen years his junior, set for summer in a plain white short-sleeved dress and with her blonde hair cut boyishly in a way that emphasised her fine looks. Pascal Bergeron introduced himself, slipping his hand into hers, and reaching to unburden her of the suitcase presented the woman accompanying him as Carine, his wife. Carine stepped forward, kissed Rebekah on both cheeks and pulled her into an embrace so secure that it made Rebekah almost sob with relief. The next couple of minutes spent themselves on the usual enquiries, the three of them standing there amid the crowd, husband and wife talking at once, in a gently bombarding tandem, filling one another's gaps as if passing a relay baton back and forth, wanting to know how she'd found the journey, and whether she was tired, or hungry, or in this weather thirsty, and about the well-being of dear Sindelar. Pascal was a director of Sochaux-Montbéliard, the newly crowned French champions, and as he steered Rebekah through the crowds towards the station's main entrance, he explained that, years earlier, while overseeing the advancement of his previous team, Reims, from amateur to professional status, he'd hosted an exhibition game against Sindelar's side, and the pair had struck up an immediate friendship. Needless to say, Reims suffered terribly when the Paper Man and his cohorts rolled into town, but it was from witnessing such drubbings that Pascal had come to understand what football really was and how it might be played when room was made for artistry. Outside, into the glaring sunlight, they wandered down a street towards where the car was waiting, he leading the way in aggressive strides and swinging the suitcase at his side as if its weight were a trifling thing, while the two women, arms linked in already-apparent closeness, followed along a few paces behind. At the border checkpoint less than half an hour later, their papers were handed over, along with a suitably solemn-toned explanation from Carine about how they were collecting their daughter's friend and taking her to Paris for a funeral. 'It's the perfect excuse,' she said, glancing back at Rebekah from the front passenger seat once they'd crossed safely into France. 'Anxiety shares a lot of traits with grief.'

Rather than staying a night in Montbéliard, which had been their original intention, they elected to instead push on for Reims, where they still kept a home, in order to shorten the onward journey, and by early the next morning Pascal had them back on the road, destined for Calais, and the boat across to Dover. News had it that the situation in the Sudetenland was reaching a bad precipice, and with the whole of France growing increasingly concerned for its own safety the thought of moving on while there was still little hindrance to doing so seemed the best and most sensible option. A loose plan had been in place for her to spend a few days in Paris, but since Pascal had to cross the Channel anyway, on business, he suggested that it would be easier, and probably safer, for them all to go now, together.

The prospect of crossing the Channel alone had been daunting, and the days and nights she'd spend in England with only the most modest grasp of a language she'd hardly spoken a word of since school; so to have Pascal and Carine as companions greatly eased her burden. Carine, in particular, had excellent English. After a night to rest in London they'd accompany her into Wales and the port of Fishguard, to board her ship, the *Innisfallen*, for the late sailing to Cork, and a whole new beginning.

By the time Rebekah disembarks the *Innisfallen*, a cold mist has settled, shrouding Cork City along its river. The crossing had been less than smooth, and in terms of comfort and accommodation the best she'd been able to manage was a corner of floor on which to curl up, using her suitcase as a pillow and covering herself as best she could with her coat. Then, eventually, due to the constant heaving and for the sake of her stomach, she was forced to sit with her back braced against a wall directly behind the steerage cabin's main doorway. And now that the ship has docked, people pack the portside in droves: most of them moving even in this poor visibility with that calmness of treading familiar ground, at ease with the way and finding themselves once again where they need to be. Others, though, are somewhat more tense, giving off an air of desperation as they seek among the crowd those faces that they expect to find waiting for them but, frighteningly, can't immediately locate. Mounds of suitcases and old leather trunks, hauled up by porters from the ship's stowage area, stand off to one side against a shed wall and beneath a carelessly rigged canvas canopy, and the few children who have made it through the barriers from outside weave among the new arrivals or see how far they can make it up the gangway, their arms fully outstretched for the rope handrails but invariably having to settle for a grip of either one side or the other, before some crewman, a heavy-coated sailor gleeful at the thought of the pain he is about to inflict, blocks off their advance and with thunderous yells and swinging open-handed blows across their ears or the backs of their heads drives them down again onto the dockside.

The constant rumble of the ship's engines drowns out even the revving of trucks and vans that have backed onto the docks and are being readied for loading, and the morning teems with so many dozen shouted conversations, in a language she can't immediately decipher but assumes is English, at least of a type, that only the loudest and most forceful of them penetrate the chaos. Gradually, though, after enough exposure, individual voices do start to gain some definition and she is able to separate one from another the calls accompanied by waving arms, the laughter that resounds like screams or a wild beast's bleating, the torrential sweep of questions and responses, and the irresistible need of those safely returned just to be filling the air of home with pleasure and relief. And after a few minutes, having become at least somewhat attuned, she starts hearing what sounds like her own name being called from somewhere out beyond the high iron railing. It penetrates in occasional but persistent stabs, delivered in a woman's voice, *Rebek-ah*, hanging most heavily on that final syllable, elongating it to a kind of music and singing it each time with the same precise cadence. Hearing it called and then lost, again and again, has something of the sense of treading water, of slipping under the waves to that dense drumming bombast and then resurfacing to more of the same precise hollering.

She searches in what she adjudges to be that direction, trying to find the source of the voice, but there are only more bodies to be seen, heads and shoulders and waving arms, with nothing to indicate that she has been in any way recognised, no one pushing into view with a raised hand and a welcoming smile. She is expected here, and over the past several weeks, dating back to when the idea was first broached, Mutzl kept going a necessary correspondence by telegram with her cousin Josef, staggering the essential details of his plan in an effort at discretion and running messages from different offices, in the various Viennese districts but also further afield. Yet while the thought of having somebody here to greet her arrival should be comforting she also understands that, since there'd been too little time for an exchange of photographs, it'll be next to impossible for anyone to pick her out of the crowd, or she them. From her place in what has turned out to be a broad and not very well-formed customs' queue, she strains to study the pack of bodies pressing the fence.

With the weather starting to thicken towards rain, the line ahead of her begins to ease forward. Fighting back her weariness, she gathers up her suitcase and makes her way slowly on with the others towards where a wide double gate has been thrown open. There are guards present, darkly uniformed men, one on either side of the queue just inside the exit, checking papers. But she sees with relief that there is little efficiency to their method, and for every person taken aside to have their credentials scoured, or at least glanced over, ten or a dozen more get to stride past, most of them stuck in conversation either with companions or those alongside them in the crowd, unaware that there is even a checkpoint in place. Everyone is in a hurry, to be home or to make a train connection or just to get out of this weather. She is caught in a tide, feeling every step dragging her further from where she most wants to be, and then someone in front of her is drawn aside and a fresh surge pushes her past the guards and through the gateway, her heart—and, too soon to even acknowledge yet, perhaps another alongside—suddenly quickening with the thrill and dread of freedom. Stunned at the ease and informality of her arrival she staggers to the far edge of a wide footpath, clear of the gate and utterly lost until, after a moment, she hears her name called again, with more urgency now, barked like an order, almost. She turns to her left just in time to see a young woman breaking from those gathered along the high iron fence and hurrying towards her at an excited half-run, one arm raised and waving vigorously in an effort to catch her eye. She raises her own hand in a gesture of shy acknowledgement that, instead of offering intended reassurance, causes the young woman to stop suddenly short and from still a few paces away repeat the name, posing it as a question now, with more of a measured softness. Rebekah nods and smiles, and whatever discomfort or awkwardness there's been is all at once gone as she is grabbed and dragged into a tight, rough hug and her cheeks tattooed in such laughing kisses that she herself can't help but start to laugh in response. And then, in a heave, tears come, violently, and she feels herself weaken towards collapse and the pallor of the morning dim to a deeper charcoal shade. Everything of who she is turns slack, muscles and limbs, and she remains upright only because she is held so. The young woman understands some of what this is but not everything, not yet, and braces to support the sudden shift in weight. It is of no consequence that this other body is roughly of a size with her own, if somewhat more frail-seeming, because young and fit and capable as she is, she possesses strength enough for both of them, and she tightens her hold and makes soft supportive shushing sounds as the suitcase slips free of Rebekah's fallen grip and drops with a clatter onto the pavement.

When the worst passes, and she is sure that the new arrival can again stand of her own volition, the young woman eases them across the footpath to take shelter for a minute or two against the high yellow brick of the old port wall. The mist is heavier, the drizzle has become rain, and they are both thoroughly drenched.

'I'm Elisabeth,' she says in English, and her smile widens to show two slightly prominent front teeth. 'But Liz for short. I'm your cousin. Joe is my dad, my father. Joseph, I mean. You probably know him as that.' She hesitates. 'Can you speak English? Do you even understand what I'm saying?'

Rebekah, numb with exhaustion, understands only some of what's said. The greater problem is how smothering the girl's voice is, and all the voices she's been hearing. So different from the clearer tightness of the talk she'd met in England, the Cork tone is oddly melodic but in the way of old whiskey dances, fast-paced and soft, the accent running sounds into one another, rounding off the corners of words, stretching vowels and blurring consonants.

'Liz,' she murmurs, repeating the name, trying the sound and feel of it and smiling in spite of her tears. She reaches for the other girl's hands and grips them in both of hers. 'Beautiful cousin.'

'Ah, would you ever stop it,' Liz says, beaming with delight. 'I'm a fine state, drenched to the bone. Call me that on a day when I'm looking my best and I might half believe you.'

But Rebekah's words are not meant as flattery. Even dishevelled from an hour out in the elements it is obvious at a glance that this girl, at sixteen years old, is coming into her own. Eyes the sharp gleaming grey of scrubbed schist and a grin that widens impishly at the least encouragement, coupling the last sweet vestiges of innocence with a kind of treacherously scheming street wisdom, this morning she is decked out in a plain blue cotton dress, men's hobnailed boots with the black leather scuffed so badly across the toes that a hint of steel capping shows through on one, and an old mackintosh to her shins but worn wide open despite the weather because the buttons, apart from a couple set low down, have been lost. Her hair is a smoky brunette shade that she keeps long, in a loose, unsophisticated style held back from her face by a simple clip that makes a little too much of her forehead but also sets the focus on the large paleness of her eyes and her full, smiling mouth.

She leans in and kisses Rebekah's cheek again. 'You're easy with your lies,' she adds happily. 'But I'm grateful, I really am.'

There is a sense that, even with the difficulties posed by language, talk will flow in tides between them. But any such surge now is quelled by the sudden presence, an imposition, almost, of two more people, a man and a woman, both of middle age but looking older: the man tallish but lessened by a slightly hunched posture, with a narrow face, long thin nose, heavy jaw and a serious-looking gash of a mouth; the woman, short at not quite five foot, and stout, with wide round hips and large bosom, wearing a headscarf tied snugly into the folds of flesh beneath her chin. While the man stands, awkward in his silence, she pushes her way forward and wraps Rebekah in another ferocious clasp. 'I'm Ruth,' she says, her face full of the same easy love so evident in the young girl. 'Welcome to Cork, my poor love. Look at you. You're soaked through. And fit to drop, I'd say. Come on, let's get you home and out of these wet things.'

As if he's been watching for a signal, Joseph stoops to pick up the fallen suitcase, and without a word, and only a nod of acknowledgement to her, not unkind but not an embrace either, starts off down the path in quick strides. The women hurry to follow, Rebekah flanked on either side and having almost to trot just to keep pace.

The Shines live a few minutes' walk from the port gate. It is raining steadily now, which makes it difficult for her to keep her bearings, but the others walk as if oblivious to the conditions, and she has no choice but to let herself be steered. They cross the bridge over the river and on the other side a road that leads away left into the dockyard, and pass a pub on the corner, the Sextant, which is already open even at this hour for those men coming off a late shift or having cut short an early one. The outer door is ajar but the place's innards have been left purposely dark so that tired souls might sit a while in peace and relative silence with their glasses of porter or, if they can afford it and to stave off the worst of the morning's chill, a tot of whiskey. Liz talks incessantly, pointing out details of note, but Rebekah only catches occasional words, and with no impression of the city beyond its apparent drabness, and nothing at all of its history, is unable to make the necessary connections. She nods her head and tries to seem interested, but Ruth, who must sense her desolation, slips a comforting and supportive arm inside hers and they continue on in the direction of the gasworks, the circular structure, all metal bones, that rises up ugly and bulking ahead of them in the near distance. Then, after a further hundred yards or so, they turn left, and in beyond a nice terraced row of red-brick houses enter a dense warren of smaller homes. Joe has waited for them to catch up. 'Just down here,' he says, his expression slightly embarrassed, and again hurries ahead, leading them along one short lane and across a wedge of open ground to a line of simple houses, narrow and plain, even shabby, their fronts consisting of nothing but a window and a door, and rising up out of the pitched roof, another longer window fronting a boxed construction, making a usable upstairs of the otherwise barely significant attic space. The door is unlocked, having been left on the latch, and Joe pushes it open and then steps back so that the women might enter first, Ruth leading the way and Rebekah, encouraged by Joe's welcoming hand, following ahead of Liz.

Inside, the house is small but comfortable enough, with a green rug thrown across the living-room floor-boards as a way of adding some warmth to the place, and along one wall a simple oak bench seat, darkly varnished, of the sort that might have been salvaged from an old church or synagogue. Beside the fire, set at a welcoming angle that is probably accidental, stands a teak-framed armchair with smoke-blue cushions to the seat and back and what looks to be wicker or raffia filling the gaps beneath the armrests. Age or misuse is evident in the fraying of the upholstery along its edges and the decorative buttons, two of them at least, missing from the backrest, but she has rarely seen a seat more inviting, and longs to just throw off her coat, flop down into it and let sleep engulf her. Even now, though, politeness dictates, and she perches instead on the edge of the bench, understanding that the armchair is not hers to occupy.

Joe notices. He says nothing, but moves to her side, touches her elbow in a way that without feeling intrusive encourages her to rise, helps her from her coat and leads her to the more comfortable chair. He doesn't smile, not yet, but doesn't need to, and because of it, of such kindness, she finds herself close yet again to tears. Instead, she takes a deep breath and, in a whisper, thanks him.

For a few minutes, Ruth and Liz keep busy in the kitchen, Ruth putting on water for tea and cutting and buttering slices of soda bread while Liz, at the stove, warms the skillet, spoons in a scoop of fat and then sets to cracking eggs, frying them slowly. In the living room, after Joe picks up her suitcase and says something about taking it upstairs for her, Rebekah is left alone. She leans back in the armchair and glances around, notes the blackened fireplace and above it, on the mantel, a small dull-faced clock set into a tambour casing cut from some pale yellowish wood, and on either side of it, tall brass candlesticks. Apart from these few objects, the rectangular oak drop-leaf table in the corner and the old wine-coloured velvet curtains, the room is bare. One wall has a couple of pictures, photographs, hanging in cheap frames at roughly eye level, but she can't see them clearly from where she is sitting and is too tired for a closer inspection. Is this what her life must from now on amount to? She thinks of home, her mother and father in Kaumberg and Mutzl in Vienna, and all of this feels impossibly small. With a sigh, she lets herself settle in the chair and, just for a few seconds, closes her eyes.

She is brought back, reawakened, by the sound of footsteps on the stairs—Joe returning, ahead of a tall, swarthy young man, introduced to her as David, who is almost of an age with her. Dressed in an old grey shirt and oversized trousers held up by braces, he has clearly just woken, and still yawning and scratching one unshaven cheek, keeps to the room's doorway and fills it, saying little but watching her as intently as he can get away with. When Liz comes through from the kitchen with the food he accepts a plate and fork but doesn't move to sit and seems at ease with eating as he is.

The egg she is given is softly fried and runs when cut open, the golden yolk seeping into the slice of buttered soda bread on which it is lying. It is salty to taste, more so than she usually likes, but its heat and sustenance immediately revive her and she eats more quickly than she should but can't help herself. Nobody says anything. Joe has taken up a low footstool, and Liz and Ruth have the bench. She is the first to finish, and uses the crust of her bread to wipe clean the plate, sweeping it meticulously until there's not a mote of either grease or egg remaining. When she looks up, Joe is watching her. 'There's nothing like the sea air for working up a hunger,' he says. And then, realising the problem, switches to the German that he hasn't spoken more than a few words of in nearly two decades but which remains perfectly fluent, it being his natural tongue, adding that after a few months spent living here in Jewtown she'll need to be letting out her skirts and dresses from the kind of eating that goes on. Such talk causes her to blush, which he registers but misunderstands, and thinking that he's been too forward with his innocent teasing, he looks away and lapses into embarrassed silence. After a few minutes, though, once the plates have been cleared and fresh tea made and poured, she starts in stumbling, broken fashion to talk, responding as best she can to Liz's stream of questions and knowing it is expected of her, attempting to tell them all about her family and to describe Kaumberg, where she'd grown up, as well as Vienna, and what's happening there now, with the soldiers, and the things that people are saying. Because she is so weary, what English she has is halting and badly broken, and at times, when her brain simply won't give up the words she needs to fully explain herself she glances at Joe and lapses into her own language, so that he has no choice but to clear his throat and once again translate. She is careful to avoid any mention of Mutzl in what she says; from their recent telegrammed correspondence, the older couple understands the situation or can likely guess, but Liz and David are young, Liz particularly so, and her sudden appearance must be upheaval enough to their lives without burdening them with further revelation.

The family hangs on every word she has to say, their gazes trained on her so tightly that when she pauses, at Joe's raised hand, so that he might translate a stretch of her story before losing the run of it, they continue to scrutinise her face for some extra give in her expression—the way she chews the innards of her lower lip or how her eyes widen as she recognises something her older cousin says, and perhaps even emphasises it with a slight affirmative nod of her head. David, fascinated as he is by the notion of foreign places, moves in from the doorway and, lacking a place to sit, drops down onto his haunches just to the left of her. Sometimes she glances across at him and sees in his eyes that, even though he may be just behind her in age, barely a year or two, he is really still just a boy, with only dreams yet of the world and what life is. And oddly, this relaxes her, so that she is able to smile at him or with equal ease to look away and start on again about her journey out of Vienna to here, the places she'd seen and passed through. And across from her, all the while, Ruth sits smiling sadly, the softness of her demeanour at least in part due to recognising a heart so torn to shreds.

This is how the time passes, minutes into an hour, the ebb and flow of speaking, attempted first in English, understanding or feeling that as a duty, before surrendering to German. Then sitting slack for the long, reluctant follow-up of Joe's translation, until they can all see her starting once again to wilt, the physical and emotional exhaustion of her recent days and the anxious sleepless nights finally overtaking her. When her eyes at last fall shut the Shine family pass sympathetic looks between them and, one by one, the men first and lastly Ruth, get up and slip quietly from the room. Each of them has work that needs attending, busy chores, even so early on a Sunday, but at least they are able to content themselves that, although they've only cracked the surface of all that wants saying, their guest has finally arrived and found a welcome place within their home.

Expecting

Cork, 1938

CORK, OF COURSE, is nothing like Vienna. This is a small, poor, hard-working city, low-set and spared grandeur, the centre of which, and bulk of, fills out an island channelled on either side by its fine river, the Lee, its one possibly great feature, which has split on the western outskirts a mile or so back, beyond the playing fields of the Mardyke, and merges again at the port, parallel with Jewtown. Their muddle of cheap terraced houses stands on the Lee's southern bank, just behind the dockyard that is the source of work for most of the men, including Joe and David. Liz works too, steadily, running the counter as assistant to one of the city's tobacconists, a small dark sickly-smelling shop tucked away on Maylor Street, just off Cork's main thoroughfare. A day seems enough to see everything on offer, yet a year of digging likely wouldn't unearth all that lies beneath.

Though she takes to the language better than anyone might have dared hope, a lack of ease with it, and particularly with the accent, proves a hindrance to Rebekah finding work. The best she can manage is an occasional day's scrubbing, arranged for her by

Joe, through the synagogue over on the South Terrace, or by Ruth, who takes such work herself a day or two a week at one of the half-dozen big houses up around the university, and who has put the word out among women she knows for anything that might be going. The little Rebekah does get is not much, but enough for her to feel that she is at least pulling her weight, and she has never in her life been afraid of hard labour or getting her hands dirty. And so, she settles in.

She grows quickly close to Liz. Of the pair of them, the youngest Shine, even at sixteen, seems the more mature and the better equipped for life. Sharing a room—and a bed—throws them together, but it is a happy arrangement and they are seldom so tired of a night that they don't pass half an hour of it tucked up together in the dark, holding hands beneath the coarse wool blankets, laughing and in whispers swapping stories of life as they've known it to be, the different facets of it, the silver in their gazes from just inches apart like tears wanting to fall. Even when a lack of words blocks the way, the give and take is somehow made sense of.

And yet, as much of a confidante as Liz has become and as dear as Rebekah holds her to her heart, there is a level of herself that simply can't be disclosed. And it is to Ruth, finally, two weeks or so on from her arrival, that she first admits her suspicions of being pregnant; Ruth, not just because she is the matriarch, the one who, it is apparent from the very beginning, holds the household together and sees to its harmony and its running, but also because, at her age, well into her forties, she has walked at least some of the same road, having brought two of her own children into the world and, she reveals, as if sharing a precious secret of her own, miscarried a couple of times more. For several mornings prior to broaching the subject with Ruth, Rebekah has woken with a turn in her stomach, a churning nausea that Liz waves away in casual dismissal as nothing more than the shift in diet or just her system struggling to adapt to the water. But as much as she wants her cousin's assessment to be correct, a deeper upset suggests that a change of greater significance and concern is taking place. She has missed a bleed, but since her period was due around the time of her arrival in Cork she has been trying to blame its absence on the trauma and exertions of travel, and she'd have probably delayed speaking of her worry, putting off acknowledging what she knows in her heart to be inevitable, if not for the ferocity of the morning sickness. Just running a spoon through her bowl of oatmeal is enough to send her hurrying away to vomit, and even the tea that in this house they drink nearly constantly is too hard for her stomach to bear.

The suggestion does not shock Ruth. The older woman sits across the table, listening and trying to understand. They have the place to themselves, a stone-coloured Tuesday morning that is nevertheless working on building its heat for the day ahead, and without Joe to translate the talk is necessarily sparse and has to be filled out with gestures. 'These things only happen the one way,' Ruth says, not unkindly, 'and if you're telling me then I'm afraid you probably already know.' She gets up, fills a mug with boiling water from the kettle, spoons in some sugar and stirs. 'Drink this,' she adds, setting it before Rebekah, and mimes the action with her hands and mouth. 'Small sips. It'll settle the stomach. An old remedy. Honey is better, but beggars can't be choosers, and we're lucky to have anything sweet at all to hand.'

An unspoken assumption is made regarding the man involved, and other than a question about when she thought it might have happened, to which Rebekah can only shrug and guess, by pointing at a cardboard sheet of printed calendar, at more than a month but less than three, the details are not further discussed.

Vagueness, it seems, is its own confirmation. And for now that is enough. The subject has been broached and will need further consideration, and Joe has to be told, but in due course, after the facts are confirmed.

In bed, that night or the night after, once she'd worked up the courage to speak of it and having got Ruth's permission to do so, she reveals the situation to Liz, whispering her news in strictest confidence, afraid of the words, acknowledging that she's not yet entirely certain, but excited by them too, and after a long embrace daring to express her belief, and hope, that he'll have to come for her now, the man responsible, that he'll have no choice, because this surely changes everything. She refrains from giving up a name—and Liz, understanding, doesn't push for one—but the moment she's sure, she says, mouthing the words against her cousin's ear, once there can be no further room for doubt, she'll write to him or send a telegram. And, whether war breaks out or not, he'll be overjoyed, and come running.

When Rebekah repeats roughly these same thoughts to Ruth, on one of the mornings after, confiding her innermost hopes, the older woman listens and smiles but can't quite keep pity from her expression, by instinct and from experience knowing so much better than the young mother-to-be the actual workings of the world.

Within a fortnight another period has been missed, leaving no further room for doubt. At Ruth's suggestion, and on an evening of her choosing, they all gather at the table, apart from David, who is out with his friends at a game of football. Joe has just returned from a shift of work on the docks and is given only time enough to wash his face and hands. Dinner, a mutton stew, is still in the pot. He knows what's coming and is calm. Between him and

Ruth there are no secrets, and she understands him, how he benefits from slow revelation. He leaves the table to the women and remains standing, leaning against the windowsill so that, until the evening light softens sufficiently, he is little more than a silhouette against the boiled white net curtains, his shirtsleeves rolled up in untidy fashion past his elbows, revealing thick forearms smothered in black hair. He grips the sill's edge and gazes at some point in the distance, his mouth tight because it is not yet his time to talk. Liz's chair puts her to the right of Joe, and she, too, is for once silent. Desperate to avoid being ordered upstairs she scrutinises the oak table's heavily marked surface, trying with all her strength to seem invisible. Beneath the table, though, in unyielding solidarity, she keeps a tight squeezing grip of Rebekah's hand.

Ruth settles opposite Rebekah and makes secrecy instantly redundant. 'Well,' she says, as if plenty has already been aired. 'There's a lot worse going on in the world at the moment than the arrival of another life into it. The situation might not be ideal, and I know you're a bundle of nerves, my poor love, being so far from home and all, but you'll be all right.' The way Rebekah stares at her makes it clear that only parts of what she's just said have been understood, but not yet wanting Joe to have to translate she explains herself better with a soft smile. 'I'm not claiming it'll be easy, but if you're to be a part of this family then your problems are our problems too, and a child's not the trouble some like to make it seem.' She glances up at her husband. 'And who knows—it might even liven things up a bit and do us all a power of good.'

'There'll be talk,' Joe says after a moment, proving he's been listening. He sounds weary, and is, after the day he's put down.

Ruth shakes her head in something close to contempt. 'A lot of right they have. Half the houses around here had babies born the wrong side of the blanket.'

'Since when has right stopped the likes of them, though? You know how they are, love. And they'll be no better across in the synagogue. It'll leave a mark. Moving forward, I mean. That's what I don't like.' The sound of his breath is heavy in the otherwise silence, like further whispers. He meets his wife's eye, and then, after a hesitation, Rebekah's. And all at once he softens. 'I'll write to your father,' he says. 'He should know that you're in good hands and that you'll be well looked after. You'll be all right now. There's enough of us here to make sure of that.'

'I've given this a good deal of thought,' Ruth says, directing her words once again to Rebekah. 'You've not been here long and won't yet have had the chance to get a proper feel of the place. The neighbours know you're here but so far they'll have only caught glimpses. They'll be curious because anyone new is always of interest, and they'll be desperate to find out your story and who you might be.' Her lips turn easy at the corners, mischievous, the way she'd been when she was young and first doing a line with Joe. Small crescents dimple her cheeks. She leans back in her chair, digs around in the pocket of her apron and after a few seconds produces a small plain gold ring, holds it up like a piece of treasure for everyone to see then sets it on the table.

Rebekah stares down at it, not understanding.

'It was my mother's,' Ruth explains, speaking slowly and using gaps of silence for effect and emphasis. 'She was slight too, at least she was when she married. By the time she died she was more my shape than yours, but let's hope you'll have that to look forward to. Anyway, when she died it came to me, but as I've never been able to get it next nor near my fingers, it's been lying in a drawer for years.'

'Try it on,' Liz says, with a prompting nudge of her shoulder, and when Rebekah doesn't stir, she reaches out for it herself, lifts her cousin's left hand into view from beneath the table and slips the band onto her ring finger. The fit is a little loose, but not so much that it can slide too easily past the knuckle. Rebekah raises her hand and considers it, straightening her fingers for full effect. The gold is thin, hardly more than a filament's worth, and of almost no weight, but it seems to fill a gap that has for too long stood empty. Again, she turns her face to Ruth.

'You're more than old enough to be wed a year or even two,' the older woman continues. 'And not at all too young for widowhood, as plenty can attest. There'll have been an accident, of course. A railway worker, I was thinking, killed on the line after falling between carriages. Pick a place. Bratislava or Prague or somewhere like that. Somewhere out of Vienna but which has a regular run. And you'll need a name that you can stick with and won't easily forget. These kinds of accidents happen all the time. Even here. Tragedies. Who'd have reason to question such a version of events? And if some do have their doubts, so what? They can't know for certain one way or the other, so any kind of talk against you will just seem like wickedness.'

Joe moves to the table and sits down on a low stool, putting himself directly opposite their guest. No; their new daughter. Without prompting, and with his voice thrust low, he translates all that has been said. Unnecessarily, since it's clear enough that she's understood, but this way no details will have been missed. And Rebekah watches his mouth as he speaks, her eyes intent. She seems to be holding her breath.

Liz thinks about it. 'It might work,' she says, after the room has once more fallen silent.

'At the very least,' says Joe, 'it muddies the water enough that what's at the bottom can't be easily determined.'

'You're still distraught, of course.' Ruth reaches for her hand and takes hold of it. 'And all the more so for being already pregnant. In

Vienna, finding yourself alone, what had promised such happiness is now a reason to be afraid. And like anyone so young, it's natural you'd look for support from the only family you have.' She pauses, and looks around. 'That makes sense, doesn't it? And it's a story we can all sell, I think.'

THE SUMMER STRETCHES and feels interminable, and the nights in particular burn to such an extent that even the most exhausted among the household can catch no more than a restless and uneasy doze. Windows are left to stand wide open, doors front and back wedged ajar with broom handles in order to allow whatever little air there is to flow through. Once Rebekah's condition starts to show and it becomes obvious that the current sleeping arrangements will no longer suffice, David, without having to be asked, simply gathers his blanket and pillow and the few books that he likes to pass the night with—westerns, mostly, or the adventure yarns of Kipling, Rider Haggard and Talbot Mundy—and settles for meeting the small hours in the questionable comfort of the downstairs armchair. Rebekah wants to refuse his bed, insisting that he needs his rest ahead of his long shifts on the docks, but he makes nothing of the gesture and says that since everyone else is rallying around, it'd be wrong for him not to help out in some small way, too. He's a quiet young man, serious, and so fresh-faced that even finding him unshaven at the weekend with a shadow of beard dirtying his cheeks, or noting the oily dark tuft of chest hair when, in response to the heat, his shirt is a couple of buttons undone from the throat, it's still difficult for her to accept that there can be so little between them in age. In terms of life experience, at least compared with all that she has seen and done, he seems a mere child. Appearances can be deceptive, though, and it is because of one girl or another—and, according to Liz, often more than one at a time, which requires some adept and careful handling—that he's so rarely around until the time comes to turn in. Her own evenings have less about them, and tend to be spent, the last hour or two of them, when the sun has burnished everything in its last fading, strolling along the riverbank with Liz, trying as best they can to stretch away the day's gathered kinks and to catch some of the water's coolness on their breath. Sometimes Ruth, and occasionally even Joe, will join them, but most nights the girls are left alone to their walk, taking things slowly, linking one another, chatting in murmurs, Liz begging everything she can of Rebekah, who she feels sure has all of the world's answers, however difficult they might be to formulate and express—such as whether being pregnant, having another life growing fast inside her, feels different and, if so, in what ways, both good and bad; asking, too, about regrets and wishes for what's to come and, with some embarrassment but also a certain bated brazenness, even bravado, what it was like being with a man, whether she'd been afraid or genuinely excited, whether it had hurt as much as some girls claim it does, and if it is something she misses and might at some point want again. Rebekah answers what she can, with hesitance at first but more openly as she starts to grow easier with the language, yet holding back just that little bit, too, afraid that if she speaks in too free a way of Mutzl, what they had together and—reading layers of meaning in the few letters she's so far received—apparently still have, that magnitude of love, even in separation, it'll be caught on the breeze and lost to her.

It is on such strolls that she grows familiar with, and even gradually attached to, her surroundings. The city is compact and distinctive, possessed of its own face and character, and apart perhaps from its English Market and few bustling mercantile streets—

Oliver Plunkett Street, North Main Street, the Coal Quay, and the main thoroughfare, Patrick's Street, which Liz only ever refers to as Pana—in a sense defined by its attitude towards impoverishment. Her impression of Cork is of a place run-down but proud, devout, if the spires and steeples that deckle the skyline are fair indications, towards the values it holds most dear, and largely good- and open-hearted. Better, greater, under the skin than on its surface. Scarcely a mile wide in any direction, it turns almost immediately and most endearingly rural along its fringes and is circled a short walk out—or a good stretch of the legs—by a series of equally compact self-contained villages—Douglas, Blackrock, Carrigaline, Blackpool, Glanmire. She promises herself that once she has her child she'll broaden the scope of her explorations and will come to know Cork properly and well, the city and everything within its relatively easy reach, just as if she were blood-connected. For now, though, satisfaction is found in simply strolling the riverbank, with Liz holding on to her for security and support. They walk as dusk overcomes the day and stop when they need to for a few minutes' rest while the sun makes tan and gold of the water, or reddens it towards the wine-dark colour of innards, she murmuring of her concern for her father and mother, and Gitta, her sister, whether they'll need to think about getting out, too, if what's bad now should continue to worsen, promising aloud to write more often, to keep in better touch. Yet because this is not the world's only shade there is also room for easier talk, and laughter, Liz prompting her to describe, in her broken way, Austria, comparing and contrasting with what she sees here, recalling the woods around Kaumberg, which in wintertime especially were truly like something from a tale by the Grimm brothers, and how things happened in that town behind closed doors and shuttered windows, just as they do everywhere, no matter how innocent and idyllic a place might seem. Liz listens, fascinated, but most desires to hear about the coffee houses of Vienna, and the dance halls, and in an attempt to seem womanly herself, talks in turn about a fella she knows from over Evergreen direction, Frank, who she actually really likes and, if he'd only stop being such an eejit, might even love. They've kissed a few times and, one evening, after they'd walked up the Mardyke to the Lee Fields, she let him put his hand up under her blouse but had to push him away and slap him, playfully so that he wouldn't feel too discouraged but hard enough for him to get the message, when he tried to get her bra open. A couple of months in, Rebekah is starting to get to grips with the language, though the accent continues to make catching the unstated inferences quite a challenge, and with regard to Frank she suggests that her cousin needn't worry too much about the slap because most young men see it as their duty to at least try and won't be so easily discouraged. But that, even so, it is better not to rush things because she'll know for certain when the situation is right, and when the man is, and most of all when she feels ready.

This summer season, the slow stateliness of the days with dawn having begun its breaking by four or so and stretching on until nearly eleven on clear nights, gives the impression of time having all but stopped, or at least slowed to a barely evident trickle. No one can recall a summer so hot. In the living room of their home, the large box wireless grumbles behind a hail of static with ruminations of coming war. Standing outside one evening somewhere towards the end of August, all of them pulling at the air in heaves, desperate for the one deep, satisfying breath that feels denied to them, they listen to a neighbour, Jeremiah, an old man now and bent nearly double over a cut-down bamboo cane but who'd spent more decades of his life at sea than on land, suggest that the stillness of the wind has the feel of the calm before a dreadful storm, and that when the weather eventually breaks, as it has to, it will happen hard. The foreboding tone delights and chills them, and the girls especially start thinking about rain and brilliant lightning; but for a long time, the summer runs on, far longer than is right, and if autumn succeeds in tightening the edges of the day, peeling back significant minutes at either end, then it does little to soften the stifling sunshine hours or the suffocating nights. What scant rain falls, forced by the surging humidity, tends to burn off before it even has a chance to soften the dirt.

And then, all of a sudden, in just the manner old Jeremiah had predicted, things change.

On the Thursday morning into the third week of October, Rebekah wakes to the sound of a hard southerly wind buffeting the front of the house. It is early, somewhere around five, and still dark, and for a few minutes, until she is no longer able to bear being on her back, she lies as still as she can hold herself, hardly even breathing, listening to the careening gusts and feeling their violence. The midwife had, at Ruth's insistence, come to the house a few nights earlier and estimated full term to be another fortnight away but suggested that with everything positioned as it was an earlier delivery seemed possible and even likely. The coming Sunday, the 23rd, if she had to stake any kind of good money on it, though it could carry through into the small hours of Monday, this being the first child and all, and with the mother such a slip of a thing. Rest was the tonic, as much of it as possible. Bed, she said, speaking plain, to Rebekah directly and then to anyone else who'd listen and who would make sure the instructions were obeyed, bed was the best and safest place for her now. 'Read a book, listen to the wireless and sleep. Make your hay while the sun shines, my lovely,' she said, her wide jowly face happy with concern—implying, with no attempt at guile, that a few days from now there'll be precious little chance to do so. In the days since, and with her time drawing increasingly near, Rebekah has been warned over and over about getting up, but it is as if the sudden weather shift has shaken something loose, and released a yearning. She struggles now from the bed, braces herself against a wall and feels her way out onto the landing and very slowly down the stairs. Below, there is already movement, and when she comes into the doorway of the living room sees the black shape of David at the window, gazing out.

'Can't sleep?' he says, without turning. His words are small but not a whisper, and delivered as a statement rather than a question. 'This wind is really something, isn't it?'

'Are you early today?'

She doesn't see him turn but catches a sense of it. The darkness is complete, but when he speaks, the clarity of his words confirm that he is facing her and has drawn closer. 'No, not till eight. But it'll be a busy day. We have ships due in this morning. Well, weather permitting, I suppose.' He hesitates. 'Shouldn't you be staying in bed?'

'Yes. But the wind. I want to feel it. For weeks the air has been so hard to catch. Do you know?'

He says he does, and she feels her arm being taken and without further discussion lets herself be led back out into the hallway. They are lashed the instant they step across the threshold. She tightens her grip on him against the night's ferocity and feels him tighten his hold in response, and after a few seconds there is something so joyful about the bombardment, a helplessness against such onslaught softened by the certainty of having the safety of the house—their home—at their back and one another to anchor to. Soon they are laughing, gently at first and then deliriously so, and the entire time that they are standing there, until the fall of further footsteps behind them announces Liz, who appears in the doorway still draped in the fog of sleep and confused as to what is going on, David holds on to her. Closer now than ever before, closer even than that evening when, in the living room, with the wireless turned up and everyone watching them and clapping along, she'd stepped into his arms while instructing him on the movements of a dance she knew well from the halls of Vienna and that he was trying, so far without much success, to learn. And while having his strength to lean against now is not the reason why, or at least not wholly the reason, for the first time since leaving her previous life she starts to feel secure, and ready for whatever is to come.

JACK IS BORN on the Sunday morning. 'Easier than I'd have expected,' the midwife says to Ruth. The women are standing outside the bedroom door, but her mouth is twisted with a smirk. 'I'm sure the father would be happy if he only knew.' Ruth's instinct is to react hard, and to attack, but she restrains herself with a slow sigh, in that heavy way of the interminably put-upon, and agrees that yes, rest his poor soul, such a proud day it would have been for him indeed. Just a few steps away, Rebekah lies in bed, with the infant in her arms and Liz in happy tears beside her, and every utterance is heard and understood. She's tired, of course, and both sad and overjoyed, and all she can think of is Sindelar, Mutzl, where he is at this moment and what he might be doing. And most of all, aching to know that he is safe and well. Over the past few months Ruth has seen the letters as they've been delivered, the ones fit to share, at least, and they've sat mornings together once the house has emptied out to pore over them, Rebekah translating as best she can, even though the handwriting is as bad as the grammar, because there's no question of Joe getting to see them, intimate as they sometimes are. She writes too, in response, dense letters filled front and back in tiny, careful script that makes the most of the paper, every week and sometimes twice a week, as well as to her parents and sister. With her family she can be a little more open, but with Sindelar she tries as much as she can to keep her story between the lines, knowing he'll understand but with a mind always towards his safety. When his letters land, they hardly acknowledge what she has had to say, but she knows his writing and searches for indications within his words, making do, telling herself, and Ruth, too, that this is how it has to be, that it is the only secure way available to them. And if with each newly arrived missive the sadness heightens, then so too does her hope, because as bad as things might be in Vienna they are clearly not yet overwhelmingly so, which still leaves room in her mind for dreams of what the future might bring. Lying in her bed now, in the first minutes of motherhood, this is what she thinks about. The gales continue to sweep across Jewtown and every taken breath tastes of the sea, which after her exertions has her desperately thirsty, and whenever she reaches out or licks her dry lips and forces a swallow, Liz, keen to be of help in any way possible, stands and feeds her small sips of water from a tall glass that has already been refilled twice in the past hour.

From the very start everyone is smitten with the child, and she, for her part, is instantly in love again. 'Jack,' she says, pushing aside all her pains and worries when Ruth asks, in a quiet moment, about a name. 'For his father's father. That's proper, I think. He was killed in the war, Mutzl said. Fighting the Italians. The name Jan is John here. And I like Jack.'

'It's a good name,' Ruth agrees, beaming at the infant until she can get him in her arms. 'I've known a few Jacks in my life and they were every one of them decent. My father had a brother with the name, though he took off years ago for America. As fine and honest a man as you could hope to meet, though. A gent.' She presses a soft kiss to the baby's cheek, and inhales deeply. 'I love the smell of a newborn. And this one here, this fine strong fella, is handsome as the day is long.'

'He won't want for mothering, anyway.' Joe has come to the bedroom door but is anxious about entering, fearing impropriety, until Ruth takes him by the wrist and drags him a few steps closer so that he can see that mother and child are well. 'But it's grand altogether that we have another man in the house, if only to restore a bit of balance. Davy and I no longer have to feel so outnumbered. Isn't that right, lad?' Out on the narrow landing, leaning against the stairs banister, David looks relieved that everything has passed off without difficulty. And it is he, the following afternoon, who arrives home from work carrying in as casual a way as he can manage, and wrapped in plain brown paper, a teddy bear, a beautiful richly honey-coloured mohair model in length and girth probably half the baby's size. He'd slipped out for it during his lunch hour, he explains, embarrassed when Rebekah breaks down in hard tears at his thoughtfulness, but pleased, too, though he tries not to show it, and he is more pleased still when Ruth takes the bear and settles it in a snug position beside the sleeping infant. 'One of the lads at work happened to mention that a bear is a good gift for a baby, and that it'll help him sleep easier. And I suppose if he will then we all will.' They can tell at a glance that it hadn't been cheap, and probably took a slice out of the few shillings' pocket money he got back every Friday after handing up his weekly wage packet to his mother, but no one remarks on it or utters a word of teasing. 'Good lad,' is all Joe says, later, when they are sitting down to their supper of liver and onions, speaking casually, as if in response to something else said, but its meaning is clear to everyone at the table. Those couple of words aren't much but they count as more than ample acknowledgement.

More letters arrive, from Vienna and from the road, and money, too, and news is sent to Kaumberg announcing the birth, singing of it, detailing the wonder, and then again, after Joe has made the necessary arrangements at the synagogue for a mohel, Shlomo Levine, to travel down from Dublin by train to perform the bris. That evening, to mark the occasion, three good bottles of red wine are produced, glasses poured and raised in toast, and offered for a good, healthy and productive life, Ruth too superstitious to chance asking for more. They drink, Rebekah, too, and even Liz, young as she is, though the women limit themselves to a single half-glass each, leaving the remainder for the men, who take turns pouring for one another, attending always first to Shlomo's glass, and speaking in slow, serious tones about things of lesser consequence, synagogue and dockyard business, mainly, until they've abruptly drunk themselves dry.

Searching

Vienna, 1980

After three days spent traipsing between library archives and government records offices, it is already time to accept defeat, for now anyway and at least in terms of a paper trail. They'd tried, given it their best. In the week prior to them leaving Cork, Samuel had put through a dozen phone calls in a German that for a few minutes at a time turned him into someone else entirely, his voice a hard, demanding bark suggestive of an elevated status that would not respond well to the disappointment of a wrong answer. Then, once they settled into their accommodation in Vienna, more calls were made, in tone much the same or similar. But to little avail. Their hotel is on Josefstaedter Strasse, just a few minutes' walk from the city's heart, the Ringstrasse, town hall and university, and almost directly across the street from one of Vienna's main theatres. It is surely this that accounts for the lobby's exaggerated opulence, beautiful mosaic-tiled floors, grand marble pillars, chandeliers, walls adorned with framed black-and-white photos, many of them inscribed in inky flourishes, representing a whole wide-spanning era's worth of notable singers, dancers and screen stars.

At the airport, a guide was waiting; Anna, a cousin of one of the old men from the synagogue, a serious and striking middle-aged woman who had an intimidating curtness about her demeanour that made casual conversation practically impossible. Her cousin Reuben—her mother's cousin, actually—had contacted her to request that she assist his friends, she explained, making it clear to them from the start that she was only doing it as a favour and out of duty. She was meticulous with arrangements, put together a list of essential places to visit with regard to seeking documentation as well as a secondary list which depended on the outcome of their initial explorations, and through the days that followed stood with Samuel at various counters and desks in cramped, overstuffed offices, arguing with clerks and on a couple of occasions, in sheer frustration, banging hard surfaces with her hand and shouting, the impenetrable bureaucracy receiving from her a bark every bit as bad as a bite, while Jack, lost because of the language, could do nothing more than hang back and wait. But by the Wednesday evening it had become clear that beyond Rebekah's birth certificate and the further newspaper cuttings that they'd succeeded in unearthing from the library archives—some reporting on notable games, others, in varying detail, on the circumstances and speculation surrounding Sindelar's death—there was nothing of any real significance to be found, nothing at least that could confirm or deny what they knew or thought they knew.

On the fourth morning, early, since it would be the last they'd spend together, Anna had driven them up into the Vienna Woods, to walk the roads of Kaumberg, a beautiful town, quaint and almost silent, if somewhat tired-looking, so they might try to catch some sense of the place that Rebekah had known as home. As they strolled, Jack carried the thought of his mother and tried hard to envision her here, and her family too, and cut adrift by his companions' discussion, in German, of what recent history had inflicted, he strayed a little ahead and at times lagged some paces behind, to peer into laneways and through shop doors at the waiting darkness. In terms of basic shape, Kaumberg was probably unchanged in a dozen generations, building itself up in a hollow of the hilly woodland and spilling out and down the slight incline from the church, so what there was to see was, likely as not, what Rebekah saw and knew. And yet, as hard as he tried, he could feel nothing of her here. The quiet stillness seemed in tune with his recollections of her, that way she had, at ease with silence but always with this sense of waiting, but no mark of her remained. They walked, Anna stopping on the couple of occasions that they encountered old men, once in a doorway along one of the narrow roads and then again, up near the church, to enquire about the address, written on a scrap of paper, which Samuel produced dutifully from his pocket. The first old man, without speaking a word or even indicating that he'd registered what had been asked, just stared at them, one by one, until they had no choice but to move on, but the second, friendlier, nodded and pointed in the direction they wanted—down this road and then a right, not far at all, the turn just beyond the shop with the red half-door that sells fabric and wool. No, he'd said, still smiling but making it more of a grimace than a grin, when Samuel had mentioned the name of Schein, the tailor. Gone a long, long time, like many. They waited, hoping for more, but nothing beyond a shrug was forthcoming, and then he turned and started off towards the church door, his long thin body leaning awkwardly rightward onto a heavy home-crafted walking stick, leaving them to make their own way. They watched him go but he did not glance back or further acknowledge them, and finally they followed the road he'd indicated and within two or three minutes found themselves in front of the house where Rebekah had first tasted the air of the world and where she'd spent the bulk of her short life. If Vienna had been adventure, and Cork sanctuary, this small house, of old stone and hard wood, two narrow storeys, was home. Nobody spoke because there was all at once far too much to say. After a minute or two, and without discussing with the others his intentions, Jack stepped forward and, for the contact as much as anything, knocked hard at the door. The silence that followed had such heft that he felt it a struggle to remain upright against it, and when he could bear the emptiness no longer he knocked again, this time without expecting an answer. Then, once it was clear that there was nobody at home, he moved round to the side of the house and peered in through the windows, one by one, trying without success to fit the woman he remembered to the interior, to an environment made up of an old polished sideboard, a table covered in a white cloth, and framed pictures on the walls of people, men and women, who could have been anybody and who, in other circumstances, might have belonged to him.

'To think of how it ended for them,' he said, back in Vienna, standing at the entrance to their hotel. Out on the street, darkness was already closing in, and the evening had turned cold. 'It's as if they'd never even existed. How can it be right that nothing of them should remain?'

'This is true of many Jews,' Anna said, her expression twisted with anger. 'So much documentation has been lost. Destroyed.' She shrugged, as that old man by the church had, and there was nothing more to say because words, even now, were not in themselves enough. Then, in low voices, and in turn, the two men thanked her, Samuel first and then Jack, and shook her hand. Samuel had earlier broached the subject of payment but, in the same brusque manner that she'd displayed with almost everything else, she had raised a hand in a halting gesture and repeated that she was only here at Reuben's request and, so, would accept nothing. Just before she took her leave now, though, Jack pressed an envelope into her hand, containing a brief letter of gratitude and five hundred schillings—merely, the note explained, to ensure that she was not left short in terms of expenses. She looked reluctant, but finally sighed and grudgingly slipped it unopened into her coat pocket. And, in return—though she'd clearly intended to give it, anyway—she held out a piece of paper to Samuel, with a name, Gustav Hartmann, and a phone number, scribbled, barely legibly, across it in blunt pencil. 'I have this for you,' she said, in a tone that felt, for the first time in their company, as if she was on their side. 'Tomorrow morning you can telephone. Wait until after nine o'clock but call before ten. And if there is no answer immediately, let it continue to ring. Mr Hartmann is old, and slow in his movements. But he is expecting to hear from you and perhaps can help with some of what you hope to know.'

The bar just off the lobby was full, as it had been every night since their arrival once darkness set in—something that seemed to happen quite early in Austria—the whole lounge area packed with beautiful people looking far too sculpted and well dressed to exist in the real world. According to the smirking waiter who brought Jack and Samuel their drinks, answering a question that Samuel had not asked and wouldn't have even if he'd thought to, quite a number of the evening's gathered lovelies were prostitutes; young women, and some men, too, apparently, who'd come to the city from rural towns or from across the border in Czechoslovakia or Hungary with fantasies of making it big but who, like so many before them, had fallen by the wayside. The old story. They mingled now among the film directors and producers, still endlessly hopeful of a break, of being spotted by the right eye as an exact type for a specific role or, failing this, being able to sleep their way into some small part, but accepting too that even if the night fell short of their dreams, it was still a chance for them to peddle their wares and earn a half-decent crust in a relatively safe environment. Jack couldn't have differentiated between the actual stars, the actresses and singers, and those working the room, and was stunned at the notion of how thin the line between them lay, but Samuel just shrugged and said that maybe there wasn't actually a line at all, because when it came to show business—and who knew how many other lines of work—nobody got anywhere easy.

They drank a couple of glasses of beer and in the restaurant next door ate a simple casserole supper and shared a half-bottle of house red, and Jack watched the street from the window, the slow crawl of the tram hauling itself past, slow against the incline. He'd expected something more, he said, sipping from his glass. Had hoped for it. A feeling of familiarity, since that place, Kaumberg, should have been such a part of him. 'Vienna, also, but cities are different in that way. They can be hard to feel a part of.'

Samuel ate slowly. 'You'll be back. Maybe in the summer. Bring the girls out. I'll come too, if you wouldn't think it intrusive. I'd be happy to. And there's so much here, so much to see. Today was just about finding our way. But we've hardly scratched the surface.'

'I almost expected to see her in the window, or walking the road. Her mother in the doorway, her father at the table. I felt sure there'd be that kind of presence, that Kaumberg would have held on to the memory of them. The house, especially. Ghosts. Whispers. I don't know. Something. But there wasn't so much as a trace of them, or of who they ever were.'

'We still know so little, Jack. That's the problem.'

'I was just months from being born here.' He spoke slowly, as if from a distance. His father-in-law listened in patient silence. 'Think about what that would have meant. What it'd have changed. My whole story would have been different. As it is, I'm entirely foreign to this place. Even if I could speak the language, I doubt I'd be able to make myself understood. Sitting here now, drinking wine, looking out this window, Cork is still all there is. And it's hundreds of miles away. I'm not sure I've ever felt more lost than I do tonight.'

THE NEXT MORNING, the last they'll spend in Vienna, Samuel makes the call. The conversation proceeds in German, the situation explained as discreetly as possible. To Jack, who can only stand alongside and watch the shift and pull of his father-in-law's expressions, the sentences sound fragmented without the intrusion of the second voice to keep things in balance. After a few minutes, Samuel hunches his shoulder and holds the phone in that way, awkwardly, against his ear, searches his pockets for a piece of paper and a pen, and with meticulous care transcribes the address of what turns out to be a cafe, repeating the facts of it twice, very slowly, so that there can be no mistake.

'Favoriten,' the desk clerk says, after pushing his round wire-framed glasses up onto the bridge of his nose to read the address. 'Yes. A poor part of the city, always and still.' He looks from one face to the other but gets nothing back, and finally does something accepting with his mouth, a kind of slatting, takes up the phone's receiver again and dials a number from memory for a taxi.

Half an hour later, they arrive on Laxenburger Strasse, a wide, bustling street, and the driver points forward beyond the windscreen's dirty glass and mutters something in disinterested gutturals, and Samuel, squinting to see what's being indicated, nods in gratitude and presses the fare into the man's hand. They get out and walk, passing buildings that look tired but not dishevelled, most of them occupied with some order of business—a cobbler's; stalls of fresh fruit and vegetables; hardware supplies; a convenience store doubling as a pharmacy; a low-rent hotel with no ground-floor windows and just its sunken doorway open onto the footpath, identifiable only by the small weak green neon sign reading some word missing half its letters that Samuel nevertheless translates at a glance as: *Vacancies*. Friday being a busy morning, people pour past in both directions, all types and ages, dressed against the weather, which is cold and frosty bright. Nobody cares that two men, with the look of a father and middle-aged son, come to a halt outside a small, murky coffee house, the Café Annahof, not lost particularly but clearly displaced.

Samuel leads the way, pushing through the door, which upon opening rings a small overhead bell. There are only a few tables, all occupied, the customers, apart from two youngish women facing one another at a table near the window, exclusively men, the white or balding heads giving them away as of a certain vintage, sixties, seventies. And it is Jack, after a moment, who notices that there is only one man in the place sitting alone, with his back to them, at a table set between a side window and the corner of the counter, hunched over a newspaper spread open beside a cup of coffee, face bowed nearly to the page.

'Mr Hartmann?'

The old man turns and considers Samuel first and then, slowly and with more intent, Jack. He has a tight, serious face, the putty-coloured flesh hanging in a way that suggests he's recently lost weight, leaving him drawn and causing his eyes, pale blue in colour, to stare. His lips tighten and make a gash of his mouth, but though he doesn't smile neither does he seem unfriendly; rather, for just a moment, he looks a mixture of uncertain and afraid, thrown into some small chaos by how forcefully the long-buried past is all at once impinging on his present. Perhaps to buy himself a few steadying seconds, he closes the pages of his newspaper, folds it neatly in half, and only now rises, awkwardly, holding on to the back of his chair for balance and offering his free hand—his wrong hand—to be shaken. He gestures for them both to sit, and turning his head a little calls the name, *Martha*, in a scraping voice, loud enough to catch the attention of the girl behind the counter, a teenager who doesn't look to be much more than fourteen or fifteen, very girlish, with a small round face, horn-rimmed glasses and long straight brown hair almost to her waist. '*Kaffee.*'

Talking is a challenge at first, because of the subject matter and the sense—on both sides—of having to open up so much to strangers, but also because Samuel has no choice but to act as translator, which until they find a better rhythm greatly impedes the flow of conversation. Hartmann is dressed precisely in a dark brown pinstripe suit quite a distance past its best day, with a more or less matching knitted tie and a white shirt washed so often as to have long since lost its sheen. Whether this effort towards appearance is part of his nature or something done for their benefit, and the occasion, the intent is touching. But it's not until the coffee arrives, accompanied by small plates of warm, sweet strudel with fresh whipped cream, Martha, the girl, moving with efficient ease, even though others are calling to her, requesting refills, that he seems able to relax. '*Meine Enkelin,*' he says, still not smiling but with pride evident in his tone, and love too, *my granddaughter*, and he nods in her direction as if complimenting her. She laughingly mutters something in response that Jack doesn't understand but somehow catches the gist of, and moves away to attend to other work.

Yes, he tells them, stirring the coffee in his cup after adding several spoonfuls of sugar. He and Matthias Sindelar were friends, and for a while the very best. His gaze hardly shifts from Jack's face, to an extent that feels quickly uncomfortable, and Jack, out of politeness, holds the stare for seconds at a time, telling himself that it is due to nothing more than the order of their places at the table, with him seated directly opposite and Samuel to the old man's right. The stare is unrelenting; as, for the most part, is the talk. Even after forty years, forty-one years now, he says, and even with all that has happened since, the memory of Mutzl has remained with him—Mutzl, yes, the name they all called him. To so many in Vienna, the war made everything before and after two existences almost, and some have shaken free of their earlier selves, but for him the past, that other lifetime, remains right there, just out of sight but always within reach. He sits in this cafe every morning and chats with whoever is around, comes in to see his granddaughter and drink her coffee, and to meet friends, but mostly to keep himself close to all that's gone. Samuel translates everything, pitching his voice to just above a murmur so that it shadows rather than intrudes on the one-sided spill of the conversation, and whenever he deems it necessary, whenever tangents threaten, leads on with a few prompting words, just to keep a steadiness to the flow, and to suggest a good direction. They'd grown up together, Hartmann explains, shared what little bit of schooling was available to the likes of them. They ran in the streets, fought and played, laughed and cried together. It wasn't always just them but it was almost always the pair of them together within a pack. And, of course, there was the football. Nobody had what Mutzl had, whether in terms of ability or appetite. Not back then, anyway. Put him in the class, if you knew anything at all about the game, with the likes of Pelé, Di Stefano, Puskás, a few more. On that level, whether you'd want to believe it or not. He lifts his hands palms open to the air, as if this gesture explains all that he is leaving out. Because even now, there are many who don't want to admit that, and many who would rather forget. He sees players now who do some of the things Mutzl used to do, but Sindelar was the best parts of all of them combined—passing, dribbling, touch, vision, scoring. If he'd been Italian there'd be statues in squares and stadiums and streets named after him, like there was with Meazza. But even that wouldn't have touched the sides of how great he was, on the field and in life, too, great in the towering sense. Not a saint, not by any means that, but aren't there enough of them already? Good-hearted, though, and nobody more full of life. Which made the ending when it came, and the manner of it, so much the harder to accept. Samuel lets the silence that follows hold for maybe twenty seconds. They sip their coffee, none of them easy about what is yet to come. 'What happened, at the end?' Hartmann asks the question of himself when it becomes clear that these visitors either can't bear to or don't dare. He glances at Samuel, then fixes his attention once again on Jack, shrugs and adds simply that there is the official version and there's his own, which tallies more with what most believed, both at the time and since, though few will speak openly of it even now. It's as he's said: most would rather forget.

Jack shifts in his chair. The story is right here, at the table with them, the things they know and so many of the missing pieces. And he can scarcely sit still.

'This cafe was his.' Hartmann continues only when satisfied that they have demonstrated sufficient surprise. 'By '38 everything had changed. Vienna as he knew it, as we all did, was no more. For the likes of us, anyway. Not so much for him, because he wasn't actually Jewish, but him, too, by association.'

'What?' Samuel is uncertain that he's heard correctly.

'No, he wasn't. His family had come from Moravia and were Catholic, though non-practising, I suppose. Not that being one thing or the other ever made any difference to him, or to those of us who knew him. Holy books aside, you are as you live. And he hated the Nazis. I mean, who doesn't now, but at the time, with the tide having turned as it did, and with no signs of it ever drawing back, most simply kept quiet, kept their heads down and tried not to attract attention. But he couldn't do that. After the *Anschluss* they wanted him in the unified team, to no avail. He played on for a while at club level, six months or so, even with his knee in such a sorry state, but he knew the end was near. And when the law changed to prohibit Jews from owning businesses, he stepped in and made an offer on this place. He'd been reared nearby and knew the owner well. Weiss. The whole family, actually, the daughters and sons, too, though they were still just children at that time. We were constant patrons, in here every morning and most nights, so it was a natural move. A hopeful one, too, looking back. Optimistic. Because as bad as things were, and with clearly worse ahead of us, he remained devoted to the city. I remember that the money was as much, at the time, as he could put a hand on in cash, and it let the Weiss family get to Budapest and, I can only hope, on from there. I remember Weiss's wife saying that her husband had relations in Yugoslavia and I think also in Greece. He'd been a wealthy man before the occupation, but money on paper is not the same as in the pocket. Later, of course, I heard talk, the kind of bad talk there always is, that he was taken advantage of, that he'd had no choice but to sell fast or give it all away for nothing, but that's not how it was. Mutzl paid the value, a considerable amount, though I don't now recall the exact figure, and Weiss had something to run with.'

Even as Samuel interprets, Hartmann remains entranced by Jack.

'You keep staring,' the younger man says, finally, more harshly than he intends. 'Is it that I remind you of someone?'

Hartmann, in getting, after a heartbeat's hesitance, the murmured translation, starts. Then, very discreetly, he smiles. 'Maybe,' he says. 'A little, perhaps. Around the eyes. Something. I can't be sure, though. I will need time to consider.' He sips coffee, for the silence. 'But, you know, you are sitting in the exact place he used to sit. Every day from the day he took ownership of this place, unless he was away somewhere with the team, he passed his hours right where you are now.'

The eyes across from Jack are yellow-tinged and rheumy, and unsettling in how they continue to scour for traces.

'I suppose it's what I want to see. You probably hoped to hear differently but if there is a resemblance to Mutzl then I am afraid it is not obvious. Maybe you have it with a ball. No? Pity.' He hesitates, though only for effect. And he is still staring. 'But I do have to say that if you had walked in here a total stranger I would still in an instant have seen a look of your mother about you. And I'd have known without a doubt who you were. Rebekah is someone I remember very well. For a few years, back before everything came apart, we were as close as families are. All of us, the whole small pack. She was a lovely girl. So sweet and gentle. I am sorry to know that her life was so short. And that she suffered such pain.'

A phone rings, an urgent, steely chiming. Martha, the girl, puts down the cup that she's been washing at the sink, wipes her hands on the front of her apron and moves without hurry to the far end of the counter. Now she seems older than she looks, perhaps late teens or even twenty, and there is something so jaded about how she speaks into the phone, and then calls out, not even 'Grandfather' but 'Gustav', waving the receiver in their general direction, that puts any notion of schoolgoing firmly in her past.

Hartmann gets up, moving with stiffness and again gripping the back of his chair for balance. A trembling about his arms looks set to spill him, but after a few seconds his strength returns, seeping through him, and with it, stability, and he feels his way along the counter on its outside, using it for support, until he can take the call. He hardly speaks beyond a few small sounds not so far from growls, and quickly ends the conversation.

Returning to the table he remains standing. 'We must go,' he tells Samuel. 'Karl, my youngest, will be here in a few minutes with his car. There are things to see.'

OUT ON THE street, Samuel and Hartmann sit in the back of an old yellow Fiat, leaving the front passenger seat for Jack. Hartmann's son, Karl, is probably thirty, with a huge black moustache that smothers his mouth and spills handlebars out across his cheeks on either side almost to his ears. He is friendly, enthusiastically so, far more animated than the older man, in an English that Jack decides within a sentence or two has to have been learned abroad. 'Indeed, yes, I spent three years in Toronto,' he says, laughing with his eyes and making a sound like stones rattling in the bottom of his throat. 'And I'd still be there now except that I knew these two sisters who had set their minds on finding a husband. They were nice enough girls as long as you didn't have great eyesight, and it did not feel right to come between siblings.' He works at the hospital now, he says, in admissions, but today is a day off.

'Where are we going?' Jack turns in his seat and directs the words at Samuel, though they are not necessarily meant for him. Hartmann answers, and it's Karl, still grinning, who translates.

'We can't give you Sindelar, but maybe we can offer you some glimpses of his world. Who he was and where he came from. How he lived. It won't be enough, of course, but it's something, the best we can do.'

◆ ◆ ◆

Very close by, just a short drive, is an old apartment building on Quellenstrasse, a wide grey four-storey complex with the look of an infirmary or a prison, set out in uniform drabness. Some of the windows have bars on them, and everything about the facade looks crumbling, left to the ruin of time. They get out of the car and stand on the footpath.

'This is the apartment building where Sindelar grew up,' Karl explains. 'This is where my father first came to know him.'

The street is quiet now but, Gustav informs Samuel, leaning in with his words, not really a place to linger long, and probably best avoided once the light is lost. A lot of unemployment in the area, a lot of disaffection, youth with nothing to do turning their minds in bad directions. Jack walks slowly from them to the building's doorway and runs a hand along the wall. With the main entrance held by a robust lock there is no way to access the flat in question, or even the stairwell and hallways, but there is a hope that the stone and timber might still carry echoes of who'd lived here. He doesn't close his eyes because he can feel the others watching, even if they are pretending not to, but he can still imagine the running boy with a ball at his feet or tucked under one arm and bristling with excitement for a game just played or one still to come. Beyond envisioning, though, there is nothing to acknowledge Sindelar's having passed this way, no notice or remembering plaque, not even his name in red- or violet-coloured spray graffitiing the blockwork. Had its people been less staunch in their denial, Vienna, old as it is and full of mood, and so densely layered in stories, might have the feel of a place raised with ghosts in mind. But old traumas continue to be felt, and it's as if the city wants this part of itself, its period of war, forgotten, even the piece of it that ought to be left to shine most brightly.

'Let's keep moving,' Karl says, finally, shepherding them back to the car. 'There's more to see. I wouldn't want to outstay my welcome here. The car might not be much to look at, but I feel an attachment to the old girl. And I've known uglier get taken. Also, the front tyres are practically new.'

Half an hour later, the four men wander on foot through some of the main city streets. 'This is the best way to see Vienna,' Hartmann's son announces. 'You have to feel the ground beneath you, and suffer the confusion. Fortunately it is not possible to get too badly lost.' He strolls beside Jack, who has already surrendered all sense of direction, talking incessantly about the area's history, while the two seniors, locked into their own conversation, lag some yards behind. Vienna between the wars was a vibrant place, Karl explains, expounding on the great intellectuals who held court here, gathering to exchange ideas and opinions in some of the more resplendent cafes, restaurants and taverns, but really lighting up on the subject of the dazzling nightlife, the elegant and cultured hedonism of the coffee-house culture and the dance halls.

At the junction of Kärntner Strasse, with its busy and expensive boutiques, and the quieter, narrower Annagasse, a side street draped in shadow and made claustrophobic by the imposing loom of high buildings on either side, they pause and wait for Samuel and Gustav to catch up. The older men do so, eventually, without a word or nod of acknowledgement or apology for their languid pace, the intensity of their chat making them oblivious to interruption. Samuel walks, head slightly bowed, prompting his companion when there's room to do so with occasional questions, requests for clarification or to have a point elaborated upon, but mostly just listening and nodding while Hartmann, in quiet tumult, recounts his stories, waving a hand between them in relentless emphasis. Most of what's said is off-topic; and even when his anecdotes do connect to Sindelar—less the man than the shining star, the legend, as if the bright surface is what has survived the decades: the great goals scored, places seen, parties attended by the great and good, since they were all around, actors, dancers, musicians, poets—they have a bad habit of slipping off in stray directions and coming undone. The war, the thick mist of it, coats almost everything, and age too has taken a heavy toll. But Samuel is patient and gentle in his efforts at steering. 'Rebekah,' he says, more than once, and Hartmann, as if startled awake, looks up, nods his head and begins to speak of times shared, in bars or in the cafe, potentially intimate moments, before losing the train of his mind again and veering away towards cup finals, country tours and the night they took turns dancing in one of the late clubs with Marlene Dietrich, even Rebekah, innocent as she was, since she so loved to dance.

'This is where he lived.'

Thirty or forty paces into the lane, on their left, is a large residential complex, six floors high and as wide as it is tall, on first consideration a blockish mediocrity, with what grandeur it might have once possessed long since rubbed away.

Karl puts a hand on Jack's shoulder.

'And where he died. Right, Pop?'

He glances back at Hartmann, and after a second, Jack does too, needing verification or assurance or something. Needing more. Suddenly, this has all become real. That Sindelar, a man he'd never even known of until recently, but in all likelihood his father, the very reason for his being, should have drawn his last breath just yards from where they are now standing, and in circumstances so tragic and terrible, impacts with unanticipated force. Ahead, to both left and right, arched old-wood doorways suggest the era, deco or nouveau, the mahogany faded and ill-maintained yet still, in shape and maybe essence too, evocative of better days and more glorious nights, and even if the front looks shabby now it requires no stretch to visualise the building in its prime.

'After the poverty Mutzl had known growing up,' Hartmann says, and Samuel, unobtrusively, voice pitched soft, once again translates, 'and the hardship, a place like this was the very definition of luxury. All the best cafes and clubs were in this area, and here, just to our right, a few doors down, was the city's finest dance hall. I remember it had a sunken floor and a terrific house orchestra. Beautiful women came from all across Europe to dance here, the rich and famous, even royalty. Some of Mutzl's teammates used to tease that him having an apartment practically on its doorstep was about the same as letting a fox guard the chicken coop. I don't know how much you know about your . . . about Sindelar, but before he met your mother it's probably fair to say that he was something of a ladies' man.'

The air is rust in Jack's mouth. If he'd had any sense of who he was seeking at the apartment building back on Quellenstrasse, it feels intensified now. He takes from his pocket the photographs that he's been carrying around these past few days, and holds them up, one in each hand, so that the others can also see, and even though they are flat and faded, and bare depictions of the man as he must have been, they add something to the moment, a kind of reverence.

Hartmann reaches for one of the pictures, the head-and-shoulders shot, the portrait. 'I can see him,' he says, smiling at a memory. 'In a way far more real than this photo. He is all over this street. We were close, as I've explained, but at the same time I couldn't help but hold him a little bit in awe. Even as kids. I looked up to him, you know. And not just because of the football. He was just so much more alive than anyone else. That's how it seemed, anyway.' He looks around, pallid and somewhat unsteady on his feet, an old man caught between disparate moments. 'It's calm here, these buildings block the breeze. But I remember that Mutzl had a kind of gale about him. Nothing was ever still when he was in sight. Just his presence made the air move. I can't explain it better than that.'

The door on their left pulls open, and from inside a man appears, maybe late-middle-aged, small-framed, in a beige raincoat and fedora. Jack finds himself holding his breath. It's as if some flicker of the past has disturbed the day, as if some veil has been torn down. The others apparently feel it too, and to a man seem capsized, knocked completely out of kilter, but Samuel is the first to rouse himself, and he hurries forward, approaching the stranger with a few unthreatening words of greeting. They speak, lowly, their backs to the others and with no acknowledgement of them, but the man's head nods in understanding to whatever Samuel is saying and after a few seconds steps away from the door and, leaving it ajar, walks off.

'We can enter,' Samuel says, ushering Jack and the other men inside. 'I explained the situation, what it is that we're doing. He used to work with a Corkman, he said. On the ships.'

'Did he?' Jack smiles, despite himself. 'Then I'm surprised he didn't barricade the door.'

A steep flight of stairs leads onto a small dark landing, and behind the landing's door, stepping out into the open air, a raised garden, an explosion of light after the murkiness of the stairwell. From the street there is nothing to indicate such a layout. The garden space is drab yet because of the season but suggestive of how it would look in fullest bloom, and apartments rise up along its entire perimeter, each level stylishly guarded by wrought-iron railings penning in a narrow circuit of gangway.

'I spent so much time here,' Hartmann tells them. 'But this is the first time I've set foot inside these doors since the morning we found him.' He gazes up and all around, and seems stunned. When he speaks again, his voice is full of air, and softened nearly to whispers. 'It's just as I remember. That's what's so odd. The years seem to have stopped with him going. At least in here they do. I almost expect him to open the door to us, and to see again that smile, the fire lighting him up. And behind him, Rebekah, on the nights she stayed, laughing in that greeting way she had, teasing me because she understood how much I enjoyed it, asking if I'd brought her anything nice.' He grins at the memory, glances at Jack and then at Samuel, and explains. 'Back then I used to carry bars of chocolate in my coat. I'd gone out for a short time with a girl whose father owned a small store in Leopoldstadt, and even when she and I finished I used to stop in once or twice a week if I was in the area to see her old man. He was a real old-style Jew, and the German he spoke was about nine parts Yiddish, just like how my folks used to talk at home, but he was crazy for football and because I'd get him tickets for games, he'd never let me leave the shop without filling my pockets. It got so that I smelled of the stuff. The kids in the neighbourhood were always chasing me.' Then, slowly, his levity is overtaken by a certain despair. 'God, it really is so strange to be back. It's as if I was just here with him, with both of them, laughing, drinking schnapps into the early hours, talking novels and politics, your mother pushing me in her gentle way about why I hadn't yet settled down and always trying to set me up with one or another of the girls from her office, and Mutzl acting playfully wistful about his own days of freedom, before a country girl had tied him down. If I close my eyes it's as if not a single day has passed since the better ones we'd known, and yet, for some reason, I can't seem to place which apartment was his. I think it's this one'—he stops, half turns and points—'above and just behind us, there, towards this corner. But I also wouldn't swear to it.'

'If nobody minds,' Jack says, at last, 'I just want to look around for a few minutes.' Samuel is watching him, and he notices and starts to blush. 'Since we've come this far,' he adds, feeling a need to explain, 'I'd like to walk the landings. That way, even if we can't say for sure which apartment was his, I'll be able to feel that I've at least followed in his footsteps and got to stand outside his door.' He hesitates, as if unsure of himself, then starts away, and a minute or so later is at the railing on the floor directly above them, gazing down. For the next quarter of an hour they watch him work his way in wide rectangles around them, and he moves without hurry, going a level higher with each round, stopping now and then to consider the view, imagining the garden in summertime, the bursts of colour, the vibrancy of that, and trying to picture too the scene in snow, the way a heavy fall turns everything so still. Nobody else appears, neither residents nor caretakers, and even though the day is cold it is pleasant to be standing here, in the open, breathing air that because of the garden's greenery feels so fresh. Perhaps the most striking detail, and something he seems to know he'll carry away with him, is how the place holds its silence, remarkable considering how close they are to the centre of the city. The noise of traffic and the bustle of passing shoppers fail to penetrate as anything more than the merest suggestion, imbuing the structure's heart with a genuine feeling of sanctuary.

By combining what he's gleaned from the letters with all that he's been so far told, life as it must have played out here during that period is finally beginning to suggest itself, hints of it anyway. But even after studying Samuel's translations of how the newspapers reported Sindelar's end, forging anything but the most tenuous connection with those final hours remains impossible. There is such tranquillity about this place, such an air of contemplation, that the notion of tragedy feels far removed. And yet that's what happened, even if the specifics remain vague. Poisoned to stillness, accidentally or by intent, whether in the apartment Hartmann pointed out or in one of these others, naked in bed of a freezing January dawn with a woman he'd known mere weeks but who he was apparently set to marry. Camilla Castagnola—an Italian prostitute, so the papers claimed, as though, even if true, that defined the entirety of who she was. Not a heart that had chased to its own beating and felt happiness, fear and hurt the same way all hearts did, but fodder for a story, and worthless beyond her sensationalised part in a sordid five-minute scandal. Thinking of this brings Jack a rush of sadness that on one level strikes as wildly overblown but on another, deeper level as thoroughly honest. Because what was her story, and what had life and the world been like for her?

Back outside, Jack takes the opportunity to once more consider the building's facade, this time with educated eyes, having seen just how much more there is to the place than a first glance might suggest. He gazes down the street towards what was once the dance hall, and lets his mind count the steps between.

'I'll never forget arriving here that morning,' Hartmann says. He shakes his head, and for a few seconds his throat won't hold words. 'Terrible. Still as a painting, the scene was, which may be why it has retained such permanence.' They wait for more but nobody pushes him, and when finally Karl proposes that they find a place to sit for a glass of something, and maybe a bite to eat, the old man nods in relieved gratitude. A couple of streets away they settle into a small tavern that hangs very dark around them, everything struck in ancient stained oak, with pictures on the walls—of men, mostly—whose faces hold no familiarity but whose names, as recounted casually by Karl—Zweig, Musil, Schnitzler, Canetti, Roth and several more—ring bells, some vague, others more resolute, with Samuel as eminent writers or at least figures of the period. This was where the likes of them would gather, Karl explains, indicating booths tucked away in little alcoves, to come and discuss literature and the time and to read from their poems, plays and novels. The finest minds of their day. Not forgotten yet, or not quite, and in one or two cases not even gone but, even so, fading from a world that is fast losing its use or need for them.

Above the table at which they are sitting is a small frosted window with thick yellow glass that might as well be bricked up for what little light it lets in. Karl orders beer, which arrives in green bottles that they pour slowly, mindful of the froth, into stemmed half-litre glasses, and the waiter returns after a minute or two with plates, a basket of bread and a wooden platter of cheese and various sliced meats. They eat, and after a while, and almost as an aside, Hartmann again begins to talk.

'In those days, I was working a two-until-ten shift, for a printing company. In Brigittenau, one of the city's outer districts. The money was good for what I had to do, though the work could at times be hard. Because I was young, the hours suited me; a ten o'clock finish was still early enough to make the best of the night, and the early-afternoon start gave me time enough to revive from even the worst schnapps hangovers. In sufferance or not, though, I was always an early riser, and had the habit of taking breakfast at Annahof. To me, seven thirty was a lie-in, even after a late finish. The nights I had a woman in tow—not as often as I'd probably have wished but often enough, I suppose, to keep me going—I'd try to see her home first, not wanting to risk putting her beside Mutzl, though if it was just a fling, a bit of fun for us, and as long as I wasn't head over heels, I'd occasionally take the chance. I know how that sounds, but what can I say? That's how Vienna was for us then. We'd sit and chat for hours, a whole small gang of us, morning and night, drinking coffee that he made himself and took great pride in, even though he had a couple of girls from the neighbourhood employed to wait the tables. Other people drifted in and out of there, almost always the same few, retired footballers and men from around who'd known him all his life, and most nights, coming off my shift, unless I had something in particular planned, a date or something, I probably went directly from the printers to the cafe. And I'd be back there first thing. That's how much a part of life it was.' He stopped, waited. 'Then one morning I arrived to find the place shut.'

'This is January you're talking about now?' Samuel has again, for Jack's benefit, slipped into the role of discreet translator, and attempts to clarify. '1939?'

'That's right. The 23rd. A couple of friends were already at the door when I got there, arms across their chests against the cold. It had snowed in the night, and I remember that my breath held white before me as I walked. It must have been eight or ten below freezing. "Closed," one of them said, when they saw me, and we smiled about that because it was a Monday, not yet seven o'clock, and the suggestion left unsaid was that Mutzl must have had good reason not to be crawling at so ungodly an hour from his bed. It was bitterly cold to be standing around, but that's what we did, waiting, expecting him to arrive any minute. He was sometimes late, but never by much, so at first it wasn't that unusual. After a while we were a crowd of five, and at half past seven one of his teammates, Stroh, appeared. By that time, not only because of the cold, the chat and good-natured ribbing had largely given way to silence, and concern was evident on every face.'

Jack feels a flush of anxiety. He knows the basic facts, from the articles Samuel has translated and from having listened while Anna, their guide these past few days, recounted the event and indulged in more than a little speculation, based on what she'd been told when she enquired among elderly neighbours and the parents of her friends, people who had been in the city at the time this story was making headline news. But this is different, this is getting the picture straight from someone who'd actually come through the apartment door and found the bodies in their bed, someone who knew Sindelar intimately, and who'd loved him. Suddenly, Jack is not at all sure that he wants to hear. And yet, he's come all this way, and if not for this then for what?

He pours the last of his beer into his glass and drinks until it is gone. Samuel notices but makes nothing of it. When the waiter passes by their table, though, he raises a hand and calls, quietly, for a second round, the same again.

'Well,' Hartmann says, perhaps understanding, too. 'All I'll say is, it was bad. The worst moment of my life, maybe. Certainly, up until that point. Of course, before the year was over we were at war, and that was fresh horror, the things that happened then, the suffering. But the morning we found him was terrible. We knocked at the door at Annagasse, banged at it with our fists, so loudly and with such violence that neighbours were roused, and it was immediately clear to everyone that something was badly wrong. Stroh and a few of the others took turns putting their shoulders to the wood, and eventually the lock gave with a sickening splintering sound that I've never forgotten. Someone else who was there, I forget who, said later that it was the sound of a leg or arm being broken. I don't know if it was, but I know what he meant because there was some of the sense of that, the same kind of stomach-churning feeling.'

'And it was immediately obvious that he was dead?' Samuel whispers.

The old man fills his cheeks with air and whistles it nearly soundlessly away. 'From the doorway, at first glance, they simply seemed asleep but when I got into the room I knew immediately. Mutzl was the colour of milk, and years had fallen off him. Once that realisation took hold I didn't want to see any more, but I couldn't bring myself to look away. He had an expression of such calm. The way he'd been back when we were young, before he made ruins of his knee. After that he was never again without some pain, and the caution he had in carrying himself always showed, in the way he furrowed his brow or as a tightness in the skin around the eyes. Sometimes, when it was particularly bad, you'd hear it catching in his voice. Even now, thinking about him makes me want to cry. I remember standing there at that bedside, every bit of whatever strength I had having drained away. It was hard to draw breath, the air in the room was so heavy, and I just couldn't believe he was gone from us. Across the bed, though, Camilla was still breathing, if only barely. It was a good minute or two, probably, before anyone noticed, because one of the men had tried, without success, for a pulse. As news of the tragedy spread through the building, others began to crowd into the room, neighbours, having hastily dressed, all wanting to see, and then the medics arrived—very quickly it seemed to me—and the police. Afterwards, nobody admitted to calling them, so we could only assume it had been someone from one of the other apartments. She was taken to hospital, but was beyond help, and she died later that day without ever regaining consciousness.' He clears his throat and looks at Jack. 'I can only tell you, if you're wondering, that the newspapers did her a cruel wrong. I knew her. Even before Mutzl did. In fact, I might have been the one who introduced them. She'd had her troubles but she was a nice girl. Kind, you know. Good in her heart. What she'd been, for a time in her life, was about survival. We never try to understand that, do we? It didn't define her, it wasn't all she was, but newspapers see lives in black and white, and only care for headlines. And most of the time we ourselves are no better. Carbon monoxide, they said, later. The official verdict. She and Mutzl, both. If you can believe that. But true or not, a tragedy. Enough to make a city weep.'

Silence takes hold then, and they finish their food and linger over the beer. Jack has questions; every new detail he's picked up has broadened the span of what he knows but also emphasised the gaps. And one gap, above all, burns away inside him. He sets down his glass and goes back into his coat pocket for the photographs. Sindelar, head and shoulders, and in full flight. He considers them, squinting in the darkness, and looks up finally to find the old man watching him intently.

'Until very recently, I'd never even heard of him,' Jack says, trying to explain. He smiles, but his sadness won't let it take. 'I wasn't told, probably because there'd not been time. If my mother had only lived a little longer, a few more years, everything might have been different. But as it is, there's just so much of the story missing. I was born in October '38, and he was dead by the January. If I could ask one question of her right this minute, it'd be whether or not he could have known of my existence, whether he'd been made aware with a letter or a phone call.'

Hartmann, beneath the yellow glass of the window, looks old and brittle, and his eyes, in trawling the dark room, have something lost about them. He listens to Samuel's translated words, barely seeming to. Then, after a pause, he takes a folded brown envelope from his inside pocket. His fingertips fumble unsteadily at the heavy paper flap before producing a palm-sized piece of card and holding it out.

Jack reaches to accept it and a shudder of air escapes him. What he has is a photograph, extremely faded, of Sindelar standing with an arm draped across the shoulders of a woman that, even allowing for the poor quality of the print, he recognises instantly as his mother. He leans into it, scouring for details, until the image is just an inch or two from his face. Sindelar, in a pale shirt and dark trousers, standing nearly a head taller than Rebekah, who is decked out in a sleeveless summer dress of some pale colour that the monochrome has to depict as white, and who has her hair down in a wild spill. They both appear to be smiling, and the closeness and ease of their pose suggests an obvious intimacy, and to see this image in a book or framed on a shelf, without knowing who they were, the assumption could only be of young and happy love.

'That's from early on, I'd guess,' Hartmann explains. ''35, '36, probably, but certainly before the city was overrun. It's them at their best, though I'm sure neither would have assumed that at the time. Anyone who knew them back then would have seen in an instant that they'd been carved each with the other in mind and that they'd only ever be shells of themselves if set apart. But I don't think any of us ever thought ahead, not really, not beyond the next game or dance, and we surely never imagined what was just beyond our horizon.'

Jack is transfixed by the image. 'I've never seen her like this,' he says, whispering it. 'Looking so content. All of a sudden, I feel as if I never knew her at all.'

'The photograph is yours.' Karl has been quiet all this time but now he begins to speak for his father, who looks on, nodding dreamily. 'It is only right that you have it. And there's something else. An answer to your question, I hope.' He takes another card from Gustav, glances at it and makes a face of understanding, and sets it down on the table before Jack.

A second picture, this one on heavier stock, thick beige card, if anything even more faded than the first and in far worse condition, the corners in particular badly creased and dented. His chest refusing air in anything more than sips, Jack stares down at it but can't yet bring himself to reach out. When he finally does, it is to feel with his fingertips the surface nicked and scratched but the image still obviously identifiable as an infant, probably not more than a couple of weeks old, eyes shut and swaddled, along with the protruding head and shoulders of a comforting teddy bear, in a heavy off-coloured blanket. On the back of the picture, close to the bottom, is an ink stamp, still legible as: *Arthur Leupold, Photographers, 6a St Patrick Street, Cork*, and above it, scrawled not quite straight in a hand he's seen before, the words, in German, *Mein Junge*—My boy.

'My father says there's not much he can tell you. He'd been in and out of Vienna during those months prior to Sindelar's death, because of a woman in Bratislava that he'd met that summer and was spending as much time with as his work at the printers allowed. In Annahof, of course, of a morning, and at night in the late clubs, that photograph was passed around again and again, and there was a lot of well-wishing and handshakes, a lot of glasses raised, to good health and peace of heart, especially with the world being as it was. But you have to understand that everything was at that time precarious. People you'd be drinking and dancing with tonight were, by tomorrow, often packed and gone, running for Switzerland or France and trying to get from there to wherever it was that they had people waiting.'

Jack is still gazing transfixed at the card in his hands, and trying to hold back the surreal weight of the moment. There are a few photos—not many, three or four, perhaps—of him as a boy, but he's never seen one of himself so young. To be glimpsing his own past like this, his own beginnings, and to think that the picture has been all of these decades in a city he'd scarcely thought of until recently, has thrown his mind into utmost chaos.

'I wish I'd talked more with him during that period,' Karl goes on, translating again directly now from his father's soft utterings, 'and if I had then maybe I could tell you what was in Mutzl's mind, what his intentions were, practical or otherwise. Because those are things you'd like to know, of course. But so much was happening, and hindsight has everything feeling muddled.'

They've reached the end, for now. Once that is accepted an exhaustion overtakes them. More has been said than they'd ever dared hope. And it is a lot to process. They finish their beer in near silence, but when at last they get up to go, after Samuel has insisted, in a way that brooks no argument, on being allowed to settle the bill, Hartmann takes Jack's arm and, still with his son as the go-between, apologises, as if he has somehow let the young man down.

'I thought this would be easy,' he says, watching to see that Karl understands, then studying Jack for the reaction. 'Talking about it after so long, I mean. Forty-one years. That's what's so hard to accept. How much the world has changed, but how much has also remained the same. If I'd been confronted with Mutzl's ghost back in that building it would have impacted me less, I think, than being made to remember. Because it's right here.' He taps his temple. Tears cause his eyes to shine. 'All of it, all the time. Everything about that morning—the dry powdery cold; the sick feeling I had on finding him, like I'd been kicked full in the balls; the dead air of the room; and the sight of the pair of them in that bed with only a thin cotton sheet across their waists, heads inclined towards one another on their white pillows, him in his usual way with his bad knee raised a little above some rolled-up towels. I see it all and yet the instant I try to focus on a single detail of his face the whole picture becomes blurred. I don't know. Maybe it's ghosts I am seeing after all. Maybe that's what ghosts are.'

Dying

Cork, 1949

BECAUSE THEY'D BEEN told that Rebekah's end was near, Ruth had been hesitant about sending Jack to school, not just on that Tuesday morning but for most of the previous fortnight. She'd given in only when the others in the house and even the neighbours insisted to her that, young as he was, the lad had to be better off with a solid routine, and that it would spare him the full picture, which he didn't need to be seeing. If nothing else, she'd know exactly where he was, and if and when the time came could easily have someone hurry the few hundred yards across to the Model School to fetch him. Some weeks earlier, the doctors and nurses had stopped talking about treatments and turned their focus, so they said, while Ruth and Joe stood by, heads hung low, on making Rebekah comfortable. Leaving no room for misunderstanding. Afterwards, on the train back from Buttevant, Ruth had cried, and she'd wept every day since, in quiet moments, and late into the night, too.

'Go on,' she'd told Jack, that morning. 'Get away with you, so. But make sure you hurry straight back home as soon as the classes let out. None of your blackguarding now, and no idling about.'

Jack hated school, didn't get on with it at all, the penned-in sufferance of the old classroom, the eagerness of Meade, the headmaster, acting on the least excuse, some slight either real or imagined, to cane the held-up palms and fingertips of even the smallest child. Ryan, his teacher, was worse still, making boys who stepped even a toe out of line pull down their trousers for lashes of a switch across the ass or the backs of the thighs, bending them over his desk in front of the blackboard and standing well to one side so that everyone could see, the girls as well as the boys, and often keeping at it until blood was drawn and he'd knocked himself nearly breathless. Learning aside, that's what school was, and Jack would have rejoiced in never again having to set foot within the shadow of the place. As much as his family tried to shield him from his mother's situation, though, news of her deterioration couldn't help but filter through, and he understood without having to be told that this wasn't a time to be acting up and causing further problems. Ruth barely slept, Joe couldn't speak above a murmur from all the burdens he was carrying, and no matter what happened in the coming days and weeks, Jack was determined that he'd not add to their heartache. If that meant doing what he was told, behaving himself and going to school without qualm or complaint, or at least no more so than usual, then that was what he'd do.

This Tuesday morning, picking up on the vibrations of what else was going on, he promised faithfully to be in the door again no more than ten minutes from the time the teacher cut him loose; but that afternoon, when the half-past-two bell finally sounded the end of what had been an interminably long school day and he was finally able to flee the old orange-brick building, tearing with the pack of other kids out through the gates and onto Anglesea Street, he found his step immediately checked by the sight of a good-sized crowd, probably forty or fifty in number, filling the footpath on his side of the road directly opposite the side entrance to the City Hall. Across the way, four uniformed soldiers and some men in dark suits stood waiting beside two long black parked cars, and as much as Jack had intended to obey his grandmother, he also knew there'd be no living with himself if he left without catching a glimpse of whatever it was that the pack, men as well as women, and seemingly of every age from his mother's on through to the stooped and practically decrepit, had gathered there to see. Jack pushed in among the pack, asking aloud to the response of gently derisive laughter if someone had been shot, thinking it only because of the military presence and, for the sake of excitement, half hoping, terrible as the notion was. Those at the front grudgingly shifted to make room, and even though his instructions had been laid out clearly, the thrill of seeing the soldiers—officers by the looks of them, from the thirty or forty yards of distance, in what appeared to be their best dress—and the cars, too, which he got into his head were limousines, since he knew the word, having read of it, was enough to persuade him that a few minutes' delay in getting home couldn't make much difference.

'Dev,' somebody said, an old man's voice, sounding annoyed, in response to something someone else must have asked. 'It'll be him. Pound to a penny. Who else would they be carting around in a wagon like that?' But a second voice, also old and male, and equally irritated, said that it wouldn't be de Valera, not with all this get-up, the soldiers especially, and it was more likely the Taoiseach, or if not Costello himself then one of his henchmen, because couldn't you nearly catch the blue stench of the shirts from where they were all standing? Probably a visitor, too, a woman added, some big-shot ambassador or foreign official. A Yank, no doubt, though whoever they were they'd mean nothing one way or the other to anyone standing here, and a desperate waste of good money, too, if you wanted her opinion, what with all this fuss.

The afternoon was raw for early May, and it had rained on and off since morning. Now, steadily, it began again, not a deluge but neither anything as soft as a drizzle. At first, no one seemed to mind; the men all had caps, and the women without exception wore head-scarves, and most of the complaints were for the ridiculous show of what they were seeing across the road, with the big cars and the army on parade. Within a minute or two, Jack was drenched, his fringe buttered to his brow, but because he was at the front of the pack, and the most keen in his watching, he was the first to notice the City Hall's side door opening and proclaimed it in a shout that sharpened everyone's attention. Across in the doorway umbrellas were raised, men in hats and dark greatcoats appeared and within seconds had hurried to the cars and once more vanished from view.

After the anticipation, the disappointment was palpable, the feeling of yet again being let down. 'Costello, I'm sure it was,' someone said. 'The fella towards the back.' But there were grumblings from others that it hadn't been him at all, that one of them might have looked a bit like Seán MacBride, who an old man standing near Jack claimed to have met a couple of times years back, in connection with the other business, and someone else said yes, that was as likely as not who they'd seen all right because weren't Clann na Poblachta in government now, propping up Fine Gael in that bloody mess of a coalition, and sure wasn't MacBride himself Minister for something or other, External Affairs, was it? And still probably with a gun in his pocket.

The crowd dispersed, and Jack, full of regret for having waited, crossed the road to where the action had happened, what little of it there'd been, and set off at a saunter in the direction of Jewtown.

The rain fell away again, but a breeze kicked up and then turned hard, and having already broken his promise to Ruth, he decided that if they were going to hang him anyway, it might as well be for a sheep as a lamb, so he crossed the next road, too, and took the way back along the side of the river, to watch for the pale flashes of pike or mullet in the tide and see how scuffed the stabs of wind could turn the water's dead grey surface.

When he eventually turned onto their terrace he saw Liz outside the door, smoking, one arm folded tight across her chest, hugging herself. The rain had put bleakness into the day. She looked up but as if in a daze, and it took her a moment to register him as something more than the thoughts in her mind. Then she stubbed out the cigarette against the brickwork of the house and slipped the butt into the left side pocket of her cardigan.

'Jack, love,' she said, her voice faraway-sounding, with that hoarseness that comes from crying. 'Where have you been?'

'School,' he answered in a whisper, guessing what had happened. 'There were soldiers at the City Hall. And big cars. I stopped for a few minutes to see them. I'm sorry.' All at once his own tears were close, but he felt some absurd need to hold them back.

'David's out looking for you.' She seemed unsure about what to do or say, and after a few awkward seconds of silence hanging between them drew the lapels of her cardigan tight again across her chest and held it fast.

'You're soaked through,' she muttered. 'Better get out of those wet clothes before Mam sees you.' Then she turned away hard and went back inside, leaving the door open for him to follow.

Rebekah's tuberculosis had been missed at first, put down initially to a bout of flu and then as bronchitis, and was only acknowledged as something serious and potentially more sinister on a Sunday morning in March of the previous year when, sitting with David in the living room, just the pair of them, he'd caught a glimpse of blood flecking the white cotton handkerchief that she had been holding to her mouth. He knew in an instant what it meant, and couldn't hide his fear for her, which only increased her state of upset and started her coughing harder, for a couple of minutes or more, until the piece of cloth was properly reddened. 'You'll have to tell,' he said, coming to her and putting an arm around her but unsure what else to say. 'There's things that can be done now,' he added, when he could, not knowing if there actually was or not, but meaning it as consolation. 'Treatments, medication. It's not like the old days, Bek. You have to tell Mam. She'll know who to see about it and how to go about getting you right.'

Rebekah looked at him and, when she was able, agreed that she would, yes, once she had the words right in her mind, but to please not say anything about it yet, if he never did anything else for her, to please grant her that.

Speaking at all of it, though, bringing it out even this much into the open, seemed to grant it new weight and urgency, and two nights later, in bed, turned onto the side that had her facing the room door and away from Liz, but sensing her cousin lying awake still, she whispered of it, as if to herself, after many hours of thinking about nothing else. 'There is blood when I cough, Liz. Do you think it might be the consumption?'

Liz didn't answer, but was afraid, and over the other's pleading slipped from bed and hurried to rouse both Ruth and Joe. The following morning a doctor confirmed the diagnosis and had Rebekah shifted, as quickly as could be arranged, to the South Infirmary. Later, though, once several days of tests had been completed and she was allowed home again, the situation seemed to ease.

Or maybe it was just that they'd all come to better terms with their dread. She spent most of her time then in the armchair in the front room, wrapped in a blanket even through the stretch of a long summer, racked by what must have been a relentless bone-deep sense of cold, and with her feet nearly in the fire that was kept permanently lit for her once the winter set in. Her coughing was largely curtailed by whatever medication the doctors at the hospital had her on, but at least part of what seemed to be an ease in her demeanour, an improvement even, stemmed from the fact that, in an effort to keep exertion so much at bay, she'd lapsed into a deep, sustained silence. Conversations hung in one-sided directions, attempting to spare her anything more than answering nods and shakes of the head, tired smiles and, only when absolutely necessary, small-worded responses.

Now a crowd packed the living room, with more still through in the kitchen, and Jack could hear cups rattling on saucers and the kettle hissing towards its boiling point, but instead of easing his way in among those who'd gathered to pay their respects he hurried up the stairs to change. Soaked and trembling, not only because of the cold, he stripped down to his vest and underpants and then, finding that the wetness had penetrated right through, peeled these away, too, and stood for some seconds naked in the room, gazing out at the day, the grey stillness of it to the eye even with the buffeting sound of the wind against the long window's glass and box frame, the street outside empty and the houses opposite undisturbed beneath a heavily bruised sky. He'd known this was coming, but as long as he didn't think too closely on the matter, death felt no different than absence, or not entirely so, and Rebekah had already been five weeks in the sanatorium with news of her progress relayed in platitudes full of false notes. At the beginning, he'd held out for any news the least bit positive, but the words that were delivered and which were meant to pass as hers so thoroughly lacked her tone and her way that he'd soon lost faith in them, though he continued, out of duty and desperation, to hope. His clothes were folded on the locker at the foot of his bed, a spare pair of trousers, a couple of old shirts and jumpers, nothing among them apart from underpants and some socks particularly clean but dry at least, and he got dressed slowly, still gazing down at the road outside, the emptiness of the world, and tried to understand what it was that made this moment now different from any of the recent weeks. He couldn't. And because he wanted to feel that she was still close by he conjured her in his mind, the best of her at first, young with laughter, but then, because that didn't fit with what was supposed to be a solemn time, how she'd been these last months, before they'd taken her away, sick and quiet, trying to be strong for him but able for no more than the smallest gesture towards that, and he pictured her watching him from her chair and repeatedly thought, *dead*, until some sense of the fact began to stick. This was permanent, yet the morning that the ambulance came for her had been just as much of a goodbye, even if everyone in the house had smiled hard, for his sake but probably for hers too, and tried to pretend otherwise.

After a few minutes, he heard someone on the stairs, and until Liz appeared in the doorway let himself imagine it to be his mother, coming to check on him, either her as he'd always known her or else her revenant, the leftover part of who she was that couldn't hope to rest easy, having left so much behind. He listened, not really believing but at the same time, in some deep-down part of himself, yearning for it, and then Liz pushed open the room door and stood there, with most of the floor between them, her heart broken for him, and all he could do was stare back even when she began to cry, because with so much that needed to be talked about he had absolutely nothing to say. His sodden shoes squelched with every shift of weight, and having this to focus on helped in an odd sort of way and he found himself wishing that she'd been drenched too, for the distraction it'd have offered her.

'You should come down,' Liz said, in a voice thin as paper. 'Everyone is asking about you, my love.' She held out a hand for him to take, and even though, at nearly eleven, he'd outgrown such gestures, he reached for her and held on, telling himself that he was doing so only because of how much she needed it, the comfort of the touch. In the weeks after, she often sobbed herself to sleep, the sound of her through the thin walls sometimes so heart-wrenching that instead of lying there, pretending not to hear, in the room he shared with David, he got up, came to sit on the edge of her bed and let himself be drawn tightly into her arms, and when, unable to help himself, he broke down too, hard, they wept together, their cheeks wetting one another. On those nights, once the hour grew late, she refused to let him back to his own bed but insisted on having him beside her, to sleep in a shared embrace that was, for him anyway, awkward at first because of his age and growing sense of the world, but then so salving that on the nights he slept alone, then as well as in years to come, after Liz had married and moved away, he found himself missing the feeling of such security and safe keeping. There had been no hint whatsoever of impropriety or questionable intent, but for how much they'd helped at a time when so deeply needed those remained the embraces that he was most glad in his heart to have known. 'You're not on your own,' she'd assured him, on one of those nights, when his tears had put his face tight into the crook of her neck. Saying the words so that they sank into him and had their truth and good nature felt to the fullest extent. 'And you'll never be. You understand that, don't you, Jackie? This house is a safe place for you, and you're loved. We're your family and you are ours. You're adored, and don't ever doubt it. So adore us back, can't you?'

He followed her down the stairs now and into the living room, and let his hand be shaken by men and women alike. Some of the women insisted on kissing him too, slobbering his cheeks with mouths that stank of tea spiked with whiskey. David had returned from his search and stood by the window, hands braced straight-armed on the sill, and as soon as the crowd parted enough Jack made his way in that direction and took up a place alongside, keeping just half an arm's reach apart. Beyond a nod of the head from one returned in kind by the other, nothing passed between them, and after a while more people arrived and some left and on it went in this fashion until finally the room was crammed and began to feel devoid of air, even though the door onto the narrow hallway—and beyond it, the front door—stood open. David caught Jack's eye again and did something, a kind of tightening, with his expression; and taking that glance as permission to escape, Jack slipped outside, into the wind.

He thought about fetching the ball that Joe had bought him on his last birthday and which he kept in their small yard, but settled instead for sitting on the roadside kerb, arms hugging his scabbed knees. The wind had more or less already blown the footpath dry, though he could feel the cold of it beneath him. He didn't cry, because he had no tears yet, but couldn't stop picturing his mother as he imagined she must have looked at the end, in that strange hospital bed, among white sheets, hair down and pale as a ghost, in the long white ward that he'd heard Ruth describing. Someone in the house, probably not noticing that he'd been standing there listening, had said that the morphine, the same stuff they'd given wounded soldiers going back to the time of the trenches, would at least have kept her pain away, meaning the words as comfort. But pain or not, she must have been afraid. Anyone would be. And for her to have died alone, with only strangers nearby, without him there to hold her hand, or Ruth, hurt so much to think about.

Then Joe was beside him, towering at first, blocking out the light, but after a moment sitting, grunting with the strain it took for him to get down onto the ground. Once he'd settled, he put an arm loosely around the boy's shoulders and said how sorry he was, but that Rebekah was loved, deeply and truly, by all of them. Talking like this was hard for Joe, but he clearly sensed just then a need.

'She brought so much brightness into our lives, Jack. From the day she got off the boat to us. And she brought you. We know how lucky that makes us. Don't ever think otherwise.'

Jack glanced at him, but fleetingly, as if that could count as a response.

'You're allowed to be sad, boy. Did Liz already tell you? And you're not too old to cry, if that's what you need to do. None of us will think any the less of you, and it does sometimes help. But you saw the pain she was in, I know you did. I won't tell you this is for the best, because that's almost always such a stupid thing to say, but it's how life can sometimes be, with neither sense nor meaning to it. She's gone much too young, and it's desperately unfair. And tragic. But we were blessed to have had her in our lives at all, and we'll remember her every day. I can promise you that.' He squeezed Jack's shoulder, and the boy, still studying the dirty gutter between his feet, nodded. 'We'll get through this. All right, lad? You need to be strong, and we will be, too.'

People continued to arrive, turning into the lane in pairs or threes and fours, women mostly, connected with the synagogue and carrying plates of sandwiches and sliced, buttered tea brack, but some men, too, holding bottles by the neck, and Jack kept his shoulders hunched and eyes set low but Joe watched the sympathisers approach, nodded acknowledgement to their greetings and utterings of condolence and gestured with a directing hand, just in case any of them were intent on further conversation, to encourage them on in through the house's still-ajar front door. 'Either we make a run for it,' he murmured to Jack, once they were again, if temporarily, alone, 'or else we'll have to go back in. Ruth will have me skinned and strung up if she looks out and sees me sitting here.'

Jack considered him, then spoke for the first time all afternoon. 'I wouldn't mind a run,' he said, the sound of his own voice, the seeming oldness of it, startling him so that he cleared his throat in an attempt to put things right. He'd had enough of crowds for one day.

THE SANATORIUM WAS in Buttevant, in the north of the county, a journey made arduous by some thirty miles of bad, twisting road even if visits to the hospice hadn't been strictly forbidden, the dread over TB, spoken of in murmurs across the whole of Cork, intensifying seemingly with every passing hour. But because the town was one of the regular stops for the Dublin train, which ran up to half a dozen times a day, Ruth was able to get herself there three times during the five weeks of Rebekah's confinement. Even though she couldn't gain entry to the building, the guard at the gate—a big ruddy-faced man of military bearing named O'Keeffe, about her own age and originally, he said, from the Boreenmanna Road, which would have made him practically a neighbour—weighed the situation and how far she'd travelled, and decided that he probably wouldn't be sacked for letting her stand a few minutes at the ward window. Rebekah's bed was three in from the window on the room's left side, which afforded her a good spill of natural light, but she was sleeping on each occasion Ruth visited. On the wall, directly above her head, hung a plain timber crucifix, the size of a crow with its wings unfurled, and painted as black, probably for emphasis against the whitewashed background.

O'Keeffe, the guard, stood alongside Ruth, so that the nurses would not make a fuss over the sight of a woman at the glass, and explained away the seemingly relentless sleeping as down to the poor creature being, for her own ease, under heavy sedation. Ruth cried the first time she visited, and he put a hand on her arm and said he had a sister inside there himself, and that it was indeed an awful thing, that if the world wasn't going from war to war it was having to deal with one kind of plague or another and there just seemed no end to any of it. His words, plain and soft, expressed sympathy without needing to state as much but spared her the disappointment of false hope.

'Are you all right about it now?' he asked, walking her back out to the gate. She had time before the train home, so there was no need to hurry. 'I mean, I know there's nothing good about any of this and no point in pretending otherwise. But your girl—your niece, is it?—has to be somewhere, if she can't be at home. And it's clean inside, and well run, and the sisters will be doing their best for her. If nothing else, they'll be keeping her pain away, which is no small thing.'

Ruth nodded and tried to smile, but felt herself close again to breaking down. 'Yes. You're right, of course. And you're very kind. It's just, we're Jewish, you see, and I suppose the sight of the crucifix above her bed caught me unawares. Seeing it on the wall just makes me realise how little she belongs here. How out of place she is.'

The guard listened, and at the gate took her hand to shake when she offered it and shrugged away her words of gratitude. 'I'll come back,' she said, by way of goodbye. 'She'll be here a while, and if you wouldn't mind and have no objections I'd like to check in on her again. Just so I don't have to feel that she's entirely alone. And maybe, next time, she'll be awake.' She thanked him once more then, and with a final glance back at the building turned and set off in the direction of town, and the train stop, a couple of miles' walk, the small platform that at least had a bench seat, and shelter, in case the rain came.

An Ending

Vienna, 1980

SLEEP COMES FITFULLY, and by six, while Samuel slumbers on, oblivious to everything, Jack has already risen, showered, shaved and dressed, and after sitting for a while on the corner of his bed nearest the door, decides on a need for air. In the hotel's lobby, the woman who has been on duty all night nods at him as he passes, offering an overtired smile.

Outside, the air is still, with an arctic cold left over from a hard north wind that is painful to breathe at first and then deliciously so, for the shock it causes the lungs. The road is empty in both directions, the surfaces of everything slathered in the distempered glow of the street lights, and after a hesitation he starts away left, with the incline, for a brisk walk, wanting to feel Vienna in solitude. His vague intention is to go as far as the *Rathaus*, the town hall, but because it is nearer than he'd realised he pushes on a little further, to one of the university's campus buildings. The lingering dark helps his mind to establish connections: most of what he passes must look just as it did for Sindelar, and Rebekah, too, and it is easy to imagine them strolling along this same stretch of road between some of the area's grand old bars and restaurants, linking arms or holding hands. Although he has never known one at all, and the other, in a relative sense, only briefly, he is grateful now that he can feel in some small but real way close to them. He is breathless on returning, but invigorated.

Breakfast is softly fried eggs, toast and coffee. He and Samuel eat, in companionable silence. This morning is the last they'll spend in Austria, but already they've been speaking of coming back. As it is, though, they have spent their time well. Despite lacking the iron-clad proof of official supporting documentation, the picture has begun to clarify itself and a lot of the blanks filled in. Thinking about home, and about his wife and daughter, and how when he gets to see them again he'll gather them in his arms and never want to let go, he butters his toast, breaks open the yolk of an egg, and can't deny himself a smile.

He is just wiping his plate clean when one of the hotel staff, a young woman with a curly black cap of hair bubbling from her head, approaches the table. She has a message, she explains to Samuel, even as she shifts her eyes back and forth between the two men. Samuel takes the offered note, slips on his glasses and reads. 'It's from Hartmann. He asks that we be ready at the hotel door at ten. There's one last thing he wants us to see.'

A CAR DRAWS up to the kerb a few minutes after the hour, with Hartmann, alone, driving. They get in, Samuel opting for the passenger seat, for ease of conversation, and Jack settling in the back, taking a position between the two seats and leaning forward a little so that, even without understanding what's being directly said, he can at least feel involved. Hartmann has the radio playing loud, somewhere within the slow central movement of a piano concerto

—by Bartók, he announces at a near shout before grudgingly lowering the volume a notch, and a piece he clearly knows well from the way he plays the beat with his fingers against the steering wheel and the snatches of it that he hums in between pointing out in passing the names of streets and areas of particular note. It is well-meant information but, lacking specific connection to Sindelar, falls somewhat flat for his audience.

'I want to take you to the grave,' he says then, with the same nonchalance, half turning his head as if addressing Jack, though speaking in German. 'The cemetery is in Simmering, not too far. You mentioned yesterday wanting to visit his burial place but I think you would struggle to find it on your own. And it did not seem right that you should miss it. What time do you return home?'

'Our flight is at seven.' Samuel glances back at Jack as if for confirmation. 'And we need to be at the airport an hour before. But we're packed and have already settled our bill, and the hotel is happy to take care of our suitcases until we collect them. So we have time. And we're grateful for this, Gustav. Genuinely. We were planning on getting a taxi. Trying, you know. But what chance we'd have had of finding the grave, I can't say.'

Hartmann nods. 'Yes. A splinter in a forest, my grandmother used to say. You won't have seen anything like the *Zentralfriedhof*. Well, maybe you know the Orson Welles film, about the spies in Vienna. The one with the zither soundtrack. The cemetery is featured in that. But even so, there is no anticipating the scale. Films show only glimpses. Millions are buried out here. They say only the cemetery in Hamburg is bigger in all of Europe. If you're interested and feel that you have the time, I can show you where Beethoven lies, and Schubert, Brahms, Strauss, even Salieri. These and so many others. In the end, we all take up the same piece of dirt, the great and the ordinary alike.'

He parks at the main entrance, a large empty flagstoned area, and leads the way in through the huge open gate. The morning is still frosty cold, even with a white sun shining, and less than a minute in among the stones Jack has already lost his sense of direction. All he can do is follow, at a few paces' lag. Ahead, Samuel keeps the conversation going, getting what further story there is to be told, and though Jack wants to know what is being said and discussed it doesn't seem right to interrupt. At a point, though, his father-in-law raises a hand, and Hartmann, understanding, halts and stands in wait while the translation takes place.

'Gustav says that on the day of the funeral more than fifteen thousand mourners gathered. That was the number the newspapers reported, which was more than had stood out for Beethoven, but he insists that the true figure, at a conservative estimate, was closer to double that, as anyone who was here would readily attest. People lined the streets all the way from the centre of Vienna, and for those few hours life in the city came to a complete standstill. The coroner had put the cause of death down as carbon monoxide poisoning, and the investigation claimed to have uncovered a cracked chimney flue. In the days prior, other residents had apparently complained of fatigue and a general feeling of staleness about the air in that part of the building.' Samuel looks at Hartmann again, and the other man nods. 'But he suggests that, at the time, few in Vienna believed this. And of those who bother to remember, few believe it still.'

The funeral, Hartmann further explains, had to be a state affair, Sindelar ranking as too significant a figure, too much a part of the country's pulse, to be simply and quietly tucked away. And since the Nazi Party was strict and very vocal in their policy of refusing such an honour to those who died either by their own hand or by another's, accidental death was the only acceptable verdict. Taking all of this into consideration and trying to view the whole sorry situation pragmatically, weighing the various likelihoods and conveniences, it was probably inevitable that rumours should quickly start to spread, even among those who were close to him.

The three men walk on. What they've just heard is, at this stage, not really news to Samuel and Jack, but with every telling a little more clarity is gained and the details, including the growing emphasis on what's been left out or merely suggested, allow for much reflection. 'Not far now,' Hartmann says, in the few words of English he can recall, smiling companionably at Jack. And then, all at once, and from a distance of several yards, they see it, prominent in its line: a chest-high slab of marble standing glassy black in the cold brightness. At its upper centre, in sculpted grey-stone bas-relief, a head-and-shoulders depiction of the man himself, every bit as vivid as the photos, three now, that Jack holds enveloped and tucked away in his coat's inside pocket. The face above a draw-string jersey collar is hawkish, sharp-eyed and seemingly alert, as if some life lay packed within. The same receding hairline and wide brow, same slender jaw. Just beneath, along with the dates, *1903–1939*, his name: *Matthias Sindelar*, carved in script, a flourish that replicates his own signature, and Jack is so instantly struck by the familiar style of it from the letters that he nudges Samuel, who looks at him, considers the stone again, and making the same connection, nods. The morning looms around them, heightened and immense.

'Nobody should have to die so young.' Now that Hartmann has begun to talk, there is a river of things to say. Perhaps he is conscious of time being short. 'Though of course too many do, at his age and far younger. Your poor mother, for one. And it's not right.' He touches Jack's arm and holds on to it a moment, and even though Jack has to await Samuel's soft interpretation of the words he is able to catch an intent of what's being said. 'Mutzl lived enough to fill a dozen lives. But his death remains terribly difficult to accept. His more so than others I've known, and I've known plenty. I'm not sure why that is. The manner of it, maybe. In the days immediately after, we kept hearing suggestions of suicide, just whispers at first but then louder and openly discussed. Of what must have been a drunken pact with Camilla. Certainly, Mutzl grieved, and in schnapps, wept, for the hard downward turn his life had taken—his playing days, which had given him such an identity, at an end; losing Rebekah, even if he'd pushed her away for her own sake, to save her; and in many ways worst of all, seeing Vienna, the city he adored, overrun by monsters. And I know he was keenly aware that as dark as those January days were, the future looked black as pitch. So I suppose suicide as a theory couldn't be entirely dismissed. But I knew him, you see, and that makes the difference. I know he'd never have taken his life. I'm certain of it, as sure as I've ever been of anything. If his thoughts had run to suicide he'd have stepped outside and fought the soldiers in the streets, put them to the trouble. He'd have stood on cafe tables and screamed his resistance.'

Jack listens, to the old man breathing the words in hissing German and Samuel making them slowly understood, and it is almost too much to have to hear. With every passing moment, Sindelar is gaining flesh and bone, becoming less of a story and more, finally, of a person. A man who felt, suffered and savoured as everyone did, who could be frightened and still fight, and who must have hoped, even in the smallest of ways but through to the very end, that better still existed somewhere and that the world wasn't just the worst side of itself. He wonders about that New Year's Eve, whether wishes had been made and some thought spared for a far-off newborn, and a love let slip away but out there still, not yet lost.

The woman, Camilla, the idea of her, is what he can't grasp. By the January, his mother hadn't been gone much more than half a year, and they'd remained in touch. And he himself was just weeks in the world. For Sindelar to have thrown all of that aside, all that potential for happiness, and taken up so fully with someone else, even committing to marriage, is beyond easy comprehension.

'Camilla?' Hartmann shrugs in helpless fashion, somehow intuiting Jack's thoughts. 'Who can say? Everything happened so fast those last few weeks. Mutzl was fond of her, I know that much, but he also barely knew her. And neither one of them was happy, having each lost their heart in another direction. But by then life had begun to feel reduced to moments, and love probably meant a lot less than it once had.'

'News of them must have broken my mother. Can you imagine how she felt, reading that? There'd have been no getting over it.'

Hartmann draws a long breath. He looks tired, not just old. Holding himself so tightly against the chill of the morning brings out all the lines in his face. 'I knew your mother very well,' he says. 'The first time I saw her and Mutzl together I knew she was the one for him. The way his breath seemed to catch around her made it obvious. Nothing could distract him when she was near. You could have set the walls of the room on fire and it wouldn't have mattered. And she was the same. Such a sweet girl. I can tell you, truly, that after she left he became a shadow of the man he'd previously been. He tried to shrug it off, but she'd changed him.

'I remember the night before she left. We'd had a small party in one of the taverns that fell mostly flat, try as we might to keep the mood upbeat, and finally we cut it short and came back to the Annahof. The place was quiet, empty except for us, just a few close friends. She sat crying, and Mutzl leaned against the window, staring at the floor, his expression stony.' The old man nods his head in the direction of the granite face ahead of them. 'Like that. Very much like it. Your mother felt it was all still just foolishness and that she'd be back with us before long because, even as some persisted with talk of imminent horrors, plenty were suggesting that the political situation had already stabilised and that the way things were now would be as bad as they'd get. She didn't want to have to leave, but felt that, as pig-headed as Mutzl could be, it might take him six months, maybe a year, to see sense. He said little in response, but now and again got up from his place by the window to refill someone's coffee, or to fetch a fresh bottle of wine or schnapps. Being as connected as he was, catching whispers from acquaintances among the news reporters, he understood enough to recognise the end in sight. So, for him, this was a wake. And eventually, after some of our group had dealt out their farewell kisses, shaken hands and drifted off into the night, he turned up the volume of the wireless, had me help him clear space on the floor, pulling tables and chairs to the walls, and took Rebekah out to dance. The few of us who were still there could have joined in, because the music, big-band stuff, 'Love Is Just a Little Bit of Heaven' and 'I Could Waltz on Forever', that kind of thing, was slow and easy, head-on-shoulder dancing, we used to call it, but our feeling was that this final time had to be theirs alone, for as long as it should last. I can hear it even now, the music, and it still chokes me up.'

Also carved on the headstone, beneath Sindelar's listing and partially concealed by the bouquets of flowers that are still, according to Hartmann, regularly laid here by admirers and old friends, as well as from the club, who acknowledge him as the finest and most gifted to ever wear their colours, are the names of his sister, *Rosi, 1904–1942*, and *Marie Sindelar, 1877–1961*, his mother.

'As wild as Mutzl could be,' Gustav tells them, 'and as hectic as his existence was, home was always for him the apartment in Favoriten.

The one we visited yesterday, the first one, the place where I'd told you he'd grown up. That was the address he gave whenever asked, his mother's address, and it was where he tried to sleep a night or two every week, even with other beds awaiting him. Being just a year apart in age, Rosi and Mutzl had grown up particularly close, though there were times in adulthood when circumstances drew them apart. She took his death particularly hard, and refused to settle for the findings of the inquest, even going so far as to hire an investigator to check into the carbon monoxide verdict. The report she got back insisted that neither the apartment's fireplace nor chimney revealed any identifiable defects, but her many letters attempting to have the case reopened went unacknowledged at official levels, and with the outbreak of war I suppose they were filed away and quickly lost. She didn't trail long behind her brother, either, just three years, as you can see, and I am sorry to say that this time the end really was suicide, after her heart, already so fragile, had been truly and finally broken by a lover.'

The three men stand together and consider the stone, these moments for one of them a remembrance, for the other two space to reflect on all that might have been.

Everything in every brightly lit direction is perfectly still, the only life about the morning the slow frailing of their breath in the air. Then, eventually, Hartmann stirs, mutters as if to himself something about how, since they are out here, he may as well take the opportunity to stop by the graves of some family members, and without further discussion starts away.

Samuel watches him go.

'It's all terribly sad,' he says, once he and Jack are alone. He means the whole thing, the entire tragic unfurling, generations wiped out, his mother's people back in Lübeck surely among them, family distant and for the most part unknown to him but still blood relatives, lost or left to ruin in either the ghettos or the camps. Within this one grave, a complete world feels buried, an immense convoluted history. Sindelar's story has made a reality of the man far beyond the few faded photographs they've seen.

'It is,' Jack says, after a long beat. 'Sad is the word. The more I learn, the worse it all seems.' The face on the headstone, sculpted so disturbingly precise, holds him transfixed. 'Would you look at him. He's not even handsome. It's hard to imagine him turning heads, isn't it? But my mother loved him. That's for certain. And maybe he loved her, too. I hope he did.' He glances at Samuel. 'You'd wonder, wouldn't you, whether he did what was best for her. Getting her out, I mean. To feel that they'd lost one another must have been unbearable.'

'I suppose, if nothing else, he saved her. And you. My daughter has a good husband because of him, and I have a granddaughter. That's a lot to be thankful for, Jack. That's the world.'

'A few weeks ago we didn't even have his name. And we knew nothing of his existence. Knowing changes everything.'

A tear spills abruptly from the inner corner of Jack's left eye, down into the channel between his cheek and nose. The wetness makes him feel the morning's chill that much more intently, and he makes as if to wipe it away, then doesn't, some part of him wanting the discomfort, the sensation something more than numbness. He stands there, at the foot of the grave, trying to steady himself. Then, from his coat's side pocket he takes out what looks to be a matchbox, and from the inside pocket withdraws, again, the folded white envelope. Samuel, curious, looks on in silence. In the envelope, tucked in behind the photographs of Sindelar, is a grey portrait, trimmed in quarter-inch white border, of Rebekah, smiling, laughing maybe, with her hair drawn back and spilling down around her shoulders.

He holds out the photo to Samuel, and the older man accepts it a moment, handling it with care, a small brittle cardboard rectangle. 'Hartmann is right,' he says, feeling that some remark of the sort is expected of him, even a statement of the obvious. 'You have a definite look of her. And I can see Hannah staring back at me, plain as day. Same eyes, same mouth the way it holds a smile.'

Jack considers the photo again, then carefully skirts the grave and brings himself beside the headstone. The bed of the grave consists of the same black marble, a solid sheet apart from a narrow channel of dirt on either side just ahead of the raised outer kerb.

'Before we left home,' he says, speaking to Samuel but also not, just needing to explain, 'I visited her grave and took a small bit of dirt from it, enough to fill a matchbox. Because if there's any truth to the notion of the dead returning to dust then why shouldn't this fistful of earth hold some essence of who she was? I've been carrying it around with me, but I said nothing because I didn't know if we'd be able to find this grave, or if there even was one. And, if I'm honest, because I felt embarrassed about it. But my thinking was that, if we did make it this far, I could in some small way reunite them.'

His eyes search the near vicinity for a rock, something with an edge that he can use to dig with, and not finding one instead makes do with his boot heel to hack at the ground and scrape a divot from the strip of soil. Samuel, slightly anxious at what might, to the wrong eyes, be taken as desecration, glances around, but aside from Hartmann, off in the distance at another grave, there is nobody to be seen in any direction.

What ought to be an easy task proves in practice quite challenging, and Jack is put to considerable effort, the dirt being frozen nearly solid, but after several hacks enough dirt has crumbled and been displaced, and enough of a groove scraped open, to suit his purposes. This is just a gesture, after all, a burial only in the most symbolic sense. He looks across at Samuel again, as if for reassurance, and from eight or ten feet away the older man grants it with an accepting shrug. Then, dropping down onto his haunches, he lays his mother's photo with great care in the ground, flat and face up, empties in the earth from the matchbox, tamps the spill until it all feels sufficiently packed, and covers this with what frozen dirt he'd dug away. Once the work is complete, the ground looks as if it has never been bothered. He lets out a satisfied breath that this time has all the weight of a sob, closes his eyes and in his mind makes a wish that might just as well count as prayerful, that these two long-gone souls should at last find peace together, and can rest. When he rejoins Samuel at the foot of the grave, his father-in-law puts an arm around his shoulders and whispers, in German first, forgetting, that he has done a fine thing, and that he's a good son.

THE FIRST STRETCH of the journey back to their hotel is silent apart from the easygoing background of Hartmann's radio, the Adagietto, from Mahler's Fifth Symphony, and the low hum of the car's engine. Samuel has again taken the passenger seat, leaving Jack to carry his own thoughts into the back. He sits, feeling the music, his eyes trained on what is chasing past his window, and it is only as they approach the city centre and the traffic turns heavy that Hartmann starts talking. The music plays on, and his voice, from where Jack is sitting, feels distant, but words pour from him with hardly a pause for breath. Samuel watches the road ahead and listens without bothering to translate, since the subject is nothing now but football. What he gets is the *Wunderteam*, mostly; unimaginably glorious during the early years of the thirties, putting the world on notice of its might with slaughters of Germany, the Swiss and a highly regarded Hungary side, and arguably peaking with a shock win—a crushing, really—of Scotland, who'd never lost to a team outside of the so-called home nations, and who were at that time widely considered one of the game's masters. Even in defeat the *Wunderteam* dazzled, far outclassing England in London, and falling short only in terms of the result. And Mutzl was the one, always. The magician, the conductor. The World Cup in '34 should have been his glory. If anything, the tournament had come a year or eighteen months too late to catch the side at its best and most dominant, with age and attrition starting to take some of the glisten from them, but they remained formidable and on their day capable of miraculous feats, since they still had Sindelar in their line-up. And for two weeks into June of that year, even on bad and stony pitches and in spite of some of the most brutal tackling anyone had seen, he'd led the way magnificently, squeezing them past France and then the Hungarians, before the semi-final against Italy, the tournament's hosts.

'Torrential rain had made a swamp of the field.' Hartmann smiles but with gritted teeth. 'I'd gone with them and wouldn't have missed it, and he made sure that they put me to work, fetching and carrying, so that I could feel involved. I remember one of the players, Viertl, on the left wing, lost a boot twice in the first half, trying to run. The game should never have gone ahead, but in better conditions they couldn't have lived with us. The mud levelled things. Mutzl had to be washed down at half-time with towels and buckets of water and the ground was red around him in the changing room from the kicks he'd taken. In the end, one goal decided the result. Platzer, our keeper, was fouled, assaulted, really, and the ball knocked from his hands. No referee anywhere would have allowed that to stand, except for a Swede who, it later emerged, had been to dinner the night before with Mussolini. But there was that in football, too, that as much as the beauty. And it cost us what should have been our crowning achievement: a final against the Czechs, a decent side but one whose number we had in our pockets. There were other days, good and great ones, cup finals and the like, and at the time, bruised and battered as our boys were, we still just assumed we'd win next time, the World Cup in '38. By the summer of '38, though, we were no longer a country, not even a name on a map. And just months after that, Mutzl was gone, and that was the story done and finished.'

When the car stops finally at their hotel, they all get out and shake hands. Amid expressions of gratitude and good wishes, Jack can feel the old Austrian staring again, trying to identify what it is that has the past pressing once more so heavily against the present, something beyond the obvious teasing reminder of Rebekah. But whatever is there proves elusive, or at least inexpressible. And then, again, it is just him and Samuel, standing on the footpath on a bright, cold lunch hour, with the road's incline dragging at them. 'We still have time until the flight,' Samuel says, leading the way out of the sunlight and in through the doorway to the hotel's shadowed lobby. 'We should have a last drink before we go.'

Jack follows him through into the bar, sits at a table near a fire that is already pleasantly ablaze and will soon be roaring, and while waiting for Samuel to bring the drinks settles back in his seat and considers the place, empty at this hour apart from the elderly bartender in white shirt and grey waistcoat. Weariness washes through him, and the heat cast by the flames makes him want to close his eyes. Even if they've proven little in terms of officially verifiable facts, he has learned a lot. And that, for now, must be enough. By tonight he'll be back in Cork, home, and sleeping in his own bed, with his wife in his arms and with his daughter tucked up in slumber in the next room. Tomorrow morning he will wake and be up and dressed before it's even properly light, ready, regardless of the weather, for the dockyard's early shift. And life, such as it is, will go on pulling with the tide.

ACKNOWLEDGMENTS

BOOKS, IN THEIR writing, need a lot of support, and *The Paper Man* is fortunate to have had plenty hands to hold on to and shoulders to cry on.

I want to acknowledge the Arts Council of Ireland/*An Chomhairle Ealaíon* for the award of a deeply appreciated literature bursary, which proved invaluable in affording me the time to fully immerse myself in getting this book written.

Sylvia Petter, a fine writer and good soul, pulled some financial strings and got me to Vienna in 2014 for the International Conference on the Short Story. I arrived with a vague idea for a novel I thought I might one day write.

Julia and Florian, and Julia's parents, Helmut and Christine Schwaninger, welcomed me into their homes and hearts and, in addition to becoming my Austrian family, gave me the Vienna I was seeking. Without their kindness and generosity, this book could not have been written.

My late friend Pete Duffy, who loved football, was a wonderful and invaluable sounding board as I began to make sense of all the bits and pieces of plot ideas and worked through the early drafts.

My deepest appreciation, always, to Robin Robertson, for all the kindness he's shown me. To Daisy Watt, a wonderful guiding hand early on, who set the ball rolling on this book. To my editor, Željka Marošević, for all the encouragement, guidance and hard work in helping to knock *The Paper Man* into shape; to all at Jonathan Cape and Vintage, from those responsible for creating the actual physical product to those who convince bookshops to make room for it on their shelves; to Jane Kirby, for getting the book stateside, and to Joshua Bodwell, my editor at Godine, for loving the story enough to want to give it a chance with American readers—my gratitude.

And finally, my love and thanks to my family, for their constant encouragement and reassurance: Martin, Kate, Liam and Ellen; Irene and Yann, who help me in more ways than I could possibly count; and my father, Liam, my first reader and the rock on whom we all exist. My mother, Regina, died in October 2021. My most ardent supporter, she was so excited that this book was going to be published. I wish she'd been able to hold a copy in her hands, but I know she's around, and brimming with pride.

A NOTE ABOUT THE AUTHOR

Billy O'Callaghan is the award-winning author of the novels *The Dead House* (long-listed for the 2019 International DUBLIN Literary Award), *My Coney Island Baby* (shortlisted for the Royal Society of Literature's Encore Award), and *Life Sentences*, as well as four short story collections: *In Exile*; *In Too Deep*; *The Things We Lose, The Things We Leave Behind*; and *The Boatman and Other Stories*. More than one hundred of his short stories have appeared in literary journals and magazines around the world, among them *Agni*, *Kenyon Review*, *London Magazine*, *Los Angeles Review*, *Ploughshares*, and the *Saturday Evening Post*. O'Callaghan was born in Ireland's County Cork and lives in Douglas, a village on the edge of Cork City.

A NOTE ON THE TYPE

The Paper Man has been set in Dante. Designed by Giovanni Mardersteig shortly after World War II, the typeface is indebted to type cut by Francesco Griffo between 1449 and 1516. Dante was first used in Boccaccio's *Trattatello in laude di Dante*, printed in 1955 by Mardersteig's famed Officina Bodoni, in Verona, Italy.

Book Design & Composition by Tammy Ackerman